HER LAST BREATH AT DAWN

INVESTIGATOR KAT CROMWELL MYSTERY - BOOK TWO

NICHOLAS HARVEY

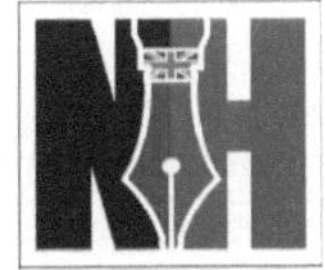

PROLOGUE

Hailey watched her date walk away toward the footbridge over the railroad tracks. The streetlights from the road cast a long, slender shadow as though the man were twenty feet tall. He didn't seem like a bad guy. Not the type she was looking for in a relationship, but then again, she couldn't define who would be. It was one of the many challenges of dating apps. *Likes?* She'd put down the features she'd enjoyed from prior relationships. There had been a few boyfriends she'd thought might be the one. She'd also had a few she'd quickly walked away from, but not as many as most women her age. Hailey prided herself on being a discerning dater.

Dislikes? Filling out annoying questionnaires had been one of her answers. What else? Assholes trolling supposedly legitimate dating sites to get laid. Bad breath. Arrogance. Excessive body hair. Expecting that a few drinks and a walk along the beach would automatically remove her underwear.

The truth, after twenty-eight years of learning, was that Hailey didn't know exactly what she wanted in a man, but she sure as hell hadn't found it yet. And the guy now getting in his car parked along Pacific Coast Highway wasn't in the running. Garrett hadn't been pushy, but halfway through their date, she'd known it was another fruitless evening. He'd seemed to sense the same, but to his credit, he'd remained engaged in their chatter.

He was a decent-looking guy. Clean-cut, well-dressed, and polite. A little shorter than she preferred, but with a trim figure, like he took care of himself without being a gym rat. At five foot six inches, Hailey was above average in height, and a slender 129 pounds. When the scales tipped to 130, she immediately added an extra fifteen minutes of cardio to her daily exercise and cut out carbs. She knew her anxiety attached to the scale's LED readout was unhealthy, but jogging was a whole lot cheaper than a shrink to sort out her self-esteem issues.

Overall, the evening had been pleasant, with only minor lapses into awkward silence, so when he'd asked, she'd agreed to a walk along Capistrano Beach with him. It was a beautiful California night, with a pleasant breeze off the Pacific Ocean. The lights of the beach cities kept the blanket of stars to occasional pinpricks, but the crashing of the waves on the sand was like a comforting soundtrack from her teenage years.

After a leisurely stroll, he'd thanked her for a nice evening and offered to walk her to her car, but she'd declined. There'd been no throwaway offer of follow-up emails or "Maybe we should do this again." Once upon a time, that would have made her feel sad and rejected, despite her own disinterest. But having endured enough dates that had amounted to nothing, it no longer bothered her.

Hailey drew in a long breath, soaking up the salt air and the cool breeze after another hot California summer's day. A vibration from her back pocket made her tense, and it took her a second to recall which phone was where. She wished she'd turned them both off, or better yet, left the one at work as usual.

She glanced at her Tissot *Le Locle* watch, a college graduation gift from her parents. It read a few minutes after eleven. Her six-thirty a.m. alarm would come too soon in the morning. She was ready to get through the final two days of the week and enjoy a quiet weekend reading, and maybe even a few hours spent at the beach. It had been a while since she and her roommate had indulged in a lazy afternoon by the ocean.

In an instant, the world went dark, and something rough smothered Hailey's face. Violently pulled backwards, she lost her balance and collapsed to the ground. Shocked and winded, pain shot through both elbows as they took the brunt of the fall. The cell phone she'd been holding clattered to the asphalt. She tried screaming, but only managed a gasp as the coarse material of the hood sucked into her open mouth. Strong hands pulled her wrists together and bound them, biting into her flesh as she heard a zipper-like sound.

Surely her date, Garrett, could see this? Had he left already? A deeper wave of panic surged through her chest as the notion presented itself. Was this him? The hands were callous and brutal, now binding her feet, crushing her ankles together.

Regaining her breath, Hailey pushed the material away with her tongue and screamed. A vicious punch whipped her head to the side and knocked her senseless. Dazed, her temple throbbing, she groaned while her clothes were tugged and pulled. As she slowly recovered, the ocean breeze tickled her skin, and she realized her stomach was now exposed. Panting in full panic, she writhed and fought, but it was hopeless. On the ground with her limbs restrained, all she could do was roll from side to side and kick both legs in the air.

A weight fell upon her thighs, and a hand pulled on the waistband of her favorite Lululemon leggings. He was going to rape her, and there was nothing she could do about it. But how could he while her ankles were tied together? The tension on her leggings released with the sound of the fabric being cut. He had a knife. The man slid toward her feet, slicing the Luon material in each leg as he moved.

Hailey felt terrifyingly vulnerable. Hopelessly exposed. The realization that she had absolutely no control or influence on what was about to happen was paralyzing. Should she simply succumb and pray it didn't last long?

The weight lifted from her legs, and with a sharp tug, her leggings were completely gone. A hand grabbed her left foot and removed her sandal. The other must have already come off, as she could feel the soft breeze brushing the soles of both feet.

"Why are you doing this?" she whispered, and flinched in anticipation of another blow.

The attacker said nothing.

A hand brushed her naked stomach and pulled at her underwear. With the swishing sound from the blade, he cut them free. Hailey pulled her shoulders together, making the only attempt she had available to protect her chest. But with another tug, along with another swipe, he'd cut her bra, leaving it pinned beneath her body.

"Please," she muttered. "Please stop."

Silence.

Was this Garrett, returning to take what he'd always intended from her? She'd shown no interest, so now he'd take his pleasure? But why wasn't he saying anything? An idea began taking shape in her mind. If he didn't speak, and kept her hooded, she couldn't say for certain it was him. Sure, he'd be the first suspect the police would interview, but if he was careful enough not to leave any damning evidence, then it would be his word against hers. Of course, he could even say it was consensual, and it would be hard to disprove. But all her frantic wondering led to a sliver of hope that maybe she'd be left alive. *Why go to any of the trouble if he intended on killing her?*

"Garrett," she ventured. "Why are you doing this?"

Feet shuffling close by was her only response.

Hailey panted deep breaths and tried to prepare herself for the inevitable. It would be like the one-night stand she'd mistakenly allowed to happen in her junior year of college. Too many drinks and a recent break-up had conspired to let her inhibitions run wild, at least by her standards. He'd been a nice-looking senior who'd said all the right things. But he'd been clumsy and rushed, and her buzz had quickly worn off. She'd ended up laying there, making appropriate noises, as though she'd been present. She'd let him finish, as it had seemed like the fastest way for the entire ordeal to be over with.

Maybe what she was about to endure would be like that, but the turmoil in her gut told her differently.

Hailey yelped as hands shuffled under her armpits and dragged her to her feet. She winced in pain as the asphalt scuffed the skin from her heels. Powerfully tossed across the man's shoulder, her panties and bra dropped away. Without a word, her captor effortlessly carried her like a sack of dog food. Naked, beyond a hood cinched around her throat, Hailey sobbed and moaned as her stomach pounded against the man's shoulder with each step.

Forcing herself to be quiet, she sensed a change in the movement. His steps were now slower and more intentional. The crashing of waves grew louder. He was moving her closer to the ocean. The sand was making his steps more difficult.

"Please tell me what you're doing," she grunted between jolts to her abdomen. "Where are you taking me?"

Without a word, the unsteady walk continued, until Hailey heard splashes below them. They'd reached the water's edge. Everything she'd steeled herself for had now changed. Why would he take her into the ocean? She listened for the sound of a boat engine, but the waves and the sloshing from her captor's staggering progress in the surf were too loud. Salt water splashed against her hood, leaving a salty tang in the now stifling air beneath the heavy fabric.

With a sudden lurch, Hailey was dropped from the man's shoulder. She held her breath, waiting to hit the water, but instead, she landed on something soft. An inflatable dinghy, perhaps? Her body was now being tossed up and down as the man pushed her through the incoming surge. To a boat? The water here was relatively shallow for a long way, and the waves, even when small like tonight, would make maneuvering a vessel incredibly tricky.

Curled up as best she could, Hailey's thoughts shifted from the rape she'd expected to the latest twist. She was being abducted for another reason. Unsure whether her new fate would be better or worse, her confusion settled on the question of why her? If he thought her family had money, he'd grabbed the wrong woman. Hailey's parents lived in the same house they'd raised her in Flagstaff, Arizona. Her father worked at the post office, and her mother was a teacher at the high school. Which surely meant she was being taken for another purpose.

Shivering with a mixture of fear and cold from the chilly water dousing her naked body, Hailey tried to think of something to ask or say that would give her any kind of clue. But before she could speak again, the inflatable bumped against something more solid. Another person? A boat? It was impossible to tell, and after being thrown around by the surf, even her sense of direction had become unanchored.

Roughly gripping her forearm, her captor tried turning her onto her back, but she'd curled her legs inside the inflatable, making it impossible. Each wave rolling underneath pulled them toward the shore, so the man had to drag them back to whatever she kept bumping against. He tugged her legs out of the little dinghy and, with a firm hold on her arm, cut the zip ties restraining her hands.

Taken by surprise, her wrists were firmly clutched before she had time to do anything. *Had that been her chance to escape?* If it was, she'd hesitated, and her uncertainty had tossed away an opportunity. Now she was being dragged from the dinghy.

Hailey screamed in pain as her back scraped across something firm and metallic. Water still splashed up against her back and legs, but she was being pulled atop bars of some sort. Above the water level. *Was this the boat?* But it wasn't moving.

The next few moments flew by in a haze of disoriented confusion. Her wrists were tied once more, but not together. She was being secured to whatever she'd been pulled on top of, her arms held straight out on either side. Her ankle bindings were cut, but quickly retied, with her legs now splayed apart.

Quivering in outright terror, Hailey felt even more exposed and vulnerable than before. Unable to move her limbs, she was completely defenseless. All she could picture was a man holding the knife he'd used to slice through her clothes and bindings. *Would her body be next?* Drops of water ran down her sides, tickling her as though a blade were being brushed across her flesh.

Hailey screamed, but her voice was hoarse and lost to the sounds of the ocean. With a sharp tug, the hood was removed, and she blinked in the darkness, salt crystals already sticking to her eyelashes. Below her, the tops of the waves danced through gaps in the metal frame and stroked her skin like the tentacles of a thousand tiny creatures.

She turned her head to either side and squinted into the darkness. Distant lights appeared to flicker and blur, distorted by the water in her eyes. Tipping her head forward, Hailey looked down at her body, taut and prickled with a fine layer of goosebumps. The lights of Pacific Coast Highway seemed so close and yet completely out of reach. Headlights of occasional cars swept by, unaware of her desperate plight. Lifting her chin, the back of her head pressing against the frame, Hailey searched the ocean behind her. Not a single light broke the blanket of darkness.

The man had vanished.

Hailey was stranded, no more than two hundred yards from civilization, yet completely alone.

1

———————

I lay on my back, blinking at the lights hanging from the gym's high ceiling. Everything was moving as though I were on the deck of a ship at sea. Indistinct music and voices droned behind the ringing in my ears. A shadow loomed over me, and I struggled to focus.

"I bloody well told you," came the booming voice of my father with his London accent.

"I'm fine, Dad, thanks," I slurred through my mouthguard.

I pushed the molded plastic out with my tongue, and he used a meaty finger to pluck it free.

"You were supposed to be blocking his uppercut," he lectured. "That was the point."

"I got the point," I breathed as another face leaned over me.

"I'm sorry, Miss Cromwell," Cisco said with a heavy Hispanic accent.

He was one of my dad's best boxers. On track to fight for the featherweight division state title. A win would be another banner to add to the collection adorning the gym's walls.

"Don't you bloody apologize," Dad told him as they both hooked a forearm and hauled me to my feet. "She asked for this."

I didn't exactly ask to be clocked in the jaw by a jackhammer. I held out a gloved hand to Cisco, and he tapped his against it.

"You okay, miss?" Cisco asked.

I nodded. "Right as rain."

He looked confused. People often were when I used British phrases. I'd inherited them growing up with English parents, despite spending most of my life in California.

"I'm fine," I said. "Got me a good one, though."

"*Sí*," he replied. "You spar very well. I forget to go easy."

"Ten minutes on the bag, then we'll hit the weights," Dad ordered Cisco before he could say anything else that would land my old man in trouble.

We all knew he told the kid to go easy on me, but it wasn't supposed to be openly mentioned. Regardless, Cisco's comment made me feel good. He'd forgotten I was the coach's daughter for a moment and treated me like any other sparring partner. The headache beginning to pound in my forehead was a reminder of that fact. Although, Cisco punished all his sparring partners, so I wasn't the first one to limp away, feeling useless.

"I'd better get showered," I said, noting it was six-thirty a.m., according to the big clock on the wall over my dad's office door.

He nodded. "You alright?"

I held out my hands, palms up, and he began unlacing my gloves. "Yeah," I replied. "I was sure he was faking again with the uppercut, to come over the top with his left."

My father chuckled, which sounded like the low rumble of a diesel engine. "Don't need word getting out about that move," he said with a grin. "It'll be a points scorer in his next fight."

I rolled my eyes. "Forgot to tell me to watch out for that, didn't you?"

He shrugged his shoulders as he pulled the gloves from my hands. "Told you to be real careful of his uppercut. What do you want me to do, box him for you?"

I worked my jaw around in circles. Despite wearing heavily padded headgear, my jaw still ached from the punch. I couldn't imagine being on the receiving end of that without any protection, especially if Cisco gave it all he had the capability of truly doing.

I looked at my dad. He was still in great shape for a man his age, and literally twice Cisco's weight. Being hit by a heavyweight champion like my dad must be equivalent to facing off with a train.

"Maybe I'll mention to Mum how you let Cisco loose on me," I said, unwinding the wrap from my wrists and grinning.

"Last sparring you'll ever do," he smiled back.

"Might be worth it to see you in the doghouse for a few weeks."

He chuckled again. "Months, more like."

"Gotta go," I said, taking my gloves and mouthguard from him.

Dad reached out and ruffled my hair like I was a twelve-year-old. "Be careful out there."

He held the ropes apart, and I ducked through the gap, stepping out of the ring. "I've been working tough cases lately," I replied as I walked toward the dressing rooms. "Stuck inside, sorting through old files. Dangerous stuff. I got a vicious paper cut the other day."

Opening my locker, I hung my sparring gloves, gave the wadded-up ball of wraps a sniff, then tossed it inside. They didn't stink too badly. I'd wash them next time. The mouthguard would get a rinse with me in the shower, but I hung the headgear on a hook. Grabbing my cell phone off the top shelf, I tilted it toward me. Two missed calls and three texts, all in the past fifteen minutes. The calls were from Sergeant Martinez and my partner, Hugo Fuentes. Same as the texts—two from Sarge, one from Hugo. I played the first voicemail.

"Kat, get to Capistrano Beach asap. We have a body."

I couldn't believe I'd just been joking around a few minutes ago about a paper cut. It was easy to get bored as a homicide investigator in a sleepy beach town, but the alternative always involved the worst form of misfortune for someone else.

The other voicemail and texts were letting me know where along the beachfront I'd find the victim, and that my partner was thirty minutes away. That was a quarter of an hour ago. Hugo lived in Laguna Beach, the sprawling town to the north.

Turning, I looked in the full-length mirror at the end of the row of lockers and blew out my cheeks. I looked like I'd just gone a few rounds in a boxing ring. A quick sniff of an armpit told me there was no way I could skip the shower. I texted Sarge and Hugo, letting them know I'd be there in ten before stripping and hurrying into the shower.

Keeping my brunette hair trimmed in a bob cut made drying faster, and I rarely used any makeup beyond eyeliner. Being a tomboy until my late teens and a surfer most of my life meant too many showers and not enough time for long hair and face paint. The downside of speed-washing was my body wasn't done perspiring from my early morning workout, so as I slid into the driver's seat of my department-issued unmarked Ford, I could feel my buttoned shirt sticking to the seat back.

My dad's boxing gym was located on Doheny Park Road, which fed into Pacific Coast Highway. In less than half a mile, I parked by the side of the road behind a red Toyota Prius. Rifling through my work backpack, I grabbed the essentials. Phone, notepad, pen, and my trusty compact instant camera. Unlike the old, traditional Polaroid units, mine was about the size of my cell phone, only twice the thickness. I slipped on my lightweight dark blue blazer and tucked the electronics into the back pockets of my black jeans. The notebook was small enough to drop in the inside pocket of the blazer. Locking the car, I walked to the metal footbridge over the rail tracks and took the steps two at a time.

Sunrise had been at 6:22 am. It was now a few minutes before seven, and the sun would be another thirty minutes before it actually appeared over the Capo Beach bluffs on the inland side of PCH. The ocean had the glassy sheen I loved when surfing during the opening minutes of the day. Sparkles twinkled from the swells in the distance, reflecting the sun still hidden from the beach by the bluffs. The long shadows kept the air cool and drew out the wonderfully peaceful feeling of first light.

Beyond the bridge and the railroad was paid beach parking, which stretched between Doheny State Beach Campground to the north and Capistrano Beach Park to the south. A small building housing public bathrooms and a locked storage room for the rangers was the only structure in sight for a quarter of a mile in either direction. A barrier of riprap rock protected the parking from extreme storm waves, then the beach itself gently sloped for a hundred feet until the sand met the cool Pacific waters.

An ambulance and three patrol cars blocked the parking area. Two sets of yellow crime scene tape stretched from the rocks to metal stakes placed at the edge of the ocean, cordoning off a section of the beach. Hugo's black Ford pulled in as I finished crossing the walkway, and he parked next to the ambulance. They'd all entered through Doheny State Park. I'd chosen the fastest route for me from the gym.

Hugo stepped from his car and straightened his dark gray tie. As usual, he looked impeccably put together in a tailored suit with perfectly groomed salt-and-pepper hair. I wondered why he didn't dye his hair, as I'm sure he'd look younger, but then it occurred to me that he might. Perhaps that sprinkling of gray was strategic. I always felt scruffy next to the man, even on mornings when I'd taken more than a handful of minutes to prepare myself.

The smell of the ocean and the beach always felt like home to me. Salty air with a hint of briny seaweed and the remnants of bonfire smoke lingering from the night before. I walked over to Hugo, who greeted me with a nod. A young deputy, Ripley, approached us with his partner, Hanson. Ripley was a good guy. Hanson, less so. The latter had tried ruining my partner with office rumors, which we'd fortunately managed to snuff out. But the tension remained.

I noticed both officers had removed their utility belts, and more curiously, they were dripping wet. Both men appeared pale and shaken.

"Vic is a white female," Ripley began as he led us between a gap in the rocks to the beach. He was struggling to keep his voice even. "Twenties, I'd say, but could be early thirties. No ID as yet." He paused and took a deep breath. "Sorry."

"You're fine," Hugo said. "Take your time. We have any tracks in the sand?"

"There's so many above the high-tide mark, sir, we can't tell what's what," Hanson said.

His voice didn't sound like his usual cocky self. I looked around the beach. No tent had been erected yet, and for the life of me, I couldn't see the victim.

"Guys," I said, still scanning the beach. "Where's the vic?"

Hugo nudged me and pointed to the water. I watched a set of waves roll toward the beach and was about to ask again when, between swells, about two hundred feet out, I saw her. The victim was naked and bound to a metal framework, which protruded above the ocean's surface. The woman disappeared from view as each wave passed over the frame, splashing water into the air as the swells struck her corpse.

2

―――――

I turned to Ripley. "You verified she's dead, right?"

The officer nodded.

Pulling my instant camera from the back pocket of my jeans, I took a picture. A moment later, the device whirred, and a slowly developing photograph appeared from a slot. Pocketing the camera, I held the picture by the corner and returned my attention to the sea. If what I was thinking happened, this was a brutal and slow way to kill someone.

"I looked up the tides, ma'am," Ripley began.

"And low tide isn't for a few hours yet," I finished for him.

All surfers kept an eye on tides, surf conditions, and moon phases. I rotated my mornings to skip the gym and hit the water based on the predictions.

"Correct, ma'am," Ripley responded. "High tide was around three-thirty a.m."

"Jesus," Hugo muttered. "When was the previous low tide?"

"A few minutes before nine p.m., sir," Ripley replied, trying not to drip on the notebook he held.

"What's the range?" I asked.

"Excuse me?" Ripley replied.

"Difference between high and low tide," I explained. "In feet."

"Oh," he said, and glanced at his notes, wiping away a droplet of seawater. "Five point one six at high tide, ma'am, down to an even foot later this morning."

"And yesterday evening's low tide?"

"Point nine-two, ma'am."

I took off my blazer and looked around for somewhere to put my clothes and electronics.

"What are you doing?" Hugo asked.

"Going to take a look," I replied, kicking off my already sandy tennis shoes.

Hugo shook his head and straightened his already straight tie. "What for? She's dead, Kat. The crime lab team will be here any minute."

I paused and looked once more at the poor woman who'd most likely drowned during the night. The rising tide would have slowly increased the waves crashing over her head. Timing it right, perhaps by the sound of the incoming swells, she would have been able to hold her breath while the waves swamped her. With gaps of twelve to fourteen seconds between most waves, she'd have had time to recover and suck in air before being engulfed once again. The process would have continued for hours until the tide rose enough that the time her nose and mouth spent submerged outweighed her opportunities to breathe. At some point, unable to spit out the seawater surging into her throat before the next swell arrived, she would have drowned. I shivered at the thought of such a slow and terrifying prelude to a horrible death.

"Any obvious injuries?" I asked Ripley instead of arguing with my partner over whether it was worth getting wet.

Ripley shook his head. "I don't think so, ma'am, but I can't say I studied her real hard."

"Wounds at the bindings," Hanson offered. "Water's washed most of the blood away, but I'm guessing she struggled."

"I dare say she did," I mumbled, handing my blazer to Hugo and unbuttoning my blouse.

I almost always wore a sports bra and briefs in case I had to run. As an investigator, that wasn't supposed to happen, as uniforms handled the arrests, but somehow I managed to occasionally find myself doing things we weren't supposed to. Hence the tennis shoes as well. Which was fine with me, as they were more comfortable than most dress shoes.

I handed Hugo my blouse. He shook his head, but didn't say anything more.

Stripped to my underwear, I took a few steps to the water, then heard a wolf whistle. I shouldn't have turned around, but I was caught by surprise. Two young guys stood on the footbridge with cell phones pointed my way. The crime lab van had pulled up, and now a bunch of civilians' cars had parked farther down from our patrol cars and on PCH.

A crowd was gathering. Perfect. It was too late now to reconsider. I was already standing in the surf in my undies.

"Maybe we can requisition you official department underwear, Kat," Hugo said with little humor in his tone. "That way, you're identified as sheriff's department for the newspaper articles."

"Sod off," I muttered in reply, and strode into the water.

As was too often the case, my partner was right. Stripping off and gallivanting into the ocean wasn't the best idea from a procedural or public relations point of view. But I needed to see her.

Contrary to popular perception, the Pacific Ocean off the California coast was downright chilly. I'd usually be striding in wearing a wetsuit and carrying my longboard under my arm. I felt goosebumps rising on my flesh, and I shivered as the water reached my crotch. Once I was in up to my waist, I dove forward and swam, ducking below the surface and swimming under each swell as they reached me. By the time I approached the metal platform, I could barely stand.

Rising and falling with the movement of the water, I alternated between kicking to keep my face above the surface, then bouncing on my tiptoes, feeling the shifting sands beneath my feet. The frame had been designed for rapid assembly with no concern over longevity. The bare, uncoated steel was already tarnished with what would rapidly become rust. Quick-release pins had been used at all the joints instead of bolts. The construction was sturdy, and certainly heavy, but had no chance of staying in place against the might of the ocean. Even combined with the woman's mass, the structure couldn't weigh more than 250-300 pounds. It had to be anchored in some manner.

I searched the base of a corner with my foot and struck a smooth, round object. With further fumbling, using my toes, I determined the corner post was embedded in a concrete-filled bucket. I ran my hand up the box tube post and felt a series of holes, one of which contained a pin. Strips of flat stock ran at forty-five degrees from the post to the top frame, creating braces, adding rigidity to the structure. Using the bucket as a step, I clung to the top frame and raised myself well clear of the water.

I could now view the victim from slightly above. The woman's flesh was unearthly pale. Several strands of seaweed had caught in her hair and across her shoulders. I noticed a small hoop earring in her left lobe, and a slender chain around her neck. She wore a watch on her left wrist.

I maneuvered closer to check the time. It was a nice-looking Tissot brand, which still read correctly. If it had stopped, it may have given us an indication of when she'd been brought into the water, but the second hand soldiered on, oblivious to the fate of its owner.

A darker shade blemished her left temple. A bruise. Hanson had been right. The zip ties securing her to the frame had cut the flesh at her wrists and ankles. Beyond that, I couldn't see any other obvious wounds. I'd hoped to see signs of strangulation, or a gunshot. Even a fatal stab wound would have meant a less agonizing death than how it appeared.

Out to sea, I heard powerful engines and looked up to spot a harbor patrol boat approaching in the distance. Turning to the beach, members of the crime lab unit had gathered at the shoreline and appeared to be discussing the situation with Hugo. They were so close, only a few hundred feet from me, and beyond them, Pacific Coast Highway a mere forty more yards. I looked at the twenty-something-year-old woman and imagined how completely helpless and isolated she must have felt. At night. Shrouded in darkness. Knowing rescue was so close and yet a lifetime away.

"Hugo!" I yelled at the top of my lungs.

He continued his conversation. Their chatter was lost to the crashing surf, as my shout had been. The cruelty of the murder was unfathomable. Someone had planned, designed, and then constructed a mechanism for the sole purpose of taking another's life. Slowly.

I fought back tears. Crying wouldn't do me or the victim any good. Berating myself, I pushed aside the trauma of the victim's murder and focused on the details. I wished I could take a few pictures to anchor my broken brain to what I was seeing. The crime lab officers would do that, but it was never the same as when I took the pictures myself.

The harbor patrol boat was approaching, but I knew they'd have a hard time remaining close. Between the surf and the relatively shallow water, the best they'd be able to do would be to anchor farther out and release rode until their stern was closer to the site.

I gave the victim one last lingering look, then started my swim back to shore.

By the time I reached the beach, a pop-up tent was being erected, and Hugo met me with a blanket to use as a towel. I think he'd gotten it from the EMTs, but I didn't ask. Still shaken from what I'd seen, I was keen to relay the information in case it slipped from my grasp without the aid of my photographs.

"We'll need the medical examiner to confirm it, but she appears to have a bruise on her left temple," I began explaining to my partner, who took notes. "No visible fatal wounds. The frame is elaborate and held together with pins for easy assembly. It's weighted with concrete-filled buckets.

The corner verticals are steel box tube embedded in the concrete. Slightly smaller box tube attaches to the top frame and slips inside the verticals. A series of holes drilled at intervals through both allows the platform to be adjusted in height."

Hugo paused writing and blew out his cheeks. "Seriously? I thought it was going to be pieces of old scaffolding. Does it look like anything someone could buy off the shelf?"

I shook my head. "I'm pretty sure it was made for exactly what it accomplished here."

Hugo groaned. "Someone went to a lot of trouble."

"And time," I agreed. "But the steel stock they used looks new, so maybe we can track down a recent purchase."

"Hardware stores?" Hugo scoffed. "There has to be one for every square mile of Orange County."

The crime lab folks had finished erecting and staking down their tent, so we moved under the cover of the three-sided shelter. My clothes sat on a folding table inside. I toweled myself dry as best I could with the blanket, then struggled into my jeans, my damp skin resisting the denim.

"I don't think you can buy box section steel that size from Lowe's or Home Depot," I responded after more thought. "We should be able to narrow it down to industrial supply places."

Hugo made another note while I slipped an arm into my shirt.

"What do we have?" came Captain Bradley's voice, startling me.

I turned and finished buttoning my shirt. She frowned.

"Did you get in the water, Cromwell?"

"Yes, ma'am."

"Why?"

The question was loaded with disapproval and challenge more than curiosity. Every time I thought I'd settled into a good place with the woman in charge of the Dana Point Orange County Sheriff's Department, she found a way of reminding me that I wasn't her favorite member of staff.

"Kat volunteered to get a first impression of the situation," Hugo answered for me.

At least he and I had found a comfortable working relationship. Having secrets about each other was a little like the Cold War. We both had our fingers hovering over buttons that would guarantee a big mess, along with our mutual destruction. But I hoped we'd moved on from unspoken threats being the reason we played nice. Respect was a far better basis for a partnership at any level.

"Good morning," Rosalia Bautista said, entering the tent.

Rosa, a lead officer with the Orange County Sheriff's Crime Lab, had her graying black hair tied back in a neat ponytail and carried a concerned look on her face. In her late forties, she was one of our best crime scene investigation officers.

"Tide going out?" she asked, looking at me.

"Yeah," I replied, welcoming the new conversation. "You've got a few hours before low tide."

Rosa nodded and stared out over the water. "Anything I should know?"

"Vic is tied to a metal frame which is weighted to the sea floor," I explained. "It's held together with quick-release pins. The waves make it difficult to do anything out there, but if harbor patrol could winch the platform off the posts, it might make it easier for you to examine her still on the frame."

Rosa nodded again. "Thanks. I'll send a pair of officers out to look." She grinned at me as I finished dressing. "I'm not as young or eager as you."

I self-consciously ran a hand through my damp hair. "You'll take pictures before you move her, yeah?"

"Of course," she replied, and I sensed Captain Bradley's eyes on me again.

It was a dumb question. Of course they'd take a bazillion pictures. They always did, but I was anxious. Most people would relish the opportunity to wipe the image of the young woman from their minds. Ironically, my broken brain might do exactly that when finding the killer may rely on an important detail I'd seen firsthand.

As a child, I'd discovered a system to overcome my rare neurological disorder by anchoring the memory with a photograph from an instant camera. Whether it was in my head or holding the photograph in my hand moments after it was taken that had something to do with it, I'd never determined, but pictures on my phone weren't as reliable. Regardless, it was a secret that, if revealed, would have me medically discharged from the sheriff's department.

A powerful secret for my partner to know.

3

I drove by the house and took my second shower of the morning. My little cottage was nestled on the hillside overlooking the Pacific Ocean along with most of the city of Dana Point. Apart from the harbor and Doheny State Park and Beach, the rest of the sleepy beach town—by Southern California standards—of 33,000 residents lived on a warren of streets built into the coastal hills, along or above Pacific Coast Highway.

I had a lovely view of the water. But only if I walked out and stood in the middle of my street, Copper Lantern. Whoever laid out the neighborhood, known as The Lantern District, either didn't have views in mind, or figured everyone would have one from their little beach cottages built up the hill. That was until real estate boomed, and the cottages were systematically bulldozed and replaced with huge multi-story homes. Except for mine and a few other holdouts.

It was still an amazing place to live, in a home I adored. And could never have afforded. My parents had been ridiculously generous in giving me one of their rental income houses.

Having not heard from anyone, I detoured via the drive-thru of PC Beans, the locally owned coffee shop, which had been in the same old building my whole life. Its full name was Pacific Coast Beans, but only tourists finding the location off the internet ever referred to the quirky little place that way.

A classmate from school, Joanna, must have been the barista as my cup came out with a sheriff's badge drawn in place of my name. I resisted the urge for one of their delicious pastries, but bought a latte for Hugo before driving the mile and a half to the station.

Rosa's first priority was identifying our victim, which, as we didn't have any new missing person's reports, required fingerprints and the hope the woman was in the system. We'd left the beach, having sent deputies in search of eyewitnesses and CCTV footage. There were several hotels, a timeshare resort, and a couple of restaurants along the base of the Capo Beach bluffs lining PCH, so maybe we'd get lucky with cameras.

I found Hugo at his desk in a small office that we shared with no one else, most of the time. The Orange County Sheriff's homicide division was based in the much larger Santa Ana station, but my partner and I were allowed to operate as a small satellite department as we both lived in the beach cities. I slid the coffee his way, and he grunted his thanks.

"Do you know how many metal suppliers there are in Orange County?" he complained.

"Maybe we start with the ones closest to the beach and work outward?" I suggested.

"That'll be San Juan Capistrano," Hugo replied, writing in his notebook. "Next would be a few options in San Clemente."

My cell phone rang, and Rosa's name came up on the caller ID.

"Cromwell," I answered.

"Hailey Carter," Rosa said without preamble. "Twenty-eight-years-old. Her red Toyota Prius was parked on PCH. It's been towed to the lab. We located her from prints. No police record, but she has a passport. I've emailed you the details."

"Thanks, Rosa. Were you able to remove her from the water?"

"Yes," she replied. "We did as you suggested, except we carried the top frame to the beach. I performed a quick examination and documented everything before we released the body to the EMTs. She's on her way to the ME's office now."

I glanced at my watch. It was a quarter after ten.

"Any reason to believe she didn't drown?" I asked.

"None so far."

"Thanks, Rosa. We'll work on contacting the family."

While saying goodbye and hanging up the call, I was already typing the woman's name into our system. DMV records gave us a home address.

"Hailey Carter," I relayed to Hugo, who was staring at me around our computer monitors. "Address is Harbor Creek off Del Obispo."

He stood and grabbed his jacket. "Do we know if she was married or single?"

"No," I replied, gathering my blazer and backpack. "You drive. I'll see what I can find out on the way over."

Harbor Creek was a smaller complex of condominiums, many of which were rented out by their owners. From Hailey's social media page I'd found on our short drive, we'd learned two things. She didn't appear to be married, but posted little online, so we couldn't be sure yet. The most recent picture was from a concert at the Forum in LA. Along with a female friend, they appeared to be having a wonderful time. The image was in stark contrast to my introduction to the victim.

I knocked on the door, doubting anyone would be home during the day on a Friday. It was possible Hailey lived alone, but with the cost of rent in Orange County as high as it was, it didn't seem likely. After a second round of knocks, the door opened, and I recognized the woman from the concert picture.

"Orange County Sheriff's investigators Kat Cromwell and Hugo Fuentes, ma'am, is this the residence of Hailey Carter?" I asked.

"Yeah. What's wrong?" the woman replied, looking bleary-eyed.

"Are you Hailey's partner, or roommate, ma'am?"

"Roommate. Has something happened?"

"May we come inside, ma'am?" I asked, and she stepped aside to let us in. "Can I get your name?" I continued as we entered the living area. It was furnished nicely with art on the walls and a pair of matching sofas.

"Melissa," the roommate said, closing the door behind us. "Melissa Sanchez. Hailey's not here."

I hated the next part for every reason. Giving a death notice was always difficult, but in no way comparable to receiving one. The other part that sucked was delaying telling the family and friends while we asked questions that the grieving would struggle to answer once they heard the news.

"When was the last time you saw Hailey?" Hugo asked, sharing the burden with me.

"Yesterday. We briefly crossed paths when she came home from work. I was just leaving. You're really freaking me out here. What's happened?"

"You work evenings?" Hugo asked.

"Restaurant manager," she replied. "Why are you here? Has something happened to Hailey?"

I glanced at Hugo, and he subtly shrugged his shoulders. Apparently, he was done sharing the load. I wondered when being the newbie would wear off, but I doubted it ever would. He'd always have twenty years more time on the job than me.

"I'm afraid Hailey was found dead at Capistrano Beach this morning," I said, knowing the recipient would never forget my words or this moment in time. "We're treating the situation as a homicide."

Melissa's face quivered, and she rocked from side to side. I stepped forward and supported her by an arm, guiding her to a sofa. Which I reminded myself I should have done before delivering the news. Hugo swooped up a box of tissues, setting them down beside the roommate.

"Who would hurt Hailey?" Melissa gasped between sobs.

"We don't know," I replied. "If you can help us with her movements last night, we'd appreciate it."

"She had a date," Melissa blurted. "She told me. It was an internet date. Someone she'd never met before."

The woman's eyes shot around the room as though she was about to leap into action. Which, of course, she wasn't. But finding anything to tear the mind from gut-wrenching news was often a way of coping. Actionable information to assist us in finding the killer could feel like a meaningful response beyond bawling her eyes out on the couch.

"So Hailey didn't have a current boyfriend?" I asked.

Melissa shook her head.

"Ever married?" Hugo asked.

Another head shake.

"When was she last in a serious relationship?" he followed up.

The roommate thought for a moment. "Until about five months ago, I think. She dated Ryan for over a year."

"Ryan's last name?" I asked.

"Kwon," Melissa replied, taking a few deep breaths. Our questions were keeping her from falling apart.

"Got a number for him?" Hugo asked.

She pulled her phone from her leggings pocket and searched for a few moments, then read off a Los Angeles area code number.

"Where does he live?" I asked.

"Laguna Beach," Melissa said hesitantly. "But he's from the LA area somewhere."

"How did things end between them?" I asked, sensing she had more to say.

She looked up at me. "He wasn't happy about the breakup, but I don't think he'd hurt Hailey. He's a nice guy. Things just didn't work out." Melissa steeled herself to ask a question. "How was she… I mean, how did she…"

"We can't say at this time," I said, saving her the pain of speaking the words aloud. "The medical examiner will give an official cause of death after the autopsy."

Melissa choked back more tears.

"What can you tell us about her date last night?" Hugo asked, with less delicacy than I would have.

She shrugged her shoulders. "I don't know anything except that she had a date."

"Did she date a lot?" he asked.

Melissa shook her head. "Maybe once or twice a month, she'd see someone, but she's particular. Was particular," she corrected herself sullenly.

"How so?" I asked.

"She didn't have to be in a relationship, you know? Hailey was gorgeous and had this way about her that guys couldn't resist," she said, and sighed. "Maybe *because* she didn't need them for her to feel okay about her life. She was strong like that."

"You say she attracted guys, so why was she using a dating site?" I asked.

Melissa scoffed. "Because the singles scene around here is brutal. Hailey wasn't looking for flings and one-night stands. She was waiting for something more meaningful."

"Do you know which internet service or app she used?" Hugo asked.

"Pretty sure it was OC Match," Melissa replied. "Last time we talked about it, she said the app seemed like the best one she'd found."

I looked at Hugo. He knew all about the various dating sites and apps, especially the ones catering to the gay community. A fact connected to my nuclear meltdown button he thought I held over him. I guess I did hold it over him, although I'd never use it.

"Local site," he replied. "Started about a year ago. It's blown up. They'll go public or sell it for a ton of money by the end of next year."

"But it's a dating site, not a hook-up site?" I asked, showing my ignorance. But the detail was important.

They both nodded at me.

"You could probably see more about it on her cell," Melissa suggested. "It's a phone-based app."

"Her phone is missing," Hugo responded. "Any chance it's here?"

Melissa quickly dialed her friend's number. "Straight to voice-mail," she said after a moment.

"Yeah. Same as when we tried," I confirmed. "Can we take a look at Hailey's room, please?"

She stood and led me to the stairs.

Hugo remained in the living room. "I'll make a start on a warrant for the dating app," he said, taking his own phone from his pocket.

I nodded and followed Melissa. "Does her family live nearby?" I asked as we reached the landing with two open doors to bedrooms and one I presumed to be a linen closet or laundry.

"Arizona," Melissa replied, walking into the first bedroom. "Hailey went to UC Irvine, which is where we met."

The room was as clean and tidy as the downstairs. A pale blue and white comforter matched the curtains, and white-painted, distressed wood furniture contrasted nicely with the light gray carpet. We were close to the same age, but Hailey had put far more thought into her décor than I ever did. My cottage was filled with mostly hand-me-down items from my parents.

"Where did Hailey work?" I asked as I searched the bedside tables.

Melissa leaned against the doorjamb and wiped tears from her cheeks. "Laguna Niguel. She's the executive assistant to the president of a tech company."

"Sounds like a good job," I commented, finding nothing more than an e-reader tablet, headphones, and a few charging cables.

It was an electronically connected world, so no diary or pictures that might have been useful. Everything would likely be on her missing phone.

"Did she enjoy her job?" I asked, moving on to the small walk-in closet.

"Mostly," Melissa replied. "I think."

I glanced at Melissa. "You two weren't that close?"

"No, no, we're best friends," she quickly responded. "It's just she works days, and I work evenings and often weekends. Seemed like we barely saw each other over the past few months."

I thumbed through the clothes hanging from the rail, and they struck me as surprisingly sensible. The left side was work attire, and the right was more casual, but the difference wasn't startling. I wouldn't describe her taste as conservative, but also not overly suggestive or attention-seeking. I pictured Hailey wearing the outfits, healthy and vibrant, ready for an evening out. And I quickly realized something was wrong.

My brain was using the concert image of the victim from her social media page. I knew I'd witnessed her pale, dead corpse that morning, but my mind had lost the image. I swam in confusion, unable to piece together any details from the beach. Still standing in the closet, out of Melissa's view, I took the one instant photograph from my pocket and stared at the image. Unable to zoom in with the camera, the platform was nothing more than a poorly defined dark patch in the water. Too far away to distinguish anything more than human flesh atop a frame with turquoise ocean all around.

With palms sweating and my anxiety building, I hurriedly searched the chest of drawers, but still didn't find a phone. Or a laptop. Back in the room, I paused by a photograph of Hailey and an older couple, who I presumed to be her parents. Everyone was smiling with the iconic image of Disneyland's Sleeping Beauty Castle in the background. I knew it was our victim, Hailey Carter, but only from the picture my brain was hanging onto from the drive over. I looked at my beach photo once more, and a visual of the pop-up tent came to me. The conversations with Captain Bradley and Rosa from the crime lab remained fresh.

But the only way I knew I'd been in the water that morning was the recollection of the captain questioning me over why I had.

I took my instant camera from my back pocket and snapped a picture of Hailey's bedroom, deliberately capturing her roommate in the edge of the shot. A whirring sound filled the silence, and Melissa looked at me with a puzzled expression.

"I didn't know they even made those things anymore," she said. "Why don't you just use your phone?"

"Taking these helps me remember details," I said, using my well-practiced line, which wasn't a lie.

But I didn't offer there was a possibility that without the instant photograph, I might not remember ever being in Hailey's room at all. Like the ocean that morning.

4

"What's up?" Hugo asked as he drove out of the Harbor Creek condos onto Del Obispo.

I'd tried not to show I was rattled, but apparently I'd failed.

"Feeling bad for the roommate, that's all," I lied, using my phone to log into the sheriff's department server.

It took me a minute to find the case file for Hailey and see what had been dropped in there. To my relief, I spotted a link to a folder of photographs from the crime lab and quickly began scrolling. The images showed a young woman tied to a metal framework in the ocean. These facts made sense to me, but it was as though I was viewing the scene for the first time. Which I knew not to be true. The tech had taken an enormous number of high-resolution shots, slowly moving around the corpse with the ocean lapping against the platform.

Scrolling down the thumbnails, I spotted a video and opened the file. I watched as the crime lab officer struggled against the incoming swells to make a lap of the structure while filming the whole time. The soundtrack was of water sloshing against his body and the metal frame, with an occasional grunt as he tried to maintain his footing. As I watched, my broken brain began inserting my own images like flashcards being thrust before the lens. I hadn't experienced anything like this before, and it was making me dizzy.

"Bugger," I muttered and hit pause, closing my eyes.

The video images were gone, but the flashcards continued as my brain pulled remnants of memories from my hippocampus. Usually, when a scene was lost to me and I referenced one of my instant photographs, the memory came back like a pair of binoculars being focused. Everything began rather blurry, but soon became clearer as the connection was restored and the memory recalled. This was different, and uncomfortable to the point of making me feel nauseous. But at least my own vision of the scene was returning. Albeit in short bursts.

Letting out a long breath to settle my stomach, I opened my eyes as I realized we weren't moving. Hugo had pulled into the parking lot for the supermarket at the corner of Del Obispo and Stonehill. And now he was staring at me.

"You look like you've seen a ghost since coming downstairs at the vic's place," he said. "What's going on?"

My first reaction was to lie again. It generally wasn't considered a great idea to hand someone more ammunition if they might turn around and shoot you with it. But I reminded myself to stop thinking of our partnership that way. Hugo hadn't given me reason to think he'd reveal my condition, and I hoped he knew by now that I'd never throw him under the bus. We'd come a long way in a short time since our first case together.

"My stupid brain decided to cut me off from this morning," I said. "But looking at the video Rosa's people took is helping bring it back."

Hugo continued staring at me. He appeared unsure what to say or ask.

"I'm fine now," I assured him with far more confidence than I felt.

He didn't look reassured. "You lost the whole morning?"

"No, just my time in the water."

"Oh, the important part," he responded.

His lips slowly curled into a grin, and I laughed.

"Yeah. That bit."

<hr>

By the time we reached the station, I'd tracked down home and cell phone numbers for Mr. and Mrs. Carter in Arizona. Making a death notice by phone was strictly against policy, for good reason, so I contacted the sheriff's office in Flagstaff, where a local officer would have the unenviable task of delivering the news. It also meant we couldn't question the parents until the visit had been accomplished.

Sergeant Derek Martinez, the officer who kept everything and everyone flowing at the Dana Point station, greeted us from behind the reception desk when we entered the lobby.

"I was about to call you two. Judge has signed your warrant," he said.

Hugo kept hold of the door and glanced at his watch. "Newport Beach?"

Sarge nodded.

"Email, or do I have to go get it?" Hugo asked.

Martinez gave my partner a neutral stare and made him wait for an answer. The drive from Dana Point to the Harbor Justice Center in Newport Beach was twenty-two miles each way. In Orange County, traffic, even taking the tollway, meant over an hour round trip.

"Email," the sergeant finally admitted. He may have grinned, but it was hard to tell with his stone-like face.

Hugo shook his head and let the door go.

"I'll make a start on the CCTV from PCH," I said. "I saw we have something in the file already."

Hugo followed me from the lobby into the hallway to our office.

"You're welcome!" Martinez shouted after us.

"Thank you, sir," I called back.

Hugo didn't respond, but muttered obscenities in Spanish as we took our seats.

I logged into the computer and found the link to the CCTV that had been loaded on our server. The footage was from the traffic lights at the pedestrian crossing on PCH, next to the footbridge over the tracks. Two cameras, one facing in each direction. The coverage on file began at five on Wednesday afternoon and ended at eight on Thursday morning, overlapping more than an hour after police first arrived. I settled in for what I knew would be a long, boring session of watching a fixed camera showing a stretch of straight road.

Starting from the moment I'd parked by the side of PCH behind Hailey's red Prius, I set the playback to double speed in reverse. But it quickly became clear that wouldn't work. PCH at dawn was four lanes of busy traffic. Our tech folks had cool software that could pull any visible license plate from the film and cross-reference to tell us the registered owner. But we'd wait weeks or possibly months to see the results. Alone, I couldn't note every plate by hand, or I'd be here just as long. So I focused on finding anyone who stood out.

Vehicles driving by slowly and parking along PCH, or vans and pickup trucks that could haul the metalwork, all grabbed my attention. As the sun returned below the horizon, the streetlights came back on, and the cars continued reversing on my screen. The traffic soon thinned, and I began picking out a few suspicious vehicles. I'd reached midnight when Martinez texted Hugo and me that the warrant should have hit our inboxes.

"Let's go," Hugo announced after reading the message and printing the paperwork.

"Give me two minutes," I responded without looking up.

Hugo didn't reply, but left the office, so I presumed he was using the bathroom and primping his hair before we left.

I increased the speed of the footage, and vehicles flew backwards across my screen until a pickup truck reversed into the spot where I'd parked that morning. Directly behind Hailey's Toyota. I slowed the film and watched a man in his late twenties disappear from view as he walked backwards toward the footbridge. I noted the time. 10:55 p.m.

"Are you coming?" Hugo asked impatiently from the doorway.

"Look at this," I responded, replaying the part I'd just watched.

Hugo leaned closer. "That's our internet-date guy?"

"Could be him leaving," I said, and continued reversing the CCTV footage.

Traffic was thin in the late evening, but several vehicles sped by. A BMW slowed and pulled over for a minute, but left again without the driver getting out. Pretty soon, two figures walked backwards into view.

"Same guy," Hugo pointed out. "That's him."

We watched as the man and the woman, both too indistinct to truly identify in the poor light and low-resolution recording, spoke briefly, backed into their cars, then reversed away. They'd both arrived together, coming from the north.

"Which way does he leave?" Hugo asked.

I played the footage forward and sped it up until the man returned to his truck and pulled away. He immediately U-turned and disappeared toward town.

"Toyota Tacoma," Hugo said, and I jotted it down, then backed up the film until the truck had just turned around.

"He's got one of those stupid tinted covers over his license plate," I noted, pointing to the screen.

"No matter," Hugo replied. "We have the warrant. We'll get a name from the dating app."

From the station, it took twenty-two minutes to drive the nine miles to the offices of OC Match in Aliso Viejo. The building was modern and stylish, with a fancy lobby. Large screens ran looping videos of smiling, happy people of all adult ages, enjoying dates in gorgeous locations. The receptionist, who could have been one of the models in the ads, greeted us with a wide smile.

"Welcome to OC Match. How can I help you?"

"OCSD Investigators Cromwell and Fuentes," I said, having learned to use the initials instead of the full department name whenever possible. "We have a warrant to access information regarding two individuals using your app."

Her smile evaporated.

"Oh. Umm, one moment, please."

She dialed an extension from her desk and relayed our request to a manager higher up the food chain.

"Someone will be right with you," she told us after hanging up. "Can I get you a bottled water or coffee?"

The coffee was tempting.

"No. Thank you," Hugo replied with a tone that implied he was answering for us both.

The receptionist nervously forced a brief smile before pretending to be busy with something on her computer. My partner had an uncanny knack for making people feel uneasy. His authoritative appearance and stern demeanor had the innocent and guilty alike feeling like they were in trouble.

Sometimes, I wished I could come across that way, but I simply wasn't very intimidating. My English accent didn't help. Everyone thought I was more likely to make them a cup of tea than haul them off to jail.

A woman in her thirties appeared from the offices behind reception. She was slightly taller than me, meticulously put together in expensive-looking business casual attire, and was quite pretty. I doubted she needed the app to find dates.

"Detectives?" the woman greeted us.

"Orange County Sheriff's Department Investigators Cromwell and Fuentes, ma'am," I responded, using the full title for the executive. It did sound more important.

We both displayed our badges.

"And you are, ma'am?" I asked.

"Sienna Monroe," she replied, as though we should already know. "I own and manage OC Match."

"With your brother," Hugo added.

She eyed him with what I perceived to be annoyance. Her expression was subtle, but a tightening of her jaw and a slight raise of one eyebrow. "Yes. He handles the coding. I do everything else."

"Is there somewhere we can talk privately?" I asked before Hugo pissed her off any further.

"You have a warrant?" she asked.

Hugo handed her a copy, which she quickly read. From the speed at which she determined it was legitimate, she'd either seen a few before, or was taking our word for it. I wondered if she'd insist on having her lawyer involved, but she turned and led us through the doorway into the offices.

A center aisleway stretched across a large area of cubicles, where dozens of mostly young people labored away on computers. Everyone wore headphones or earbuds, and the dress code appeared to be anything goes, providing it covered the essential body parts. I'd never seen so many colors of dyed hair in one place.

Sienna continued to the back, where a row of actual offices looked out over the street and surrounding hills. Her office was in the corner, and she offered us seats opposite her desk.

"You understand privacy laws restrict us with what information we can share," she said, sitting in her high-tech-looking office chair.

"This is a murder inquiry," Hugo said. "The woman named in the warrant, Hailey Carter, is dead, and the man she met last night through your dating app could well be her killer. At a minimum, he was the last person to see her alive, apart from the killer."

Sienna appeared noticeably stunned. "Okay, well, of course we'll help you in any way we can. I was merely pointing out the limitations legally placed upon us."

I noted she'd switched from "my company" to "us" and "we" now she'd learned someone was dead.

"We need the name of the man she arranged to meet," I said.

Sienna nodded and focused on her computer. We waited. A few

moments later, I heard a ding, like a message had arrived. Sienna studied her screen and typed a reply. We waited awkwardly for another minute until finally, a printer whirred on a credenza, and a sheet of paper fed into the tray.

"Do you need Miss Carter's contact information?" Sienna asked.

"Yes," Hugo responded.

We had most of her details, but it was a good idea to check the email address she'd used. With another warrant, we should be able to access her email records from a computer. Although we hadn't found a laptop at her condo, so she may have used her phone for everything. Or her work computer. We'd need to check that, too.

The printer whirred again.

"How about the messages between the two of them?" Hugo asked.

"You know that would violate our privacy agreement," Sienna replied.

"Can you tell us where they'd arranged to meet?" Hugo asked.

"That information would be in the messages, detective."

"Investigator," Hugo corrected sharply.

He was usually better at charming the pants off pretty ladies, but something about Sienna Monroe must have irritated him from the get-go.

"If you happened to mention a spot some of your app users like to frequent on first dates, Miss Monroe, you'd be saving us an enormous amount of time," I said. "I'm presuming the expedited arrest of someone who may be targeting users of your dating app would be in your best interests?"

Sienna did the slight eyebrow raise in my direction, then turned her attention to her computer screen.

"I've heard Seabreeze Cellars in Dana Point is popular these days," she said, then got up from her chair and handed Hugo the two sheets from the printer.

He gave me a questioning look. I nodded. I knew the wine and cocktail bar on Del Prado.

"Thank you for your help, Miss Monroe," I said. "We can show ourselves out."

She nodded and returned to her chair. "Good luck with your investigation."

"One more thing," I said from the doorway. "Mind if I snap a quick picture?"

Sienna shrugged her shoulders. "I suppose that's okay."

I quickly took the picture of the fancy office with the owner of OC Match looking at me with a puzzled expression.

"Why do you need that?" she asked.

"So we can show who we served the warrant to," I said.

Which was true. Just not a legal requirement on our part.

"Garrett Caldwell," Hugo said, reading from one of the pages as we left the building.

I took out my cell phone and called Sarge.

"Martinez," he answered.

"Sir, can you run a name through DMV for us?"

The silence I took to mean yes.

"Garrett Caldwell. We have an address on Via Valle in Dana Point, sir."

We'd reached the car with the sound of distant typing in my ears before Sarge said anything.

"2023 Toyota Tacoma four-door. That your guy?"

"Matches the vehicle that arrived with Hailey and left just before eleven p.m. He's suspect number one, sir."

"Bring him in," Martinez responded, and hung up.

5

Hugo's a foodie. I'm not. That's not to say I don't like food, because I do, but I'm a fussy eater, which makes ordering everything except dessert a pain in the ass. He took the freeway back and detoured into San Juan Capistrano, stopping at a food truck he liked. He chatted away to the woman in Spanish, the cook waved to him with familiarity, and they both seemed quite excited about his visit.

I ordered Baja fish tacos with only fish and cheese, and they both looked at me like I'd ruined their day. Hugo just shrugged his shoulders. My Spanish wasn't fluent, especially when they spoke really fast, but I got the gist of the banter that came next and had the three of them laughing. Something about the weird *chica* with the funny accent.

It was a little after two p.m. when we parked outside a house on the south side of Dana Point. I'd always thought all the homes on the bluffs overlooking PCH and the water were considered Capistrano Beach, but Garrett Caldwell's place had a Dana Point address. Regardless, it was about a quarter of a mile as a crow flies from where we found Hailey Carter's body.

The home looked to have three or four bedrooms in the typical stucco and wood style of beach homes built in the '60s and '70s. A single garage door filled half the lower level, with an entry porch to the left. Upstairs, sliding glass doors opened to a balcony overlooking the street. We got out, and I snapped a picture, leaving it in the car to process.

We both unclipped the security straps on our sidearms as we approached the front door. The Toyota Tacoma was parked in the driveway, along with a Honda Accord. I rang the bell, and we waited. After a few moments, I heard two male voices shout something incoherent before the door opened.

"Hey," said a young man who didn't look like the DMV picture we had of Garrett Caldwell. This guy wore board shorts, a short-sleeved checkered pattern, a collared shirt, and no shoes.

"Is Garrett Caldwell home?" I asked.

The man, who was probably around my age, eyed Hugo's hand resting on his holstered sidearm.

"Umm, yeah. Who are you guys?"

We slowly pulled out our badges and held them up.

"OCSD Investigators Cromwell and Fuentes. Caldwell?" I reiterated.

"Okay," he said before turning around. "Garrett! Dude, there are a couple of cops down here looking for you, man."

I listened carefully for sounds of a back door opening, but after a few minutes, footsteps plodded down the stairs, and Caldwell appeared. He also wore board shorts along with a surf company T-shirt, and I noticed a silver chain around his neck with a small pendant. It looked like the letters P and K, but it was almost hidden by the hem at the neckline of his shirt, so I couldn't be certain.

"Who's here?" he asked.

"OCSD Investigators Cromwell and Fuentes," I repeated. "Are you Garrett Caldwell?"

"Yeah," he replied. "Shit. Are my parents okay?"

"This isn't about a family member," I assured him. "Were you at the Seabreeze Cellars wine bar last night?"

"Yeah, why?"

"You were there with Hailey Carter?" I continued.

He nodded, frowning. "Umm, yeah. I think that was her name. What is this about?"

"Miss Hailey Carter was found dead this morning at Capo Beach, sir. We need you to come with us."

It wasn't Hugo-level intimidation, but I think I sold the line pretty well. Caldwell looked nearly as shocked as his friend.

"Dead? Are you serious? How?" Caldwell asked.

"Wait, are you arresting him?" the roommate asked.

"No," I said firmly. "We're asking Mr. Caldwell to come to the station with us to discuss the matter."

"So he doesn't have to go with you?" the roommate persisted.

Caldwell held up a hand. "It's okay, man. I didn't do anything wrong, so I've nothing to hide. She was perfectly fine when I left her."

"Can we see some ID?" Hugo directed at the roommate.

"Mine? What do I have to do with any of this?"

"You seem eager to put yourself right in the middle of our discussion with Mr. Caldwell," Hugo replied. "ID."

"It's cool, Brandon," Caldwell said. "I need to grab my wallet, anyway."

He started back inside the house, with Brandon following. Hugo and I looked at each other. Caldwell didn't appear like a guy about to run, but this would be his chance. The house backed up to a slope leading down to Via Canon, which led to the freeway exit onto PCH. Plenty of places to hide, but we'd have the area swarming with deputies pretty quickly.

It didn't matter, as he returned right away, tucking a wallet into his pocket. While the roommate showed Hugo his ID, I stepped back and snapped another photograph. This time of the entryway and all three men.

"Am I coming with you or following in my car?" Caldwell asked.

I liked the idea of having his pickup at the station for an easy inspection if the inquiry required, but it was also another opportunity for him to make a break. The last thing we needed was a high-speed car chase across Orange County, and he was currently our primary suspect. Our only suspect.

"Come with us," Hugo replied, obviously on the same page. "Someone will run you home afterwards."

On the ride to the station, we learned Caldwell worked from home, doing ad copy for an advertising agency based in LA. He probed us for details regarding the murder, but we remained vague and waited until we were all seated in the interview room, where we'd be recorded. After Hugo made the usual introductions and comments for the tape, we began.

"Walk us through yesterday evening, please, Mr. Caldwell," my partner said.

The suspect didn't appear to be nervous at all. Concerned, maybe. I couldn't distinguish if that was empathy for the victim, or worry for himself. Either way, he was appropriately somber and polite.

"It was a first date," Caldwell began. "We met through an online app. Had drinks at a wine bar in town, then dinner, and finally a short walk on the beach. I left from there."

"Can you give us times and locations?" I asked. "We're constructing a timeline of Hailey's movements throughout the evening."

"Sure. As best I can recall," he replied. "We met at seven-thirty at Seabreeze Cellars on Del Prado. I think it was about an hour later when we walked around the corner to Surfside Grill." He paused and thought for a moment. "I'm guessing it was around ten when we left for Capo Beach. It was definitely a little after eleven when I went back to Seabreeze for a nightcap. I remember because they close at eleven thirty, so I sat at the bar for a while, had one drink, then went home."

"Did you drive separately for all of this?" Hugo asked.

Caldwell nodded. "Yeah. I had my truck, and she drove a…" He frowned and thought again. "I guess I don't remember what it was. A small car. Red, I remember that. It was red."

"Where did you park for the wine bar?" Hugo asked.

"Which time?" Caldwell countered.

"Both."

"Violet Lantern the first time," the suspect replied. "But farther down across Santa Clara. When I came back, I snagged a spot out front on Del Prado."

"What about Hailey?" Hugo asked. "Did you see where she parked?"

"Umm, I'm not sure. On Del Prado I think. That's right, when we walked back from the restaurant, we passed her car, and I jogged to mine as it was a lot farther away. Then I followed her to the beach."

"Where did you park there?" Hugo asked.

My partner was keeping his tone conversational, as though he was simply recording details of Hailey's movements. Sticking to the reasoning we'd given Caldwell. Naturally, we were actually looking for holes or flaws in his story. So far, everything had happened exactly as he said from the little we knew.

"Near the footbridge."

"And this was after ten?" Hugo asked.

Caldwell nodded. "I can't be certain, but I'd say it was sometime just after ten."

"Beach closes at ten," Hugo pointed out.

Caldwell shrugged. "If you lock up everyone who sneaks down to the state beach after ten, half of Dana Point will be behind bars."

I laughed. "No kidding, huh? So, whose idea was the walk?"

"Hers," he replied.

"But you left before her. Alone," Hugo said.

"Yes."

"So, what happened during the walk?"

"We walked to the RV park and back."

"And then?" Hugo continued.

"We said goodnight, and I left," Caldwell replied. "She told me she wanted to chill for a few minutes." He took a couple of breaths and rubbed his brow. "Man, I guess I should have insisted on staying, but I didn't want to appear pushy, you know?"

"Did you make plans to see each other again?" I asked.

He shook his head. "No. I mean, she was cool, and a pretty girl. But there didn't seem like there was any spark from her side. Honestly, I was surprised she suggested the walk. I thought maybe I'd misread the vibe, but I think she was mostly interested in my house."

"Your house?" Hugo questioned.

"Yeah. It came up over dinner that I'd bought the place with a few friends. She seemed real interested in how that had worked out, what with house prices being insane around here. Only way we could buy anything was to do it as a group."

"Great idea," I responded. "Must be tricky finding enough friends you trust who also qualify for the loans and whatnot."

He nodded, so I moved on to the question I was working toward.

"Have you done any work on the place yourself? Are you handy like that?"

Caldwell laughed. "No chance. I can barely hang a picture without help."

We spent another hour going through his story over and over in different ways. He even showed us the message exchange he'd had with Hailey in the OC Match app. It was close to five by the time we asked Sarge for a deputy to run Caldwell home. All we could do was thank him and let him know we may have more questions.

"So he had plenty of time to kill her, right?" Captain Bradley asked when we sat opposite her desk for the debrief she requested.

"They're at the beach for forty minutes before Caldwell leaves alone," Hugo replied. "So, yes. In theory, he has plenty of time to knock her out, drag her out to the framework, and tie her down. But not enough time for him to set up the structure. Not to mention, where did any of it come from?"

"Maybe he set up all that beforehand," Bradley suggested. "So all he had to do was take her out to it."

I'd printed off a copy of Rosa's picture of the crime scene, and now it was bringing back my memory of Hailey on the frame all too clearly. I shuddered.

"He's dressed exactly the same when he leaves, and his hair doesn't appear to be wet," I pointed out. "We double-checked, and his pickup doesn't come back later. It wasn't parked on PCH yesterday, either."

"People would have spotted the framework in the water if it was erected before dark," Hugo added. "Which means it had to have been placed there between sunset and 10:15 p.m. when the two of them show up. People using the fire pits and the bathrooms nearby would make it impossible to carry anything into the water for most of the evening."

"But the metal and concrete-filled buckets could have been brought in anytime through the state park entrance," Bradley said. "Caldwell could have been there earlier in the evening. Maybe he set it all up before their date."

"Those buckets are five-gallon contractor size, ma'am," I replied. "Filled with concrete, they weigh around one hundred pounds each. It's not like he was running up and down Capo Beach with these things flung over his shoulder."

She frowned at me.

"So he had help," Hugo said, which was good, as the captain didn't appear to be too happy with me. As usual.

"Or the supplies were brought in by boat," I suggested.

"Isn't it too shallow there?" Hugo asked, looking at me.

"Not too shallow for the draft of a small boat, but the swells rolling would make it challenging," I replied. "It wouldn't be easy moving hundred-pound buckets and metal sections into the water, but it would be possible."

"So we should see if Caldwell has a boat, or access to one," Hugo suggested.

Captain Bradley sighed. "And there's always the chance Caldwell's telling the truth, and she was fine when he left her."

Hugo and I looked at each other. Bradley was echoing a point we'd already discussed after the suspect had left. Which, if true, left us absolutely nowhere with the case.

6

It was past eight by the time I'd dropped by Seabreeze Cellars and Surfside Grill on my way home. Both had made their CCTV available for me to look at without requiring a warrant. I'd send someone back with paperwork to make copies later, but we needed to corroborate Caldwell's story as soon as possible. Which I was able to do. Hailey appeared to be relaxed in her date's presence, and while neither's body language suggested things were moving along quickly, there was laughter and conversation from what I could see. All the times matched what Caldwell had told us.

I hung my blazer on a peg by the door and switched the lights on. Furious scurrying from across the living room was followed by dead silence. I laughed.

"It's me, Roger. It's okay."

I walked over to a rustic wood credenza, an addition to my little cottage in the past few weeks. Along with the ten-week-old harlequin cross rabbit.

"Hey, mate, how was your day?" I asked, gently opening the right side door.

He stepped to the edge of the cupboard, then hopped down to the rug, lifting his little front paws onto my knee. His cute little nose twitched, and I petted his head while he looked up at me with his dark brown eyes. Each time I gently stroked my hand over him, his long ears sprung back up. He was not much bigger than the palm of my hand. I picked him up and took him with me to the kitchen.

"Ready for some greens?"

Cradling the rabbit in one arm against my chest, I opened the refrigerator door to see what we both had available for dinner. It looked like Roger had more options than I did. That wasn't surprising. He was the first pet who I was solely responsible for, and I was paranoid I'd find some bizarre way to prematurely end his life.

I'd stewed over the idea of having a dog or a cat for ages. I craved company, but I was avoiding members of the opposite sex. Mainly for their safety. My fiancé had ended up at the bottom of the Pacific Ocean after a boating accident. At least most of him had. A piece of Paul had washed up earlier this year. Regardless, I'd concluded that a dog would be perfect from my point of view, but not theirs. I was gone far too much to leave a mutt alone all day in the house. A cat would be fine, but I already had plenty of people in my life who barely tolerated me, and I didn't need to come home to another. Hence the rabbit.

After seeing an ad for a rescue center in Fountain Valley called the Bunny Bunch, I went by on my day off, and Roger chose me. A little ball of fur came straight over when his brothers and sisters remained wary over the other side of the run. The lady then explained what it took to look after a rabbit in the house, and none of it seemed to conflict too badly with my unpredictable schedule. The fact that they were easily litter box-trained and their poops were little pellets of recycled vegetables was the clincher.

The woman then sent me away to rabbit-proof my house, purchase all the necessary equipment, and fill out an alarming amount of paperwork designed to scare off uncommitted adopters. By the time I returned to collect my bunny, I'd protected every accessible electrical wire in plastic wrap, bought a very fancy hutch disguised as a credenza, and stocked up on alfalfa hay, pellets, greens, carrots, and an assortment of toys.

So now Roger, who weighed a couple of pounds, had food to last him through the apocalypse, and I was staring at a frozen cheese pizza or slightly stale cereal.

Setting him down on the hardwood floor, he slipped and slid around while I tore off a few lettuce leaves. I put them in a ceramic dessert bowl and placed it on the large area rug in the living room. Roger struggled for grip with his furry feet on the hardwood, but flew to the bowl once he found traction on the woven rug. With his little front feet in the bowl, he munched away like he hadn't been fed for days.

Turning on my toaster oven, I unwrapped the pizza while I kept an eye on the rabbit. Just watching the little guy made me smile. We were only a fortnight into our roommate situation, but so far he'd brightened my mood when I came through the front door each evening. I just hoped he wasn't too bored home alone all day after being with his siblings since birth. Of course, that also involved some shithead dumping the litter in a cardboard box by a dumpster, so life wasn't all fun and games before me. The big test would come when he was old enough to be neutered. If he forgave me for having his manhood removed, then we should be able to overcome anything.

Popping the pizza into the preheated toaster oven, I pulled my laptop from my backpack, set it on the dining table, which doubled as a desk, and turned it on. While it booted I poured myself a glass of wine from the cheap box in the fridge. Roger was still eagerly mowing through his lettuce, so I sat at the table and logged into the sheriff's office secure server.

My intention had been to go over the little information we had so far on Hailey Carter's murder, but as often happened, I found myself pondering another case. I had very few recollections of what happened during the storm in which my fiancé, Paul, went over the side of his family's Four Winns cuddy cabin cruiser. For a long time, my stupid brain refused to release any memories beyond the fact we'd gone out on the water for the day and been caught in a storm with engine trouble. An unfortunate blow to the head during an altercation with a suspect had jarred loose a few more details, but introduced a whole new set of questions. Mainly around Gabriella Castillo.

The Castillo family had played the role of Orange County's mafia for decades. Her grandfather was in jail for a series of charges, from tax evasion to handling stolen property. The district attorney had stacked up everything and anything they had on the man to get him convicted for so many minor offenses, he'd ended up with a twelve-year sentence. He was guilty of far worse crimes, but at least he was off the streets. Which put his son, Gabriella's father, Ramon Castillo, in charge of the family's businesses.

The Criminal Investigation Bureau was continually chasing Ramon, but he was slipperier than his father. He maintained a strong presence with his legitimate businesses and let his lieutenants handle the illegal stuff. But how his daughter fit into all of this was the part that interested me.

"It had to be her," Paul told me when I'd asked why he'd cheated on me with Gabriella Castillo. A girl I'd gone to school with.

At least, they were the words my fragmented mind allowed me to hear. When I'd still been a deputy, I'd seen his car outside her house while I'd been helping CIB with a stake-out, so I knew there'd been something going on. But the confrontation on the boat trip was a shattered mess of memories. Also, pursuing any inquiries about their relationship had been a double-edged sword for me. People like Captain Bradley already suspected me of having more to do with Paul's death than met the eye, and my lack of recollection didn't help. If it came out that he'd been seeing Castillo, I had a major motive, and the fingers would start pointing once again. But I had to know.

I ran a check on Gabriella Castillo to see if anything had come up since the last time I'd looked into her DMV and police records. She'd been arrested a few times in college, but nothing had ever stuck. Her attorneys had made a DUI go away, which wasn't easy to do.

One new item popped up. She had a speeding ticket. Sixty-five in a fifty-five on PCH. Which meant she was really going at least seventy. She'd asked for a court date instead of doing traffic school, no doubt hoping the citing officer wouldn't show up. Or, knowing Daddy would make sure he didn't. The hearing was on Monday.

From the other side of the room, Roger took off running at breakneck speed. He was a furry blur, shooting over the large living room area rug before turning and using the bedroom wall and door like a wall of death, banking before flying back across the room behind the couch. Running out of rug, he slithered across the hardwood toward the front door, his little legs unsuccessfully fighting for traction. He finally slowed to a stop and changed direction, feet still thrashing like a four-wheel-drive car on ice as he clawed his way back to the rug.

Once on the grippy surface, he leaped in the air and kicked his back legs, spinning around and landing facing the other way. He hopped a 180 and came over to me. I reached down and picked him up, setting him in my lap. His little heart was pounding a million miles an hour.

"Get that out of your system?" I asked him as he panted for breath.

The first time he'd done a crazy session around the house, I figured he was terrified of something, and I ran to the computer in search of answers. Apparently, it was common for young rabbits to tear around, and it was good for them. The goofy leaps in the air were called "binkies" and suggested the bunny was happy and content in his environment. I'd gone from scared I'd done something to freak Roger out to incredibly happy.

The toaster dinged, so I got up and set Roger in his litter box on the way to the kitchen. He was doing well with his house training, but I noticed he tended to pop out a pellet or ten sometimes after he'd run around. Cutting the pizza into four slices, I slid dinner onto a plate and tore off a section of paper towel. After topping off my wine, I headed for the couch.

"Did you do your business, mate?" I asked the rabbit.

It appeared he had because he hopped out and followed me. Sitting down, I scooped him up and placed him on my lap, then turned on the TV with the remote. The local nine p.m. news was on, and they were leading with the mysterious drowning death of Hailey Carter at Capo Beach. I groaned. The television news was usually good about waiting until we released the name, so I presumed her parents had been given the awful news. The talking head carried on with the story, consisting of nothing more than the headline, followed by a bunch of questioning statements and a bit of background on Hailey.

Roger settled in and began nibbling the hem of my shirt.

"Oi. Quit that," I urged as the TV switched to an interview with Hailey's roommate.

Melissa Sanchez spoke through teary eyes, wearing a UC Irvine sweatshirt. She said the usual stuff about it being unbelievable and what a wonderful woman her best friend was. So far, the beach footage was of the Crime Unit's tent, and not of the platform in the water. I was sure it would surface later, but for now, the channel was being respectful to the victim, and our investigation. "Woman strapped to frame and slowly drowned in coastal waters" would start a panic up and down the beach cities.

Promising to bring the viewers more information as soon as they had it, the news moved on to something else, and so did I. Finding a rerun of an old weekly show from when I was a kid, I ate pizza, sipped wine, and talked to the rabbit who'd fallen asleep in my lap. Eventually, my mind circled back to Hailey, and my stomach tightened. The image of her in the water was staying with me now, and I wondered what would motivate a person to do that to her. If it was Garrett Caldwell, then he'd planned it long before he'd secured a date with Hailey. So did that mean it had nothing to do with her personally, and she'd simply drawn the short straw?

But Caldwell had told us the walk on the beach had been her

idea. Which, if it was, may have been the worst decision of her soon-to-be-ended life, and he was innocent. If he'd lied, then he was probably the killer. Yet, we still couldn't explain any of the timing.

It was 2:13 a.m., according to the clock on the microwave, when I woke to find the TV on a 1960s western, drool down my chin, and a damp spot in my lap where Roger had peed.

7

———————

Running in Dana Point wasn't much fun. The city was built on a hillside, and my house was halfway up it. No matter which direction I went, I faced a large amount of elevation change. The good part at this time of year was I could enjoy the dawn as I made the three-and-a-half-mile loop around town. We had an amazing climate, where even in the summer months, the overnight dipped into the mid-sixties. A perfect temperature to go running with distant views of the ocean from various points on my route.

When I made it home, I let Roger out while I showered and ate breakfast, then put him away in his fancy credenza hutch with a good supply of hay. When he was older, I hoped to leave him roaming the house all day, but for now I didn't trust that I'd rabbit-proofed everything needed, or that he wouldn't chew my couch to death. Feeling an urgency to get to the station, I skipped my PC Beans drive-thru in favor of a second cup from my single-serve coffee maker at home.

With backpack and travel mug in hand, I strode into the office, ready to attack Hailey Carter's case. Five minutes after arriving, having read the summation of the autopsy report that had been delivered overnight, I felt the same sense of despair as when I'd been next to the victim's body in the water.

"Anything new?" Hugo asked, breezing past me and taking his seat.

"Autopsy," I replied.

"Cliff notes," he requested as he logged into his computer.

"Drowned, as we thought. Lots of small abrasions on the back of her shoulders, torso, and thighs. Probably from being dragged onto the frame. Bruising on her temple was most likely from a punch."

"Caldwell didn't have any cuts or bruising on his knuckles," Hugo said, peeking around our monitors.

"You looked?" I asked, annoyed I hadn't thought to pay more attention.

He nodded. "He had well-kept nails, too. Doubt he did any metal work lately."

"Traces of a black fabric in her hair being sent for analysis," I continued. "No skin under fingernails. No defensive wounds. The damage around her wrists and ankles was from struggling against the zip ties."

"Sexual assault?" Hugo asked.

I shook my head. "Thankfully, no. And no evidence of recent sexual activity."

"Time of death?"

"Between midnight and two a.m."

"Hmm," Hugo grunted as though he were about to say more, but sat back instead.

"What?" I asked, sliding my chair to the side to keep his face in view. I wanted to see his expression.

He tapped his pen on his notepad and swiveled slowly back and forth in his chair. "I don't see how Caldwell did this."

I desperately wanted to offer a counterargument, but my partner was right. The young man had opportunity, but not the means or any obvious motive. And there was something else that didn't make sense for Garrett Caldwell to be guilty.

"He'd have to either be the cockiest bugger of all time, or not nearly as clever as his university degree suggests," I said. "Whoever killed this poor woman put a lot of planning into her murder. Why would he then make himself the most obvious suspect?"

Hugo nodded. "Be a lot harder and take more planning to make it look like Caldwell did it."

"Not to mention he left the beach before eleven," I pointed out. "Although his alibi only checks out until he leaves the wine bar at eleven thirty. We can't be sure he went home."

"So he disabled the victim and hid her at the beach. Went to the wine bar for half an hour, then picked up ridiculously heavy buckets of concrete and metal framework, returned to the beach in some manner we can't see him, set it all up, and left her to drown."

"Maybe he's a good multitasker," I replied with a weak attempt at levity.

"Then left again without being seen," Hugo added.

I blew out my cheeks and retrieved my instant pictures and the print from the Crime Unit from my backpack. I spread them out on my desk. An idea I hadn't tried before came to me, and I snapped a picture of the Crime Unit photo I'd printed. Seeing as it was my brain trying to trick itself, I assumed having the instant pic wouldn't make any difference. But on the other hand, the various departments in my jumbled skull could be like most organizations and not communicate very well.

"Okay. Priorities?" Hugo asked, wheeling his chair to the side to face me. I watched his eyes scan my pictures. "You good?" he added.

"Yeah," I replied, a little too quickly. I took a breath and lowered my voice, although we were the only two in the room. "The crime scene got a bit wobbly, but Rosa's pictures seem to be keeping me straight."

I could see the concern in his eyes. My system minimized the issue, but it couldn't be easy working with a partner who, at any given time, may or may not have a full grasp of the case. It was hard not to wonder if the only reason he didn't request another partner or turn me in was my knowledge of his personal life. I hoped not. I'd come to rely on and trust Hugo.

"Good," he said. "So, what are our priorities?"

I scanned my pictures to make sure everything felt anchored, and then checked my notes.

"We need access to her work computer," I began. "Talk to a co-worker and her boss. See if there were any issues there."

"The roommate seemed to think Hailey's ex was a great guy, but we need to follow up," Hugo added. "We'll need help with the metal supply companies. There's too many for us to cover alone."

"And we can't forget the boat angle," I said.

He looked at me. Hugo was not a boater, but I'd grown up spending plenty of time in and on the local waters.

"Where do we start?" he asked.

I shook my head. "I've no idea, to be honest. We should talk to harbor patrol and see if they have any thoughts on how we can trace small-boat traffic."

"Alright," he said. "I'll talk to Bradley about help on the metal. You handle harbor patrol, and get a warrant for her work computer. I'll get background on Kwon and see if we can interview him."

Hugo shuffled his chair back behind his monitor before getting up and heading for Captain Bradley's office. I looked up the number of my friend I knew with Dana Point's harbor patrol and called him.

"Yeah," came a sleepy voice.

"Oh, bollocks, Nate, did I wake you up?"

"This Kat?"

"Only if I didn't wake you."

He laughed. "You're fine. Day off, but I gotta get up, anyway. What's up?"

"Did you hear about the body on Capo Beach yesterday?"

"I think everybody did, Kat," he replied, sounding far more awake. "That kinda shit is big news around here. Heard she wasn't exactly *on* Capo Beach. You get the case?"

"Yeah, that's why I'm calling."

"How can I help?"

"We think there's a chance the perp may have used a boat. Is there any way to track small-boat traffic in the area during the night?"

Nate took a moment. "I assume you mean track, as in recorded data instead of real-time radar?"

"Yeah. We need to know if a small boat was near the beach on Wednesday night."

"Unless it had AIS, the Automatic Identification System used on larger ocean-going vessels, I don't know of any way, Kat."

"That's what I figured," I replied. "I'll request the CCTV footage, but we don't know where the boat could have originated from. Heck, we don't even know whether there was a boat, so it's all a shot in the dark."

"I hear you," he said. "Sorry I can't be more help, but maybe you'll get lucky with the jetty cam. It does record everything leaving the harbor."

"We'll check it out. Thanks, Nate."

"You surfing this weekend?"

I groaned. "Unlikely, unless we put this case to bed. Maybe first thing tomorrow if I get up extra early. Cheers, Nate."

We hung up, and I started a request for the CCTV footage from the harbor, beginning with any camera with a view of the entrance. Hugo came back and didn't look pleased.

"She in a mood?" I asked.

He rolled his eyes. "She's pissed we let Caldwell walk out of here."

"What could we hold him on?" I scoffed.

"She knows we couldn't," he said, taking his seat. "I'm sure she's got the brass up her ass over it. Anyway, she's getting us help to visit the various metal supply companies in each city. I have to send her a picture of the framework so they know what would have been ordered."

"Bloody hell," I muttered. "We don't need pictures of the execution frame getting out there."

"How else do we let them know what to look for?" Hugo asked.

"A materials list," I replied.

He peeked around the monitors and frowned.

"X number of feet of three-inch, quarter wall, box tube steel, etcetera," I explained.

"Was that in English?" Hugo grinned.

"Have you ever cut a piece of metal or sawed a two-by-four in your life?" I asked, shaking my head.

"I suppose you have?" he responded.

"I helped my dad refit and modify the gym a few times. We built him a new office, made steel frames to hang punching bags, and I helped remodel the bathroom in my cottage."

"Then you handle the list for Bradley, and I'll do whatever you were about to do."

"Warrant for the computer," I said.

"On it," he replied, so I went back to my phone and called Rosa Bautista at the crime lab. It rang a long time, and I expected voicemail.

"Hey, Kat," she said, taking me by surprise.

"Rosa, sorry to bother you. I know you must be buried, but has anyone measured the framework yet?"

"I think so, but nothing's in a report. We won't get finished with it until probably tomorrow."

"I just need the sizes of the box tube so we can look into suppliers," I said.

"Okay, can I have one of my crew measure everything and email you the dimensions?" Rosa offered.

"Perfect. Give them my mobile number if they have questions."

"Alright. It should only take him fifteen minutes or so. Any leads, Kat?"

"Nothing much. Her date was with her on the beach, but he left, and we don't see how or when he could have constructed all this frame business. No priors. Regular working bloke. First date, so no history. We have an ex we're going to talk to."

"Sounds like you've got your work cut out," Rosa said glumly. "I'll get my tech working on the dimensions."

"Thanks," I replied, and we hung up.

Hugo was on the phone, talking to someone about a warrant for Hailey's computer, so I searched our database for Ryan Kwon. Three options came up, and I matched the phone number Hailey's roommate, Melissa, had given us. Kwon's home address was in Laguna Beach, as she'd said. I considered calling him, but that would give him too much warning if he was involved. But we'd also waste a lot of time driving to Laguna and back if he wasn't there.

I searched for his profile on social media and found one with a picture that appeared to be the same guy as on the driver's license. His feed was mainly full of paintings and sculptures, with a few shots of him with other people at what looked like a gallery. I checked the tags. Shoreline Gallery of Laguna Beach. Next came an internet search for the gallery, and after clicking around, I found several pictures of Ryan Kwon. He appeared to be a member of the sales staff. I checked the gallery's address. It was the same street number as his license address, except it had a "B" after it. He lived in an apartment in the same building.

"I have an address for Kwon," I told Hugo once he was off the phone.

"Want to see him first, or get the vic's computer?"

I thought for a moment while I looked back at Ryan Kwon's DMV record.

"Oh, bugger," I muttered, and thumbed through the notes I'd made while checking CCTV from PCH.

"What?" Hugo asked.

"Kwon drives a 2022 metallic blue bimmer," I replied, still double-checking myself.

"Okay. Sounds nice," Hugo said, standing and gathering his things.

"Remember when we were watching the CCTV yesterday?" I asked as I hunted for the footage on the server, then fast-forwarded to the spot I was looking for. "Look," I told him, pointing to my screen.

As I'd recalled, a BMW briefly pulled in at 10:36 p.m. It stayed there for less than a minute before driving away again.

I checked the license plate one more time. "That's Ryan Kwon's car."

"I vote we see him first," Hugo said as he walked toward the door.

"Seconded," I added, scrambling to gather up my pictures.

8

———————

The gallery opened at ten a.m. It was a few minutes to the hour when we arrived after trundling along in traffic on Pacific Coast Highway. The building was on the inland side of PCH, built into the steep hillside like most of Laguna Beach. An older wooden structure, the ground floor housed the gallery, with steps to the side leading to a thrift store above. On top of that were what appeared to be several apartments, which were undoubtedly accessed from the back of the building on Ramona Avenue.

"We could call the locals to cover the back," Hugo suggested after parking across the road from the gallery.

We were both amazed we'd found an open spot on PCH. Parking was notoriously difficult in the town built along the highway next to the sea. Homes and businesses packed every square inch, shoulder to shoulder, filling all buildable space, and in some cases, using tall pilings to create that footprint on an otherwise impossible grade.

"Or we wait for him to open the shop," I countered, looking at my watch.

Hugo pulled out of the precious parking spot and blended into traffic.

"We have time," he said. "Let's take a lap."

He turned left on Cleo, but had to continue to the second street back, Glenneyre. Ramona dead-ended at the Holiday Inn building, which occupied most of the end of the block. Heading north on Glenneyre, he turned left on Legion, accessing Ramona halfway down the hill to PCH. The back street was narrow, serving garages on top of the buildings along our right, and underneath many of the homes upslope on our left. The gallery building was easy to find as Kwon's metallic blue BMW sat in the short drive, nosed against one of two ancient-looking garage doors.

Hugo turned the car around and looped back to Pacific Coast Highway, where, needless to say, we'd lost our prime parking spot. He found another several hundred yards up the road. It was now after ten, so we crossed PCH at the Cleo crosswalk and approached on the gallery's side of the road to avoid being seen. An open sign now hung on the glass front door, so we strolled inside.

Unlike the spacious galleries with entire walls dedicated to one painting, Shoreline Gallery was packed full of art. Certain sections were dedicated to particular artists, and others appeared to be a mixture of examples from various people. We heard a cheery male voice from the back.

"Good morning! Please look around. I'll be right with you."

I checked for cameras, counting at least four covering every angle of the store. Hugo nodded toward the back, and we moved that way. A long counter divided the store from offices, one of which had a one-way glass window. The door was slightly ajar.

"Mr. Kwon?" Hugo asked.

"Yes, I'm just booting up the computer systems," the voice replied. "I'll be right there."

Hugo looked at me again and shrugged his shoulders, so we waited. I picked up a business card from a dispenser on the counter.

"Ryan Kwon - Manager," it said.

I pocketed the card and took the opportunity to snap an instant photo of the counter and office area. Hugo nudged me and pointed to a sign that said, "No photographs or video, please."

"Oops," I said, shaking the new photograph as it developed.

"I should arrest you," Hugo said, barely cracking a grin.

"Bloody hell, Hugo. You almost showed a sense of humor there," I replied with a smile.

He turned to the office. "Mr. Kwon, we're with the Orange County Sheriff's Department. Would you mind coming out here, please?"

This time, we were met with silence.

"You're kidding me," Hugo mumbled and strode behind the counter, pushing the office door open.

I followed my partner. The office was empty. I tried a side door, and it opened into a stairwell leading up.

"The bugger ran," I confirmed. "This must go to the apartments," I added, gesturing to the stairwell.

"Let's get the car," Hugo said, and started for the door.

"Call it in," I responded. "I'll go after him."

"No, Kat. Not alone," Hugo called back.

He was right, as usual. Protocol dictated we operated in pairs, but the guy had no priors, no gun license, and we were in Laguna Beach, not Central City, Santa Ana. He sold paintings for a living. He may also have maliciously drowned his ex-girlfriend, but we were two hundred yards from the ocean, so I didn't feel threatened.

"Get the car!" I shouted back. "Meet me up top."

I heard Hugo swearing in Spanish, but he didn't come after me. I bound up the stairs to a short hallway with three doors. One seemed to continue up the slope. The other two had the letters A and B on them. Unclipping the strap on my sidearm, I banged on each door.

"Orange County Sheriff's. Open up."

I banged again, and apartment A's door opened.

"What on earth is going on?" a middle-aged woman in a bathrobe demanded.

"Ryan Kwon?" I asked, keeping a hand on my service weapon.

"He's in B," she replied. "What's all this about?"

I banged on the other apartment door again. "Ryan Kwon. This is OCSD Investigator Cromwell. Open the door. Now."

"Oh my Lord," the woman babbled. "What has Ryan done?"

"Go back inside, ma'am," I said, and banged on the door to B once more.

No response.

I pointed at the only other door. "Where does that lead?" I asked the woman, who'd ignored my order and stayed in the hall.

"To the parking," she replied.

I ran to the door and pulled it open, expecting to see steps. What I found instead was a blur of human rushing my way. Before I could set my feet, I was bowled backwards, landing hard on my tailbone and sliding across the tile floor. I grasped at the wall, but my fingers found nothing to grab hold of.

The floor suddenly disappeared below my butt. Tumbling backwards, I rolled down the wooden stairs, coming to a stop halfway down when my feet jammed against one wall and my shoulder into the other.

The woman screamed. Ryan Kwon looked down at me in horror, then turned and ran. With all the chaos and distraction of Hailey Carter's case, I'd forgotten about the smack I'd taken to the jaw in the boxing ring. Now, crumpled in a heap in a stairwell, a hundred other aches and pains joined my jaw in one painful surge.

Untwisting myself, I scrambled up the steps past the woman, who was clutching her face in disbelief. Running through the open door, I bounded up the steps, exiting through another wooden door into the bright sunshine. I was standing next to the garages, and the blue BMW was gone. Running the few steps to the road, I saw the car disappear from view at the end of Ramona, turning left toward PCH.

Fumbling for my phone, I dialed 911 and asked to be put through to local dispatch.

Across the road from the Holiday Inn was a little place aptly named The Taco Stand. I was ready for a couple of Baja fish tacos by the time we were done dealing with the bathrobe woman, who turned out to be the gallery owner. She swore up and down that Kwon was a wonderful, reliable fellow, but couldn't explain why he'd run from us.

My body felt battered and bruised, and my ego had taken a further bashing from Hugo, who reminded me why we didn't go running after suspects on our own. I resisted telling him he could have come with me, but we both knew calling it in and letting uniforms do the chasing would have been by the book. Contrary to just about every TV detective show, we weren't supposed to bash in doors and chase criminals. We show up afterwards and investigate, keeping our suits neatly pressed and our bodies unscathed. Which was the way Hugo liked it.

"We've got it," he said, looking at his email on his phone.

I swallowed the rest of my taco and took a gulp of Diet Coke before throwing the rubbish away, then chasing after Hugo down the street. We'd been waiting on the formality of a search warrant for Kwon's apartment, so while the rest of Orange County's law enforcement watched for the blue BMW, we could finally look through his place.

Camille Langley was still frustrated by the earlier mayhem and having to work her own gallery alone, but she gave us the key to apartment B. We used the internal stairwell, climbing past the scuff marks my limbs had left on the walls.

Kwon's apartment was a small studio. Only two windows faced south, but the angled view of the ocean made up for the diminutive size. Working for the landlady undoubtedly made it affordable as well. I'm not sure what we thought we might find inside, but there certainly weren't any scraps of steel box tube or welders hidden in the closet. Ryan kept his place clean, tidy, and well-organized. His kitchen was stocked, and from the food in the fridge and cupboards, he clearly cooked for himself at least some of the time.

Unsurprisingly, the art on the walls were all originals by artists

I'd never heard of, although unless they were the *Mona Lisa* or a Monet, I wouldn't know them, anyway. At a guess, I'd say the art was worth far more than the furniture, which looked like nice hand-me-down stuff that vaguely matched a modern theme.

"Look at this," Hugo said from beside the queen-size bed.

He was pointing to a small framed picture, turned face-down. Using a nitrile-gloved hand, he picked up the frame, and we both studied the photograph of Ryan, his arms wrapped around Hailey Carter. They were laughing outside a restaurant I recognized in Laguna Beach.

"How long did the roommate say they'd been broken up?" Hugo asked.

"Five months," I replied.

Along with my crazy neurological issue of dropping certain memories came the opposing ability of successfully remembering details that stayed put in my mind.

"Long time to still have her picture on his bedside table," Hugo commented.

"Somebody hasn't moved on," I agreed.

I crouched down and peered underneath the bed. Two long, low plastic storage bins on wheels narrowly fit below the bedframe. I reached under and rolled them out. The first contained clothes, which at first I figured were winter-season outfits for Kwon, but then I realized they weren't his size. And they were women's clothes.

"Isn't this the jacket she's wearing in that picture?" I asked Hugo, holding up the garment.

He checked the picture. "Looks like it."

Things weren't stacking in Ryan Kwon's favor. He had motive as the jealous ex-boyfriend who witnessed Hailey out on a date, and his presence on PCH gave him the opportunity. We still lacked means, and any form of actual evidence tying him to her murder, but running from us made him look guilty as hell.

I returned the jacket to the storage bin and opened the second lid. This one was full of general odds and ends we all accumulate in the home. I found assorted cables, extension cords, an external hard drive, a bundle of pens held together with an elastic band, and a Ziploc stuffed with various office supplies. Plus, one more clear plastic bag.

"Hardly a smoking gun," I said to Hugo. "But worth comparing."

"What have you got?" he asked, having moved to the closet.

I held up the bag of zip ties I'd pulled from the storage bin.

He shrugged his shoulders. "Even I have some of those things at home."

I frowned at him. "Really? You know you need a pair of side cutters to trim the ends of them. You don't do tools."

He shook his head. "I've no idea what you just said, but the ones I have are reusable so they don't get cut."

I looked at the bag in my gloved hand. "These things are everywhere, aren't they?" I asked absentmindedly as I thought about zip ties. "But most of them that are readily available are cheap, shitty ones with plastic pawls."

"Plastic what?"

"The little tab that locks in place," I explained. "It's called a pawl."

He shook his head. "How would you possibly know that, Kat?"

"My dad whined about the lousy types he found locally and had to order some special from an aircraft supply place. They had stainless-steel pawls and were much stronger."

"You think the killer used these double-throw-down zip ties?" Hugo asked.

It was my turn to shrug my shoulders. "I don't know, but he meticulously planned everything else."

"Okay, but Kwon has the cheap kind, right?"

I nodded. "Yeah, and looking at these again, they're too small."

"Doesn't mean he didn't have more," Hugo pointed out.

"True," I agreed, looking over at the photograph Hugo had left upright on the bedside table.

The happy version of Hailey Carter stood in stark contrast to the other image now welded in my brain. I stood and stepped to the doorway from where I could capture most of the small studio apartment with my instant camera. I then sent Rosa an email asking for specifications on the zip ties used to strap the young woman down to the execution frame.

9

Kwon was still in the wind, and we were waiting to hear on everything else, so we drove to the offices of GilTech in Laguna Niguel after calling ahead. The city of Laguna Niguel touched the water between the northern part of Dana Point and the southern reaches of Laguna Beach. From there, it stretched inland, nestled in the rolling San Joaquin Hills before blending into Aliso Viejo, Mission Viejo, and Laguna Hills, creating an endless sea of housing and commercial development.

At the corner of Pacific Island Drive and Alicia Parkway, we found a standalone modern building of glass and block. We walked by the cars parked in front of the building to the side of two handicapped spots. The receptionist was expecting us and quickly led us upstairs, passing us off to another woman in a small cubicle in front of the corner office.

"Mr. Gil is expecting you," the second woman said, echoing the words of the receptionist. "Go right in," she offered, gesticulating to the open double doors.

A man I figured to be in his mid-thirties stood behind a large glass desk and greeted us. He was tall, slender, with a tanned, clean-shaven face. He wore business slacks and a crisp white button shirt with the sleeves rolled up to his elbows.

"Enrique Gil," he said, shaking our hands. "This is a dreadful reason to be meeting. We're all devastated here in the office."

We introduced ourselves and took the seats he offered across from his desk.

"Can I get you coffee? A water?" he offered.

"No, thank you," Hugo replied. "What is it you do here?"

We'd already looked up the company, but it was always good to hear it from the man himself.

"We specialize in surveillance technology. Mainly government-contract-type stuff we can't talk about," he replied.

"Cameras and listening devices?" I questioned.

He smiled at me. "Something like that. Our niche is drone-mounted equipment."

"You make the drones?" I asked.

Gil shook his head. "No, we outfit drones and other items with various forms of innovative surveillance technology."

I found the subject partly fascinating, but mostly terrifying. It would be interesting and eye-opening to learn more, but I suspected he couldn't tell us much, and it wasn't why we were there.

"What did Hailey do for the company?" Hugo asked.

"She was my executive assistant," he replied, pointing to the door. "She sat right outside my office. Hailey handled my calendar, travel, meeting schedule. Frankly, I'm lost without her."

Hugo glanced over his shoulder toward the cubicle we'd passed by. "Looks like you've filled the role already."

"Grace was our receptionist. She's filling in and trying to help me manage. The woman at the front desk is a temp." He lowered his voice, his brow creased. "I'm hoping Grace will work out, but she has big shoes to fill."

"How long did Hailey work for you?" I asked.

"A couple of years now," Gil replied. "I hired her when we expanded and moved into this building."

"A good employee, you'd say?" I asked.

"Absolutely. Like I said, I'm lost right now without her, and we're in the midst of delivering a big contract, so it's all go." He rubbed his forehead. "Do you have any idea who did this?"

"That's stuff we can't talk about," Hugo took a little too much delight in replying.

"Of course. Forgive me. It's all just such a shock."

"Hailey was here at work on Wednesday?" I asked.

Gil nodded.

"Normal day? Anything unusual?"

"Not that I noticed," he replied. "But like I said, we're swamped, so I may have been distracted."

"Are the employees currently working overtime?" Hugo asked.

"Some of us are, yes."

"Hailey?" Hugo asked.

"No, the office staff keep regular hours. It's been the development team, my manager, and me. We've been burning the midnight oil."

"Do you make everything here?" I asked.

"Oh no, we handle research, development, and testing. Once we go into production, it's all outsourced."

I tried picturing what that work might entail. My mind's eye conjured boffins in lab coats soldering wires in intricate circuit boards, but I doubted I was even close. The circuitry was probably CAD-designed and constructed in a series of automated machines.

"What do you know of Hailey's personal life, Mr. Gil?" Hugo was asking as I refocused.

"Not much, really," he replied. "We're a relatively small company, so everyone knows everyone here, but I try to maintain a professional relationship with my employees."

"To your knowledge, did she ever date anyone from the company?" Hugo pressed.

Gil rubbed his brow again. "Not that I know of, but my attention isn't on that sort of thing."

Hugo and I looked at each other and exchanged a subtle nod.

"I think that's all for now, Mr. Gil," I said. "We appreciate you seeing us on short notice. We'll collect Hailey's laptop and leave you in peace."

He stood. "If I can help in any other way, please let me know. Obviously, we can't bring Hailey back, but the culprit needs to pay for taking her from us."

I handed him one of my cards. "Mind if I take a picture?"

"Of me?" he asked, taking the card.

"Your office," I said, stepping back to the doorway.

"I guess that's okay," he said. "Although I don't know what that has to do—"

I took a quick picture before he could finish and retract his permission.

"Okay. Well, Grace has Hailey's laptop," he remarked. "Obviously, my IT team has wiped all the GilTech-related data and access. We left anything personal."

I frowned. "So her work email has been removed?"

He nodded. "Of course. It would be a violation of our NDA contracts to leave that on there."

"Our warrant was for the computer, not whatever you deemed okay to leave on the computer," Hugo retorted.

"Actually, according to my attorney, your warrant is for any personal data belonging to Hailey Carter, which is what we've left on the computer," Gil said.

His voice remained amiable, but his expression took on a challenging edge.

"What if she'd used her work email for personal communication?" Hugo asked.

"That would be against our company policy," Gil quickly responded.

"Okay," Hugo continued. "But what if she did use it for something personal?"

"Then I'll have her email account checked and will release anything deemed personal communications to you within forty-eight hours."

Hugo took a half-step forward.

"Thank you," I said. "Please let us know if you find anything."

Hugo hesitated, but then followed me out of the office. We weren't about to win an argument over the intricacies of the lawful extent of warrants in regards to intellectual property. That was above our pay grade, and we'd need to consult our own legal department.

Grace handed me a laptop with its power supply.

"Thanks," I said, and held her gaze for a moment.

Her hand lingered on the laptop. "You're welcome. Anything we can do to help."

We walked down the stairs and across the reception. I waited until we were outside to say anything.

"He give you a weird vibe?"

"Smarmy bastard," Hugo replied.

"Wedding ring," I said, relaying my observations. "Wife, no kids in the picture on the credenza."

We walked to the car, where I turned and snapped another picture. I then retrieved a large, clear plastic evidence bag from the trunk. As I was about to slip the laptop inside, I noticed the edge of a bright yellow sticky note protruding from between the screen and the body of the computer. I walked around to the passenger side and got into the car. Once hidden from view of the corner office, I hinged the laptop open and retrieved the note.

"Look at this," I said as Hugo slid into the driver's seat.

"A phone number?" he questioned.

"Grace must have put it in there," I replied.

"In case we had questions, I guess," Hugo said, closing his door.

"I don't know," I replied hesitantly, recalling her engaging stare and the way her fingers had purposefully held the computer a few seconds longer than necessary. "I think she has something to tell us."

Hugo started the car. "Text her and ask."

"Yeah," I said, keeping the sticky note and sealing the laptop in the evidence bag.

Hugo turned around, and I reached over to the back seat, setting down the bag.

"Hey," I blurted, glancing out the back window. "Hold up for a sec."

"What's up?" Hugo asked, braking to a stop.

"Can you reverse alongside the building?"

Hugo looked in the mirror. "I guess. Why?"

"Back up. You'll see."

He reversed beside the building to where a tall roll-up door was open with a van parked outside. Hugo stopped short so we could see around the van. Inside the building on the left was a counter for shipping and receiving, and farther into the building were partitioned-off rooms with sturdy doors, suggesting they protected hermetically sealed areas.

"Pull beyond the van," I said, and Hugo did so.

From the new vantage point, we could see the right side of the warehouse section. Benches lined two sides of a rectangular bay with a large tool chest atop a rolling cabinet at one end. The third side housed a series of metalworking equipment, including a bandsaw, a drill press, and a MIG welder.

"That's not the equipment I was expecting for a tech company making surveillance devices," I commented. "Looks more like an automotive or industrial workshop."

"Hardly rare for someone to be into off-road racing or motocross here in Southern California," Hugo said as he slowly pulled away. "But looks like Gil does have the gear needed to build a metal framework."

"We should get this address to whoever Bradley has hunting down the metal suppliers," I said, taking out my phone. "See if they had a delivery lately."

"Maybe they have those fancy zip ties, too," Hugo said, and grinned at me.

I rolled my eyes and typed a text to the number on the sticky note.

"Grace, this is OCSD Investigator Kat Cromwell. Call me on this number whenever you can."

I waited, watching the three dots fading in and out as she typed a reply, or at least contemplated one with the cursor in the text box. Hugo drove us to Crown Valley Parkway, heading south. After a few minutes, I gave up watching the screen.

"This feels like every possible suspect adds an element to the case, but none of them fit all the criteria," I complained.

"What does Gil drive?" Hugo asked. "See if we can place him at PCH in Capistrano Beach on Wednesday night."

I hadn't brought my laptop along, so I called the station and put it on speaker.

"Martinez."

"Sir, it's Kat and Hugo. Could you run a DMV search on Enrique Gil, please?"

"Address?" the sergeant asked.

"Good question. We only have a business address, sir."

"Stand by."

I waited while keyboard tapping filled our ears.

"I've got twenty-six Enrique Gils in Orange County, Kat."

"Between age thirty and forty, sir."

More typing.

"Gets you eleven."

"Between five-eleven and six-one, sir."

I waited.

"Three. Fullerton, Santa Ana, and Dana Point."

"Dana Point for a hundred," I replied, mimicking a TV game show I couldn't recall the name of.

Martinez didn't laugh.

"2023 Porsche Cayenne and a 2024 Aston Martin Vantage Roadster."

I looked at Hugo. "You see either of those in the car park?"

Hugo shook his head. "It was a white full-size in the primo spot."

I reached into my pocket with my free hand and pulled out the instant pictures I'd taken, selecting the one of the building.

"Almost looks like a rental," I commented. "Says '300' on the back."

"Chrysler 300," Hugo confirmed.

"Should I continue standing by for your next request, Cromwell?" Martinez asked. "Or may I go back to playing Candy Crush, as apparently that's all you think I do between your phone calls?"

I cringed. "Sorry, sir. We have a picture, but it's from an angle where I can't quite see all the plate."

"Then I suggest you get a better picture," Martinez replied.

"Yeah, of—" I began, but he'd already hung up.

"He didn't get to answer the two-hundred-dollar question," Hugo quipped dryly.

"He hates me," I muttered.

"He wouldn't take your call if he hated you," Hugo replied. "He tolerates you, which is as good as it gets with Martinez."

My phone chirped, and I unlocked it to see the sergeant's message. But it wasn't from him.

"Grace replied."

"What'd she say?" Hugo asked.

"'Can we meet after work?'" I relayed.

"Somebody wants to tell tales out of school," Hugo commented, drumming his fingers on the wheel. "I'll bet you a lunch that Gil either was or tried to be more than co-workers with Hailey."

"Yeah," I mumbled, busy typing a reply. "I'm not stupid enough to take that bet."

10

———————

Heading south on Crown Valley Parkway, we decided to return to the station to drop off the laptop and dig a little deeper into Enrique Gil. It was now mid-afternoon, two days after discovering Hailey Carter's body, and we had nothing but loose connections. Kwon had elevated himself to the top of the suspect list simply because he'd run from us, but so far the only thing tying him to the murder was his brief presence on PCH Wednesday night.

"We can't rule out the date," Hugo said as we approached the light for Camino Del Avion. "He can't account for his whereabouts during the night, and the vic never left the beach after he'd been with her."

"He didn't return by car," I added, thinking it through. "At least he didn't on PCH, and the park was closed, so he couldn't have driven inside."

"Walked in, or maybe your boat idea," Hugo added.

My phone rang, and I saw it was the station number.

"Cromwell," I answered, putting the call on speaker.

"Your man's been spotted," Martinez said without preamble. "Parking lot outside Gelson's in Monarch Plaza. Ripley and

Hanson are on-site. Turn your radio on and tell them what you want them to do."

"Will do. Thanks, Sarge," I replied to a dead line.

We usually kept the police radio in the car turned down or off to avoid hearing all the regular chatter, but Hugo turned it up, and I grabbed the mic.

"Ripley and Hanson, this is Sam 54 and 23. Over," I said, using our call signs.

"Ripley here, ma'am. We have the suspect's car under observation. Haven't seen suspect as yet. Over."

Hugo had already aborted the left turn on Camino Del Avion and was continuing to PCH.

"Observe and only apprehend if trying to leave. We're less than five minutes out. Over."

"Copy," came the brief response.

"Grocery shopping wouldn't be top of my priority list if I was on the lam," Hugo commented, switching on the grille lights but leaving the siren off.

"Stocking up for a road trip," I suggested.

Crown Valley curved right, then left down the hill, jogging around the Monarch Bay Plaza Shopping Center. Hugo turned left onto the entry road, where we drove behind a restaurant, a gas station, and an office building to the main parking for the grocery store and other businesses in the plaza. I spotted a patrol car by a Pilates studio, and Hugo pulled up alongside. I powered down my window, and the summer heat quickly swept inside the car.

"Over there," Hanson said from the passenger seat, pointing toward Gelson's. "Spotted the BMW and checked the plate, but haven't seen your guy."

"How long have you been here?" I asked.

"Thirty minutes or so," he replied. "We picked up food from Ichibiri. Noticed the BMW when we came out."

I looked over at Hugo. "What do you think?"

He shrugged his shoulders. "Think he saw you this morning?"

I scoffed. "Yeah. As he bowled me down the bloody stairs."

"That's right. Because you went after him alone, if I recall," he responded.

I rolled my eyes.

"I'll do a sweep inside Gelson's," Hugo said. "Have the deputies move closer to the exit of the parking lot. You watch Kwon's car in case he's not in the market."

I nodded and relayed the plan to the two patrol officers as Hugo took his handheld radio and got out, walking toward the grocery store.

"This is Sam 23 to team at Monarch Bay, switch to operations channel. Over," Hugo said over the radio.

Reaching back, I rifled through my backpack until I found my handheld and turned it on. It now echoed the broadcasts coming over the car's radio as dispatch squawked about other police matters around town. I turned the car's radio down again to lessen the distracting noise and switched the handheld to the operations channel.

"Cromwell here. Over."

"Ripley and Hanson on this channel. Over."

After letting Ripley reverse out of the spot next to me, I did the same thing, but turned around and backed into the same spot for an easy exit if needed. I saw Hugo enter Gelson's, then scanned the various businesses and pathways to make sure I didn't miss Kwon.

It was hard to argue with Hugo's statement about Garrett Caldwell, Hailey's internet date. The man had been the last person seen with Hailey, after which she never left the beach they'd visited together. Until the EMTs took her body away. But I still couldn't make sense of why Ryan Kwon had decided to flee. Of course, he had no way of knowing why we were arriving at his work to ask questions, but he appeared to have assumed the worst. Clearly, he was guilty of something.

When I made another scan of the parking lot, I spotted a man hurrying from the pharmacy in the far corner. He was immediately suspicious. No one in their right mind wore a hoodie in the middle of the afternoon on a California summer's day.

Getting out of the car, I keyed the radio mic. "Possible sighting walking toward Gelson's from CVS. Gray hoodie. Carrying a plastic bag."

"No visual from our position," came Ripley's voice.

I began walking between the parked cars, angling slightly away from the suspect, hoping he wouldn't notice me. The hood over his head shadowed his face, and at fifty yards, I couldn't make a positive ID.

"Is it him?" Hugo asked over the radio.

My partner was likely deciding whether to abandon his grocery store search and join me outside, or continue his sweep, but I couldn't answer for certain. I also didn't want to raise the radio to my mouth and give myself away. But it didn't matter. I didn't get the radio volume turned down in time, and the crackly voice from the speaker must have alerted Kwon. He stopped dead in his tracks and stared at me. I could now see it was him.

I quickly looked away and continued, hoping he'd search elsewhere for the source of the radio chatter, but he must have recognized me. He ran toward the BMW, still four rows of vehicles away. I gave up my ruse and sprinted his way, keying the mic on the radio.

"It's him. Pursuing on foot. He's trying to reach his car."

"On my way," Hugo quickly replied.

I could tell I'd arrive at the BMW a few seconds after Kwon, which should give me time to apprehend him, or at least have him trapped inside his vehicle. He must have realized the same thing, as he changed directions and aimed for the corner of the shopping center. The angle gave him a head start.

A car horn pierced the peaceful afternoon as a driver slammed on his brakes to avoid hitting Kwon. Our suspect crossed the lane and disappeared in the gap between the grocery store and the row of shops where I'd parked.

"Ripley, get to PCH!" I called over the radio. "He's going behind the shops in that direction."

"Copy," came the reply, which I barely registered as I dodged behind the stopped car and made for the corner.

Beyond the gap, the area opened up into grass and pathways surrounding picnic tables, where a handful of workers enjoyed their break. Clearly startled, they stared at me, unsure what to do.

"Police!" I announced. "Which way did he go?"

They all pointed toward the embankment on the far side of the service lane behind the buildings. I ran across the narrow road and found a gap in the shrubs and trees. The slope was steep, plunging down to Pacific Coast Highway, where all four lanes were busy with traffic. Slightly south of where I stood, Kwon slithered down the grassy hill toward the sidewalk.

"He's on PCH!" I relayed through the radio as I ventured down the hill, trying not to break my neck.

"At the light," Hanson's voice responded as Ripley was likely driving.

"Bugger the light," I cursed. "Put the siren on and get here!"

My body ached from the bumps and bruises courtesy of my date with the stairwell earlier in the day, and I cursed some more under my breath. More horns sounded and tires screeched as the suspect ran across the first two lanes of the highway. In the distance, I heard a police siren, so Ripley must have given up waiting for a green light.

Sliding to the sidewalk, I broke into a run, trying to catch the drivers' attention, but most were busy looking at the madman who'd dashed across in front of them. I pulled up just in time for a woman in her SUV looking down at her cell phone to roll by me. I heard her scream when I slapped the side window as I ducked behind her and made it to the center section.

Kwon had already cleared the southbound lanes. He glanced over his shoulder. The cars were now hearing the siren and, having seen the suspect running, were easing to the right-hand lane, making it easy for me to cross. I sprinted down the sidewalk in pursuit. Kwon checked for me again, then slowed and scrambled up the embankment on his right. The slope on this side was much shorter, and he quickly reached the top where a four-foot fancy metal fence bordered a home.

Angling along the face of the slope, I quickly gained ground as Kwon scaled the fence, pausing at the top. He turned and swung the plastic bag at me as I reached for him. The bag glanced off my outstretched arm, then hit the top of my head. I was glad he hadn't caught me around the ear, as whatever he had in the bag weighed more than I'd expected. The delay was enough for him to drop over the fence, and as I recovered and reached the same point, I saw why he'd been reluctant.

The metal fence topped a six-foot retaining wall at the bottom of a garden, and the suspect lay on the ground, catching his breath from the ten-foot drop. I looked around for a better way down, but didn't see another option. He was now getting back to his feet. I clipped the radio to my belt.

"You're making this much worse for yourself, Ryan," I called out, but he was running across the backyard, determined to keep running.

Scrambling over the metal fence, I lowered my feet to the top of the block wall, then crouched down until I could hold the lowest bar of the fence with my hands. Awkwardly, I shuffled my body over the edge and walked my feet down the face of the wall until I hung from my hands at full stretch. When I released, I still dropped farther than I'd anticipated, and even with bent knees, I tumbled over onto the grass.

"What the hell are you doing in my backyard?" came a man's voice as a door opened from the house.

I picked myself up. "Police. Go back inside," I ordered, but the old man just glared at me.

"I'm in pursuit of a suspect," I barked. "Get back in the house!"

"I need to see some ID," he retorted.

"What part of 'in pursuit' do you not bloody understand?" I shouted as I ran by and continued up a path alongside the house to where the side gate had been swung open.

Kwon was just disappearing down the side of another home on the opposite side of the cul-de-sac. I retrieved the radio as I ran.

"He's in the south section of Monarch Bay, heading down the hill," I gasped. "Where are you, Hugo?"

I carried on running down the hillside, following the route I guessed the suspect had taken through the trees alongside the border fence for the gated community.

"Coming your way," was all Hugo replied.

I pictured him still sitting in the car outside Gelson's, sipping on a fresh coffee he'd just bought, while I chased our suspect all over the place.

"We've turned around and are entering Monarch Bay community now," Hanson announced.

"Take the road to the Beach Club," I responded, hoping they could cut him off if he ran along the beach.

His other choice was the golf course to the south, but he'd need to hop the boundary fence to reach it, and I could hear the rustling of undergrowth ahead of me. I reached another home, followed by the road looping in a hairpin as it zig-zagged down the steep hillside. The Pacific Ocean opened up before me as I rounded the corner, and I spotted Kwon veering onto a concrete footpath leading directly down to the beach.

Where the hell did he think he was going?

Cutting right, I dashed behind a row of cars parked in the lot overlooking the beach, gambling on him taking the north option to the sand. South meant crossing the spillway, and while it hadn't rained in weeks, every sprinkler from the nearby neighborhoods, and especially the Monarch Beach Golf Club, drained through the spillway into the ocean. Even in the summer, a stream divided Salt Creek Beach, separating the popular surf spot from the northern section below the wealthy Monarch Bay community.

A path led from the parking lot to the patio, which I crossed in a full sprint. Kwon was now slogging through the soft, powdery sand, trying to make a call on his phone. The lifeguard stand screened me from view for a few moments, giving me enough time to scamper down the broad steps to the beach.

"Excuse me!" a restaurant employee called out, and the scattering of beachgoers all turned to see what the fuss was about.

Kwon turned, too, and immediately spotted me bearing down on him. He launched his cell phone into the air a split-second before I lowered my shoulder and bowled him over. Kwon groaned with the air expelled from his lungs as I crashed him into the ground. Looking up, I caught the splash as his phone landed in the surf.

"You're under arrest, dipshit," I muttered, and pulled the handcuffs from my belt.

11

————

The sun was about to set by the time Ryan Kwon's hurriedly employed lawyer showed up. They talked, and finally we sat down in the interview room, where Hugo read them the usual disclaimers and rights information. I had my instant pictures in my pocket, but had gone through them several times before we entered the room. Everything felt firmly anchored regarding the suspect.

"You drive a metallic blue BMW 330i, correct?" I asked.

Kwon nodded.

"Verbal answers for the recording, please," I said impatiently. I was happy for him to feel outsmarted and vulnerable.

"Yes," he responded.

"Which you drove away from your apartment in Laguna Beach shortly after ten a.m. this morning."

I looked at his lawyer when he didn't respond. Before he could urge his client to answer, Kwon spoke up. "Yes."

"And you'll recall, that was moments after you told my partner and I that you were booting up the computers in the gallery downstairs where you work. Sound right?"

"Yes."

"And why was it you drove off in a big hurry to avoid talking to us, Ryan?"

"I had an emergency come up," he replied.

Hugo scoffed.

"An emergency?" I echoed. "What kind of emergency was this?"

"A friend needed help with something," he replied.

He was sitting up straight in his chair and spoke clearly when he answered. We knew from his records that he'd obtained a bachelor of arts degree in art history, so he was obviously a reasonably intelligent individual. Why he was choosing a bullshit path of excuses further baffled me.

"And you knew this, how?" I asked.

"He called me."

"On your cell phone?"

"Yes."

I noticed Hugo shaking his head and grinning. Another great way of letting a suspect know he was screwed.

"Perfect," I responded brightly. "I'll grab your phone, and you can show us. We managed to retrieve it from the ocean, where you no doubt *accidentally* dropped it during our little jog on the beach this afternoon. Good job it's one of those expensive, waterproof types."

I began to rise.

"I deleted my call history," Kwon said.

"Really?" I questioned, sitting back down. "Is that something you usually do?"

"There's no law against deleting anything from a personal cell phone," the lawyer who'd introduced himself as Collins said, holding up a hand in front of his client so Kwon didn't answer.

"You're absolutely correct, sir," I replied. "No law against launching a thousand-dollar phone into the ocean, either, but it is rather unusual behavior. As is deleting call history after running from the police."

Kwon looked at me. Not in the eye, but a vague stare in the general direction of my face.

"Okay, let's move on to why you pushed me down the stairs outside your apartment?"

Kwon cleared his throat, buying himself time to construct his answer. "You surprised me. I thought you were an intruder."

"We'd announced ourselves as being with the Orange County Sheriff's Department, Ryan. Twice," I pointed out.

"I didn't hear that."

"You came back inside through the back door to shove me down the stairs," I continued. "If you were surprised, why did you come back in?"

"I'd forgotten something, so I was coming back. That's when you opened the door and surprised me," he replied.

"What had you forgotten?" I asked.

"A note I left in my apartment."

"Then why didn't you get it after assaulting me?"

A hand went up again. "My client has already explained the misunderstanding, which unfortunately resulted in you tripping down the stairwell, investigator. He had no intention of assaulting you."

I ignored the lawyer and kept my eyes on Kwon. "The note, Ryan."

"I realized I had it after all," he replied.

"Gotcha," I said. "So, after *misunderstanding* me backwards down a stairwell, and recalling that you had this note after all, you decided to jump in your car and leave to help your friend. Do I have this right?"

He nodded.

"Verbal responses, please."

"Yes."

"Perfect. Thank you for straightening that out for us. Just as a formality, we'll request your phone records, which will verify your friend's call. Then we'll speak to the friend, of course. What's his name, please?"

Kwon leaned over and whispered something to the lawyer. The hushed conversation went back and forth several times before they both sat back.

"My client can provide a name and contact number for you at the end of this interview, which, as he's answered all your questions, I assume is now."

I slowly shook my head. "Not even close."

Hugo leaned forward. "My partner's been incredibly patient with you, Kwon, but I've had enough of your bullshit."

The suspect's eyes widened, and Collins held up both hands.

"My client has cooperated completely with—" he began, but Hugo cut him off.

"What were you doing on PCH Wednesday night at ten o'clock?"

"What does this have to do with the gallery this morning?" the lawyer asked.

"It gave us the reason to visit your client," Hugo responded. "Why were you stopped by the side of the road at the beach where your ex-girlfriend was murdered around the same time?"

All the color drained from Kwon's face, and Collins stuttered a few times before forming a sentence.

"This is all new to us," Collins said. "We need a few minutes to confer."

"It's new to you," I pointed out. "Not to Ryan."

Hugo let out a disgusted sigh. "Pausing interview at 7:23 p.m."

We left the room rather than allowing them to chat in a conference room. We could hopefully get back to it much quicker this way. I followed Hugo to the coffee pot, where we treated ourselves to the tar like dregs left in the carafe.

"What do you think, Kat?" Hugo asked.

"I think this coffee's terrible," I replied after taking a sip.

He raised one eyebrow at me.

"Kwon's guilty as hell of something," I said. "But hard to know what. Stalking his ex-girlfriend, I suspect."

Hugo nodded and glanced at his watch. "Think Rosa is still at the crime lab?"

I took out my phone. "Probably," I replied as I dialed her cell phone number.

"You've got thirty seconds, Kat. I'm just heading out the door," Rosa answered.

"Yeah, sorry for calling so late, but we're questioning a suspect," I explained.

"In the Carter case?" Rosa asked with more interest.

"Yeah."

"What do you need?"

"Has your team had a chance to go through Hailey's Prius yet?"

"Umm, they started late this afternoon, so they haven't got very far yet. Anything in particular you're after?"

"We think someone may have put a tracker on it," I said.

There was a long pause, and I heard a door swing open. I presumed she had been making her way out of the lab on her way home.

"Just let us know tomorrow when they've checked, Rosa."

"Hold on," she said, and I heard a scuffling noise. "Really need the car on a lift to check properly," she muttered.

I covered the phone. "She's looking now," I told Hugo.

"Excuse me," came Collins's voice through the hallways. "We're ready when you are."

"We'll be there in just a minute," Hugo called back.

Through the phone, I heard more grunts and bumps as Rosa presumably scooted around on her back and examined the underside of the Toyota.

"Got it," she said, her voice some distance from wherever she'd left the phone.

"She's found something," I relayed to Hugo.

He mimed the action of taking a photograph, and I nodded.

"Hello, Kat?" Rosa said, having gathered up her phone.

"What have you found?" I asked.

"There's something stuck on the bottom of her car by magnet, it appears," she replied. "I don't want to touch it before we've dusted for prints."

"Does it look like a bug?" I asked.

"It certainly could be," she replied. "But they come in all shapes and sizes these days. Once we pluck it off, we'll be able to find a brand and perhaps a serial number."

"That's good enough for now," I said. "Can you text me a picture of it?"

"Yup. As soon as we hang up. And I'll have the team prioritize it first thing in the morning."

"Thank you, Rosa. Now get out of there so no one can bother you anymore."

She chuckled. "Night."

As we walked back to the interview room with our lousy coffee in hand, my phone buzzed, and we stopped.

"I can't tell what that is," Hugo commented as he looked at the poorly lit picture Rosa had taken.

A second shot came through. This time, she'd used a flash.

"Looks like what I think a tracking device might look like," I said.

"Let's roll with it," Hugo replied, and we returned to the interview room.

"Resuming interview with Ryan Kwon at 7:49 p.m.," Hugo said after starting the tape. "Same people present."

"My client wishes to cooperate in every way possible," Collins began. "Are we satisfied that this morning's misunderstanding was an unfortunate overreaction on my client's part?"

"I don't feel particularly satisfied," I replied. "How about you, Hugo?"

"Not for a moment," Hugo added, and gave me a subtle nod.

I unlocked my phone and showed Collins Rosa's picture.

"What is this?" he asked, putting on his reading glasses to study the image. "Am I supposed to know what I'm looking at?"

I turned the phone toward Kwon, who blinked several times as he turned pale once more.

"This is the tracking device recovered from Hailey Carter's Toyota Prius at our crime lab," I explained, turning the picture toward Collins once more. "A tracking device which your client used to stalk his former girlfriend."

"What proof do you have that my client had anything to do with whatever you think this is in the picture?" the lawyer asked.

"Pretty sure we'll find the corresponding app on Ryan's phone that'll be paired to this device," I explained. "And once we trace the serial number on the tracker, it shouldn't be difficult to follow the trail to the customer."

"So, Kwon," Hugo demanded. "What were you doing on PCH Wednesday night at ten o'clock after you tracked your ex-girlfriend's car to the beach?"

The suspect closed his eyes and shook his head. When he finally opened them, he looked scared.

"I wasn't stalking her."

"So she gave you permission to use the tracker?" Hugo asked.

Kwon shook his head.

"Verbal responses," Hugo barked.

"Please, let's keep this civil, sir," Collins said.

Hugo shoved his chair back and stood. "Civil? We had to pluck a young woman from the ocean who'd been slowly drowned in the most horrific way. And right now, your client is looking mighty good for it."

Kwon vigorously shook his head. "No, no, no. I could never hurt Hailey," he seethed, slipping into anger to keep tears at bay. "Yes, I drove by the beach because we'd been talking again. It wasn't completely over between us. But I could never hurt her. You should be looking at the guy she was with at Capo. I never even got out of my car."

"Then why all the running?" I asked. "You can spout all this bollocks about misunderstandings, but you ran from the police twice today. You left the gallery unattended. Those are not the actions of an innocent man."

Kwon muttered and swore under his breath.

"We should talk about this before you say anything more, Ryan," Collins urged, and turned to me. "So far, all I've heard is circumstantial evidence of my client being briefly in the vicinity of the crime scene. And I'm assuming he was there before the time when you believe she was killed, correct?"

"Where did you go after you left Capo Beach?" Hugo asked Kwon, ignoring Collins.

"Home," Kwon replied.

"Who can verify that?" he persisted.

The suspect shook his head. "I live alone, man. But you'll see my car on any CCTV along PCH."

"We'll certainly check that," Hugo responded, taking his seat. "Meanwhile, you'll remain our guest here."

"On what charges?" Collins asked. "You've no reason to hold my client. He should be released unless you have anything more substantial to hold him."

I frowned at the lawyer. "Assaulting a police officer, resisting arrest, unlawfully tracking an individual without their permission," I listed before turning to Kwon. "And, of course, for ripping the gallery off."

It was spur of the moment, but it fit. It didn't mean he hadn't killed his ex-girlfriend. All the running was making him appear guilty of that. But why run before even knowing why we were banging on his door? I guessed it was because we'd sought him out at the gallery.

And the look on his face confirmed my theory.

"I don't know what you mean," he said, with little conviction.

12

It was eight-thirty p.m., I hadn't eaten dinner, and I'd missed two calls and a text from Grace at GilTech. With all the running around after Ryan Kwon, I'd honestly forgotten about her. As I left the station and walked to my car, I tried calling back. She answered almost immediately.

"Investigator Cromwell?"

"My apologies for missing you earlier," I responded. "I was tied up all afternoon and evening."

"Where are you?" she asked in an urgent tone.

"The sheriff's station in Dana Point."

"Can I meet you?"

"Tonight?" I replied, looking at my watch again. "It's late. Can you tell me over the phone?"

"No," she quickly replied. "I mean, it would be better in person. You asked for some background information on what it was like working with Hailey, and I'm happy to talk with you about that."

I was confused. I didn't recall asking her that, but there again, I couldn't always rely on knowing what situations were floating untethered in my brain.

"Okay," I replied, playing along. "Where works for you?"

"I'm not far away. I'll come to Dana Point."

"Okay, I'll wait at the station on Golden Lantern."

There was silence for a few moments. "I'll be there in fifteen minutes."

We hung up, and I groaned. I certainly wanted to hear what Grace had to say, but fifteen minutes was the worst timing. Not long enough to run out for food, or to have something delivered. Our little station didn't even have a vending machine. The city offices in the same building did, but that section had been locked up since 5:01 p.m.

I settled for making a fresh pot of coffee and pondered my brief call with Grace. Her urgency had been strange. It was most likely that she wanted to be involved at some level and was using her work relationship with Hailey as a way to get attention. It was no longer surprising to me how virtual strangers became close friends of the deceased after their passing. A product of modern society where everyone is looking for social media content, regardless of how they get it.

Grace arrived, wearing sweatpants and a loose-fitting T-shirt. A far cry from her office attire. She stood nervously in the reception while I came around the counter from where I'd been sharing a coffee and chatting with the overnight desk sergeant.

"Thanks for coming by," I greeted her.

"Sorry it's so late," she replied, looking around the empty reception. "It's quiet here at night."

"We hope it is," I replied, and opened a door to the hallway leading to a conference room. "We can chat down here."

Grace hesitated, then went to the counter and handed over the cell phone she carried in her hand.

"Can you keep this for me?" she asked the sergeant.

He shrugged and glanced at me. "Sure."

I shrugged at him in return and waited for Grace to follow me down the hall to a conference room.

"Have a seat. Coffee?"

"I'm fine, thank you," she said, sitting down and fidgeting in the chair.

Taking a seat across the table from her, I set my coffee down. I really didn't need any more caffeine in my day. What I needed was something to eat and an early night, but that would have to wait.

"Tell me about working with Hailey," I asked, although I thoroughly recalled our visit to the GilTech offices, and everything felt sequential with nothing missing. I was confident I hadn't asked her this before.

"Yeah, sorry about that over the phone, but I have to be cautious."

"Cautious of what?" I asked, at least relieved that I hadn't forgotten a moment from our earlier encounter.

Grace looked at me in surprise. "You know what GilTech does, right?"

"Only what Mr. Gil told me," I replied, starting to understand where Grace was coming from.

"Military top-secret-level surveillance," she whispered.

"And you think your phone is bugged?" I asked. "That would be illegal."

She raised her eyebrows. "I'm not taking any chances. It's a company phone."

Now I understood the reason she'd given me over the phone for the meeting. Which had caused me fifteen minutes of self-doubt, but she wasn't to know that.

"Then I assume you don't trust Enrique Gil?"

She shook her head.

"And how does this relate to Hailey?" I asked.

"I don't know exactly," Grace replied, shifting anxiously in the chair. "But I do know she was talking about leaving."

That didn't jive with Hailey's roommate Melissa's version, but she'd admitted they hadn't seen much of each other lately.

"Was this a new thing?" I asked. "Her thinking of leaving?"

Grace nodded. "We're all on edge. I'd leave if I had something else to go to, but Enrique pays well. I can't afford to be without work. You know how expensive it is to live in Southern California."

"What's got everyone upset at the company?"

"Enrique," she replied. "He's been a different man since his wife left him."

"Different how?"

"Late coming in, missed meetings. Some days, he shows up looking like he never went to bed."

I could see how employees would be nervous, but I still wasn't sure how this related to Hailey's murder.

"And this had Hailey thinking about leaving?" I asked.

Grace leaned closer. "He hit on her."

"Did anything come of it?" I asked.

"How do you mean?"

"Did they go out? Or did she go to HR about it?"

"No, no, she was bothered by it and worried how it would affect things at work, but she turned him down," Grace replied. "I'm certain she didn't say anything to HR."

"Hailey told you she didn't?"

"Didn't have to. HR is Enrique's wife, Julia. No way she could risk pissing her off."

My mind raced. I was dead-tired but jittery from the caffeine, and I knew I was processing the information slower than usual. The certainty I'd had regarding Kwon having planted the tracker was now in question. Thinking back, he'd never admitted to tracking her. Only following her. Probably because the interview room had become so familiar to me, I found the discussions within those walls stayed with me, and I could remember the details very clearly. He'd denied putting the tracker on her car. *Then how did he know she was at the beach Wednesday night?* Maybe he'd followed her all evening.

Enrique Gil certainly had the technology to track Hailey, and plenty of opportunity to plant the bug on her car at work each day. But why, if he was already tracking company phones?

"Did Hailey have a company phone?" I asked.

"Yeah," Grace replied. "But she didn't use it for anything personal at all. She left it in her desk when she went home each day."

That would explain the need for a tracker on her car, but made the company phone somewhat superfluous.

"Isn't the point of having a company phone that you can be reached at any time?"

Grace nodded. "But Hailey insisted she worked from eight 'til five. If she needed to do overtime, she'd stay later at the office. Once she left, it was her time, so she didn't need the company phone. Enrique never pushed her on the issue."

"But no one else did the same thing?" I asked.

"Shit, I turned in my personal phone," Grace replied. "Saved me over a hundred bucks a month. But that was before I was scared he was listening in or tracking us."

I still hadn't heard a good reason why Enrique Gil would track all his employees, but I was beginning to see why he might have been stalking Hailey.

"Did Enrique know Hailey was thinking of leaving?" I asked.

"I doubt it," Grace replied, then considered her next words carefully. "But I wouldn't put it past him to bug the offices. He may have listened to our conversations."

My face must have reflected my skepticism.

"You don't understand the shit we work on at GilTech," Grace insisted. "It's not just the means of acquiring footage, data, and audio; it's the processing of the information. Gil doesn't have to listen to any of the recordings. He's developed software that scans real-time alerts when certain words or phrases are used, and presents the results in customizable reports."

I knew this kind of technology had existed for years. I'd even been shown demonstrations of software the sheriff's office had access to. But from what Grace was describing, it would still require one man to search through a ton of reports.

"I'm violating the nondisclosure even talking about this," Grace said, blowing out her cheeks. "But believe me when I say this is next-level stuff. Enrique could easily set it up so he'd know if we talked about him, leaving the company, wages, whatever it might be. It's AI technology determining whether it's what he wants to know, based on parameters he sets up in ten minutes."

Maybe she was right. The company had military contracts, so I didn't doubt the technology was there.

"Okay, Grace," I said with more finality than I'd intended. "What exactly is it you think Enrique has done that we need to be concerned about?"

She sat back in the chair and chewed her lip. "Shit. I don't know Investigator Crom—"

"Kat is fine. The whole investigator title is a pain in the arse."

"It's funny how you say 'arrrse,'" she mimicked.

"Blame my parents," I said with a grin, and waited for her to get back to the point.

"Maybe I'm wasting your time, in which case I'm really sorry. But Enrique went from being a good, professional boss to a creepy guy, and he had a major thing for Hailey. I thought it was worth mentioning, but perhaps I'm blowing it all out of proportion."

"Did Hailey talk to you about dating?" I asked, thinking about the things Melissa had told us.

"Some. I know she broke up with her boyfriend earlier this year, and I don't think she'd dated anyone since. Not seriously."

"Anyone else at work interested in Hailey?"

Grace laughed. "Every straight guy, and she could probably turn the gay guys hetero."

"She was a pretty girl," I remarked.

"She was, but it wasn't just that. Hailey had this air about her like she had time for everyone, you know? Just nice, and she didn't have a bitch button she'd turn on, even when guys were being obnoxious. It was like it rolled right off her. She would laugh it all away." Grace stood. "I should let you go home."

"One more question while you're here," I said, also rising from my chair. "The warehouse and workshop area downstairs at GilTech. What goes on down there?"

"In the labs?" she responded.

"I saw what looked like sealed laboratories, but there's also a shipping area and a workshop."

"The labs are for all our hardware testing and development. They're strictly off-limits except for the R&D staff. Then, like you say, there's a shipping and receiving desk and some other machinery. In the back, there's a row of 3D printers, too."

"But why the metalworking equipment?" I asked. "Hardly much use for that sort of thing on drones, computers, cameras, and software."

"I don't know," she replied. "It was brought over from the old building, which was before my time. Someone told me Enrique tried developing remote-controlled, driverless robots for bomb squads at one time. Maybe it was for that."

"So Enrique knows how to use the welder and other machinery?"

"I guess so. In the beginning, it was him and a partner. Some guy he met in college. From what I was told, Enrique kept the surveillance side of the business, and the other guy took the remote robot part."

"But Enrique still got the metalworking equipment," I commented.

She shrugged her shoulders. "I suppose."

"Mind if I snap a quick pic?" I asked, taking out my camera.

"What for?" she asked suspiciously.

Hardly surprising after our discussion on hi-tech surveillance.

"Just for my notes," I explained. "Helps me keep who, what, and where clear. Sometimes it's months later when we're looking back on these things."

"You think this might take that long to solve?" she asked.

"Hopefully not, but the court case will be months away even if we caught a suspect today."

She nodded. "I suppose so. Sure, go ahead."

I took a picture, then we walked out to the reception, where Grace retrieved her phone.

"Thank you for filling me in on Hailey. Sounds like she was a lovely lady to work with," I said, partly for Grace's peace of mind, but partly because she'd convinced me that Enrique certainly had the capability of listening in through the cell phone, even if he wasn't actually doing it.

It was 9:37 p.m. when I walked through my front door, pizza in hand. Another raging Friday night for me. Roger startled in his credenza, and when I turned on the light, I spotted his little twitching nose peeking through the wire mesh on the door.

"Sorry it's so late, mate," I called to him, and he hopped into view.

I dropped the pizza box on the kitchen counter and walked over, opening Roger's door. He took one look to make sure I wasn't an imposter, then leaped out onto the carpet. Without further delay, he sprang in the air a few times, then raced around the living room like he'd been waiting for this moment all day.

Watching the furry blur whisk around the room, I couldn't help but laugh and wondered if a man could ever make me this happy when I came through the door after a long day. Someone had, once upon a time, but that had turned out to be a lie. It was only later, when I discovered Paul's infidelity, that I realized I should never have felt that way when I looked at him standing in my kitchen. Smiling at me.

Roger came to a stop near my feet, his little sides heaving in and out as he panted for breath.

"You'll never do that to me, will you?" I said, picking him up and cuddling him to my chest. "You and me have a good thing going on, mate."

Roger ground his teeth. Which was another thing that had terrified me at first, but I'd learned was a sign of contentment. I accepted his teeth grinding now as wholehearted agreement.

13

I stood looking out over the water at Doheny Beach, the ocean lapping around my ankles as I pulled the back zipper closed on my wetsuit. The sun wouldn't appear above the hills for a while, but the pale light of dawn cast a muted light across the Pacific. Two-foot rollers made their way across the gently sloping sea floor, carrying surfers on longboards toward the beach. I picked out my mother, her lean, tall figure, a picture of elegance as she deftly rode a wave until it broke fifty feet in front of me. Instead of turning and paddling back out, she lay on the waxed fiberglass and let the white water bring her toward me. Striding into the ocean, we met in thigh-deep water, holding our nine-foot boards apart, and hugged.

"Beautiful morning," I said, staring at the glassy water and perfect waves for riding longboards.

"I just got here," she replied. "That was my first wave."

"Looking good," I complimented. "I can't stay long, so if my first's like that, I may ride it to the beach."

"Busy?" she asked as we slid onto our boards and began paddling out.

"Yeah. The woman at Capo Beach."

"Of course. How awful. Do you think you can wrap it up quickly?" she asked.

My mother knew I couldn't share details of a case. Unlike my dad, who'd ask anyway, she carefully inquired without putting me on the spot. Her sympathy was for the victim, but her concern was for me.

"We have a suspect who was with her at the beach, but it looks like he couldn't have done it," I replied, then paused as we both dipped the noses of our boards and rode under an incoming wave. "Two other suspects, but they're unlikely the culprit, either. I have a bad feeling about this case, Mum. It's an ugly one, too."

As she always did, my mother considered her response for a few moments before speaking. Another trait not shared with my father.

"I'm sure you and Hugo will figure it out," she said, choosing the supportive path. "It's still early days, right?"

"Yeah," I grunted.

No two cases were ever exactly the same, but they did tend to fall into categories of complexity and time they took to solve. The first few days were always critical for gathering forensic evidence, witness statements, and establishing obvious suspects. In Hailey Carter's case, the ocean had removed most of the forensics, there were no eyewitnesses, and the obvious suspects all had alibis or circumstances that made it logistically impossible for them to have murdered her.

We reached the lineup where the waves built, and I said hi to a few of the other surfers, most of whom I'd known most of my life. My mum had taught me to surf at Doheny, and it was the closest, easiest break near my parents' house and my cottage. In high school, I'd surfed shortboards a bunch because that's what most of the kids preferred. Longboards were for veterans who liked to cruise the waves. But sometime during college, I'd been happy to switch to my nine-foot Robert August Wingnut and hang out with my mum instead of fighting for waves at the crowded spots. I wanted to relax and enjoy the ocean, not scramble in a frenzied charge to get position on a wave.

I looked over my shoulder at the swells rolling our way, studying their form as they built momentum.

"Which one?" my mum asked.

It was a game we played. Which wave in the set would be the best one? She was unpredictable and picked anything that took her fancy, even if the wave didn't look like it would have the best form. I almost always took number three, which she knew all too well.

We let two waves roll under us, with several surfers around us taking them, or at least attempting to. I remained straddled on my board, trying to look disinterested. My mum laughed at me.

"You're not fooling anyone, Katherine."

I laughed with her and began paddling as wave three approached. I could still hear her chuckling as I stood up, the powerful wave of water carrying my board toward shore. For the next thirty seconds, my mind was free of police cases, dead boyfriends, and neurological disorders. I was one with the ocean, which cradled my board and guided me smoothly along as I adjusted my stance and balance to stay nestled in the face of the wave.

It was a perfect ride, and true to my word, I dropped to my board and rode the whitewater into shallow water. Back into the daunting clutches of reality.

I was fifteen minutes into searching CCTV along PCH for Kwon's BMW when Hugo arrived at the office.

"Morning," he said, taking his seat and setting his large to-go cup of coffee down on the desk.

I stared at the cardboard cup in jealousy. I'd dropped by PC Beans and picked up a cup on my way in, but it was long gone, and I was ready for more. At least my brain was keen on the idea. My body more likely yearned for a caffeine fast for a day or two.

Long enough to allow there to be more blood than coffee in my veins.

"I met with Grace last night," I said, then proceeded to debrief Hugo on the main points I'd learned.

By the time I'd finished, I'd also seen the metallic blue BMW on enough cameras to know Kwon had told us the truth. Which I also relayed to my partner.

"And it's definitely him in the car?" he asked.

"Yeah. There's one view where the street lights are just right. You can see it's Kwon."

"He could have gone back," Hugo suggested.

"Sure. Maybe he dropped by home to pick up the metal framework he magically compressed into the boot of a BMW."

Hugo slid his chair to one side and raised an eyebrow at me. "It's a trunk, Cromwell. You're in America, and I'm just saying it doesn't rule him out completely."

I sighed. "Yeah. Sorry. I'm frustrated is all. Grace reiterated what Melissa told us about Hailey. She attracted men. We've got Caldwell, Kwon, and possibly Gil all interested in her, and two of them were even at the location, yet we can't see how any of them killed her."

His expression softened. "I know. It kept me awake last night. On one hand, the method in which she was killed seems clinical. Almost surgical in its precision."

"More engineered," I interjected. "Precise, but in a mechanical sense."

Hugo nodded. "Okay, but what I was going to say is, it also feels like an incredibly personal way to kill someone. Slow. Cruel. Like the killer was making a point."

I thought it over for a minute, and Hugo sat patiently waiting. The fact that he wanted to continue the conversation was a major step forward since our first case together, when he considered me chewing gum on his shoe. I looked at my pictures I had spread out next to my keyboard.

"We know Gil has the equipment," I said, "and, we believe, the ability to construct the execution frame. All three seem smart enough, although I question Kwon's decision-making."

"We have him held without bail based on him being a murder suspect," Hugo said. "Because of the weekend, he won't be arraigned until Monday. But if he can't be Hailey's killer, we need to let him post bail for the other charges."

"Let me check first that he didn't drive back to Dana Point," I replied, and Hugo nodded.

My partner was right, and we didn't need to burden the system unnecessarily, but I had little sympathy for Kwon. He'd shoved me down a flight of stairs, and my sore limbs wouldn't let me forget.

"What does Caldwell do for a living?" Hugo asked.

"Works remotely for an advertising agency in LA. He has the pretty nails, remember?"

Hugo frowned. "I don't believe that's the adjective I used."

"So what do we do about Enrique Gil?" I asked.

He shrugged. "Nothing. Yet. We need some kind of evidence that places him in the vicinity or connects him to Hailey beyond asking her out on a date."

"We need the plate on that car he's using. We could call around the rental companies and see if his name pops up, then check the PCH footage again."

Hugo blew out his cheeks and ran a hand through his neatly groomed hair. Each strand seemed to spring back into perfect place like soldiers on a parade ground.

"We'll be hunting through CCTV for weeks."

"It's that or wait for support to run the search for us, and they'll take even longer," I pointed out. "Wait, why don't we just ask Grace? She probably booked it for him. Or has access to his email and the confirmation."

I picked up my phone and texted the woman I'd met at the station.

"Finish up with Kwon," Hugo said when I was done typing. "I'm looking through old cases using a few different parameters.

Making sure we haven't missed anything that might tie this to another case. After that, we'll both tackle more footage."

I nodded my agreement and returned to my screen. Picking the junction near where we'd arrested Kwon, at Crown Valley Parkway and PCH, meant I could see if he returned to Dana Point by the most obvious route. Which was the same way he'd gone home. He could also have taken Laguna Canyon Road out of Laguna Beach just north of his apartment, but that route was nearly twice as far.

I sat there, staring at cars rushing by or abruptly stopping as the fast-forwarded video raced along for the rest of the night. I had to pause a dozen times to make sure the blue sedans I spotted weren't Kwon's BMW, but none were, and I quit when the timestamp read four in the morning, as we knew Hailey had drowned well before then.

My cell phone buzzed, and I read the message.

"Grace got back to me about Gil's rental," I relayed to Hugo. "He's had it since Wednesday while his car is in the shop. She's taken a screenshot of the confirmation email. I have a plate number."

I texted her my thanks, then ran the plate in the system. One speeding ticket and one parking violation came up, but neither was recent.

"I need another coffee before I search anymore CCTV," I announced, and got up to reload my cup.

"Hey, just a minute," Hugo called to me.

"What you got?"

"Come look," he muttered, focused on his screen.

I walked around his side and peered over his shoulder. "What's the case?" I asked, scanning the report.

"A vic in her late twenties, Taylor Davis, drowned off Corona Del Mar State Beach Park eight months ago," Hugo replied. "Ruled an accident."

"Got caught up in an old mooring line while swimming alone at night," I said, reading aloud from the official findings. "While the circumstances were strange, no evidence of foul play could be determined."

"Yeah," Hugo scoffed. "But why was she swimming naked in the middle of the night alone?"

"That'll be the *strange* part, I suppose."

"Or was it our killer testing out the method?" Hugo responded, scrolling down from the conclusion section. "Says here she likely drowned hours after becoming entangled, but no one heard any cries for help."

A shiver ran through me as I pictured a woman ensnared in an old line and struggling against it until becoming exhausted. Finally, she would have been unable to keep her head above water.

"Does it say why she was even at the beach?" I asked.

Hugo tapped the screen, pointing to a section of text farther down the report. "She'd been on an internet date."

"No bloody way. Really?"

Hugo looked up at me. "Through OC Match."

"Seriously?" I muttered, frantically reading.

"But the guy was cleared," Hugo continued. "They'd had dinner in town. Seen on restaurant cameras. Then bought coffee and strolled down to Inspiration Point. He swore she stayed there when he left. He's seen on CCTV driving away forty minutes after buying the coffee, and hours before her estimated time of death."

I searched the report for the name of her date. "Devin Williams. No priors."

"Looks like they had no choice but to call it an accidental drowning," Hugo said. "They had nothing."

"What about her clothes?" I asked, scanning again to find any reference in the report.

"Never found," Hugo replied.

"Yeah, that's bollocks, then," I replied, standing up straight. "How did they explain her clothes missing?"

Hugo scrolled down farther and tapped on the screen again. "Their theory was that she went in the water during the incoming tide, which then reached her pile of clothes on the beach. She drowned in the night, and the outgoing tide took all her clothes with it."

"Shoes and all?" I questioned suspiciously.

Hugo searched the report again, looking for a reference to what Taylor Davis had been wearing that night.

"Jeans, blouse, lightweight jacket, socks, and Converse high-tops. She can be seen wearing all that in the video. Williams also described her outfit in his statement."

"Assuming she was wearing underwear too, that's a lot of items to be dragged out, never to be seen again," I said. "Something's not right with this. Who had the case?"

"Fitzpatrick," Hugo groaned.

"Is that bad?" I asked. "I don't know him."

"He's a detective with Newport Beach PD."

"I got that much, Hugo. Is he a lousy detective?"

"No, he's a good detective. Very good, actually."

"So, let's reach out to him," I persisted.

"You'd better do that."

"Okay," I replied. "But what's your problem with him?"

Hugo looked around the room, then sighed at me. I had no idea what he was trying to convey for several moments.

"Oh, bugger," I blurted. "Is he an ex of yours?" I whispered.

He gave me the *no shit* face, and in this instance, I wished I'd used a different English swear word.

14

Evidence or murder boards look good on TV shows, but modern police forces have computer software to accomplish the same task. Although, sometimes I thought a board would be faster and easier. For someone with a neurological screw loose like me, who relied on visual aids to keep things straight, I was constantly scanning and adding my pictures. The upside of the software was being able to hyperlink each suspect to evidence or forensic files saved somewhere else on the server.

By the time I'd updated the case on the computer, left a message for Detective Chase Fitzpatrick, read through the entire Taylor Davis file myself, and put Ryan Kwon's release in motion, an email arrived with the CCTV from the harbor. More footage to plow through. The exotic and exciting life of an OCSD investigator continued.

"Have you started looking for Gil's rental car?" I asked Hugo.

"Hmm," he grunted, which I took as an affirmative.

"I'll dive into this marina footage, then."

"Hmm."

I checked my watch. Half the morning had already flown by, and I'd spent it all staring at grainy nighttime CCTV video. And drinking coffee. With more of both in my future. With a fresh cup of crappy station coffee, I settled in for another session.

The camera was mounted near the harbor patrol building on the central island in the harbor and was aimed at the dogleg exit to the ocean. By starting before sunset, I could read the names on the stern of the boats, and often the registration numbers along the hulls. Once darkness descended, it became more difficult. The parking lot lighting cast a faint glow over the water, but the size, color, and style of the lettering determined whether I could make it out or not. I noted each one I could read and took screenshots of the ones I couldn't.

The good news was that not many boaters were heading out after nightfall. Most cruised the coastline for an hour or two before returning, and I could see which direction any that turned just outside the harbor went. West meant they would clear the headland to continue north, and east would follow the coastline south. I only cared about boats going south toward Capo Beach.

Nearing midday, I had a list of three boats that had returned before 10:15 p.m. when we knew Hailey and her date had arrived at the beach. Two boats had come back later, but one of them had traveled north. That left a sleek, white sport fisher, which I guessed to be around thirty-five to forty feet, with dark-tinted glass around the cabin and two people on the flybridge. The name on the stern was part of a stylized logo or fancy lettering I couldn't read.

My friend at the harbor patrol, Nate, had asked about surfing this weekend, so I guessed he wasn't working. But if the sport fisher was local, there was a good chance he'd know it. I texted him a screenshot, and a few moments later, my desk phone rang.

"Kwon's being released now," Sergeant Martinez informed me.

"Thanks, Sarge. I'll be right there."

"Ryan Kwon is being released," I relayed to Hugo, who didn't respond. "Want to have a word before he leaves?" I added.

"Go ahead," he replied without looking up.

I wasn't sure what I had to say to the suspect, but something told me I should see his face before he left. Or maybe I was avoiding more excruciatingly boring CCTV-surfing.

I'd made it to the door when Hugo called to me. "Hold up, Kat."

I paused and looked back.

He stood from behind his desk. "We have confirmation it is a tracking device pulled from Hailey's car. The unit is 29.95 from Amazon and requires a subscription to the tracking service, so we'll get a warrant to see who owns the subscription. But that's just a formality."

"Fingerprints?" I asked.

"Yeah. Kwon's."

I thought for a moment.

"Doesn't change anything, Kat," Hugo said from across the room.

I nodded. "I suppose not. We already have the stalking and illegal-tracking charges on him."

"Which are misdemeanors. But more importantly, you just proved he was in Laguna Beach when Hailey was murdered."

"Yeah," I agreed. "At least he was in Laguna Beach when we think she was strapped to the execution frame."

Hugo frowned. "You keep calling it that. It's a horrible name for it."

"Got a better one?"

Hugo opened his mouth to reply, but then reconsidered for a moment. "No."

"Exactly. Makes you uncomfortable hearing it referred to that way, yeah?"

Hugo sighed. "As it should," he said, and sat down.

I walked to the reception, where Ryan Kwon was being handed his belongings.

"Mr. Kwon," I greeted him, and he looked my way.

He appeared tired and disheveled. He quickly turned away and started for the front door.

"Before you leave, sir," I said, and he stopped. His shoulders sagged, and he slowly turned. "Your fingerprints are on the tracking device, and the service will verify your account with them on Monday. I also have an appointment with your boss next week."

His expression tightened at the last part.

"If you'd care to make a statement regarding what you've been up to in the gallery, you might get ahead of that problem," I said, fishing more than anything. I didn't have an appointment, or anything more than a suspicion regarding his work-life transgressions.

He nervously stared at me with one hand on the door.

"Your call," I continued. "I'll be handing that side of things over to the Economic Crimes Squad, so you'll be getting a visit from them."

"Fuck," he muttered, then pushed the door open and left the building.

Now I was the one unsure what to do. I should have had a better plan. Ultimately, it wasn't Hugo's and my problem to worry about how the guy was swindling Bathrobe Lady, but the more charges we stacked on Kwon, the more bargaining chips we had if it turned out he was involved in killing Hailey. It appeared he needed a time machine or an invisible helicopter to have murdered his ex-girlfriend. But it felt like we were missing something big with the case, so maybe he did.

"Thanks, Sarge," I said to Martinez behind the counter, then returned to my desk.

My body ached, and I wondered why I was so sore after surfing that morning. Then I remembered being clobbered by Cisco a few days ago and rubbed my jaw. But that still didn't explain the dull pain in my thigh and shoulder.

And that's how these things often hit me. Our brains have these little worker bees who run downstairs and retrieve memories from the basement, bringing them back up to our conscious minds when needed. The older the memories, the farther down the stairs they're stored. Everyone else had enough worker bees to cover for their mates when they took a tea break, but apparently my brain was short-staffed. I could sense I was missing an event, but there was no one to bring the memory upstairs.

Sitting down, I quickly scanned my pictures, and each of them supplied an instant recognition in my mind, yet the feeling persisted. An anxiety swelled in my throat. I stood up again, rolling my shoulders to feel the ache one more time, hoping the pain would get my worker off his arse. Nothing.

"Hugo?" I whispered, moving next to him.

"What?" he asked, still engrossed in his computer screen.

"Did I get into a…" I struggled to find the right words. I felt stupid asking my partner to tell me what happened.

"What?" he repeated, looking up this time.

"Nothing," I replied, now chewing on the anxiety.

My issue made me feel so weak and vulnerable, but I'd fought the problem my whole life, and put in place a system to success-fully function around it. Most of the time. I decided to hunt through the case notes before succumbing to asking what felt like such a dumb question.

"Are you okay?" Hugo asked, now concerned.

I nodded. "Yeah."

"Bullshit," he responded. "Something's up, Kat."

I let out a long sigh. "My shoulder hurts."

He laughed. "I'm not surprised."

Bollocks. So it was something work-related. Or at least he knew about it.

"Do you need to get it looked at?" he asked.

No, I thought. *I need my head looked at by someone from the future who can help with the myriad of odd and weird neurological issues people suffer from.* I hadn't seen a specialist in a long while to keep my medical file clear, but I doubted they'd come up with a fix. I'd been on the path to having a disorder named after me the last time I'd been prodded and scanned like a lab rat.

I shook my head. "I'll be fine."

Hugo stood so he could see me as I sat back down in my chair.

"What are you missing?" he asked in a quiet and surprisingly sympathetic tone.

On the one hand, I liked the fact that my partner could read me well enough to know something was wrong. I just wished it had involved buying me a coffee instead of figuring out my brain had misfired. I rubbed my shoulder.

"He knocked you down the stairs, Kat."

"Right, of course," I replied, but my mind remained blank.

My expression must have, too, as Hugo continued.

"Kwon. Outside his apartment above the gallery in Laguna. You ran upstairs after him, and he surprised you. Knocked you backwards, and you tumbled halfway down the stairwell."

One of the worker bees must have finished his cuppa and sauntered in the right direction. An image of looking up at a sloped ceiling flashed through my mind. I sensed I was lying awkwardly on a flight of steps.

"Okay," I muttered, letting the information return in clips and short bursts of memories. "I've got it now. Thanks, Hugo."

He remained standing and didn't look convinced. I wasn't, either. Sometimes an explanation could recover an event for me, but only if it was very recent. Once the package had slipped down into pure long-term memory, I needed one of my pictures to retrieve it. Or a bang to the head had been known to shake things loose.

"It's back," I lied. "But I need a pic from the scene, or you may have to help me again," I added, which was true.

"We can drop by the gallery this week," Hugo said, and finally sat down.

His words reminded me of what had just taken place with Ryan Kwon, and I searched the internet for the gallery's number. It rang about five times before a woman answered.

"Shoreline Gallery of Laguna Beach."

"Hi... Mrs. Langley," I responded, pulling her name from my notes just in time. "This is OCSD Investigator Cromwell, ma'am. We met the other day."

Why my stupid brain would hang onto the details of meeting the woman in her bathrobe while ditching the important incident of being shoved down the stairs was beyond me, but I could picture her clearly.

"What's going on with Ryan?" she asked. "I've had to cover for him. Is he really in trouble?"

"I can't discuss his involvement in our murder case at this stage, ma'am, but I do have another question for you."

"Oh, okay. What's your question?"

"Have you noticed any anomalies in the gallery lately?"

"Anomalies? What do you mean?"

"Funds missing, items missing, strange people coming by to see Ryan, that sort of thing, ma'am," I explained.

"No, I don't think so," she replied. "But I leave most of it to Ryan. That's why I'm really at a loss without him here. I had a man come by this morning to pick up a piece, and I had no clue whether he'd paid us or not. It's so embarrassing, and frankly unprofessional, to ask."

Camille Langley had just described the perfect environment in which an employee could embezzle funds. But I had to tread carefully. With no evidence whatsoever, I was basing my suspicions purely upon Kwon's reaction to us showing up, and his expression on the two occasions I'd mentioned fraud.

"Mrs. Langley, based on something that's come to light during our questioning of Ryan, I would suggest you have someone other than him take a look at your accounting and inventory."

There was a brief silence. "What on earth do you mean?"

"Just what I said, ma'am. You'd be wise to make sure everything is in order."

"He would never…" she began, but trailed off.

"You can reach me through the Dana Point Sheriff's station if you need anything, ma'am. Have a lovely day."

I ended the call and heard a grumble from Hugo.

"What?"

"Have a lovely day," he mimicked in a terrible highbrow English accent.

"'Have a good day' is corny and sounds cliched coming from a copper," I replied defensively.

My cell phone buzzed with a message, which I read rather than listening to Hugo's standard comeback about being in America.

"Bloody hell," I muttered, looking at the text from Nate with the Marine Patrol. "The boat which left Dana Point marina on Wednesday night and went somewhere south during the time period of the murder is called *Shore Code*."

Hugo stopped giving me a hard time. "*Shore Code*?"

"Yeah, like a play on words with 'sure' as in certain, and 'shore' as in coastline."

"I hate boat-name puns," Hugo responded. "Who's it registered to?"

"Dylan Monroe."

"Monroe... Monroe..." Hugo thought aloud. "Where did we come across a Monroe?"

It never ceased to amaze me how my brain could mislay an entire event, yet recall details about something else. "OC bloody Match," I replied, tapping a finger on my instant photo of Sienna Monroe in her office. "Dylan is the coding-genius brother."

15

"I feel like we're in a bloody pinball machine," I said, standing up and running a hand through my hair.

Hugo stood, too. "We need to prioritize here. It's becoming a mess."

"Too bloody right," I mumbled in reply. "We keep adding suspects and still can't find anyone with the opportunity along with a motive."

"Then maybe Monroe's our guy," Hugo responded. "You brought up the idea of a boat involved. Let's see if we can find a connection between Monroe and Hailey outside of her using the app."

"Yeah," I agreed, then looked at the whiteboard on the wall we rarely used for anything more than leaving reminders for each other. I wasn't abandoning our software, but sometimes it helped me to see an old-fashioned list.

It took me three tries to find a dry-erase marker that wasn't dead. I then began by writing Caldwell's name on the board.

"You auditioning for a TV show?" Hugo joked.

"Sometimes it's better to see these things in large print instead of a computer screen," I replied, adding more names.

"Fine," he said, moving closer, "but if you start with the red string, I'm asking the captain for a new partner."

I finished writing and took a step back. "Okay. Caldwell."

"Had opportunity. Sort of," Hugo said. "But then he didn't, and unless he's a closet serial killer hiding in plain sight, then I don't see a motive."

I wrote "alibi" next to his name, and "motive" with a question mark.

"Kwon," I said, writing "alibi" next to his name, then "ex."

"Motive but solid alibi," Hugo added.

"Enrique Gil," I said, writing "alibi" next to his name and adding a question mark. "He wasn't a suspect at the time, so we didn't ask him where he was Wednesday night."

Hugo walked thoughtfully in a circle. "But he may have a motive if he took the rejection hard enough."

"I doubt the guy is used to being told no," I commented. "But staking a woman out on a custom-made frame to drown her is taking 'no' to a first date a bit far."

"Agreed," Hugo said. "And I don't see any of the vehicles associated with Gil on the CCTV. We can't place him at the scene."

"New on the menu is Dylan Monroe," I said, writing "opportunity" next to his name. "But again, it's hard to see a motive unless there's a connection we're unaware of. Or he's nutty as a fruitcake."

"Nutty as a fruitcake?" Hugo teased.

"One of my dad's favorite sayings," I replied, writing a fifth name. "Let's add Devin Williams to the list. Maybe he'll be removed if we can't tie the Corona Del Mar drowning to ours, but worth keeping on our radar."

"So," Hugo pondered. "Our priorities right now should be Monroe, and finding out more about Fitz's case."

My partner caught my grin. "Everyone calls him Fitz," he said defensively. "It wasn't a… you know, special name or anything."

"How long were you seeing him?" I asked quietly.

"I don't know. Four, maybe five months."

"It ended badly?"

Hugo looked incredibly uncomfortable and returned to his desk, shuffling paperwork around. "He was upset. And he had a right to be. Let's get back to the case, Kat."

Naturally, I was now even more curious, but I knew when I'd prodded one of our taboo subjects as hard as he could stand. I owned the other two off-limit subjects we tiptoed around. My neurological disorder, and my fiancé's death. All three were treacherous ground, only trodden upon with great delicacy and respect. Those were the rules we appeared to have established without any discussion on the matter.

"I'm waiting for Fitzpatrick to call me back," I said, avoiding the use of "Fitz," although my satirical side was dying to amuse itself. "So why don't we start with Monroe? I'll call the offices and see if he's there."

"Or we could show up and surprise him," Hugo suggested.

"Long way to go to find out he's not there or choosing to be unavailable," I countered.

He nodded. "True. I'd much rather sit here and look through more CCTV."

I laughed. "Fair point." Then an idea came to me. "Let's give him a reason to talk to us."

"What do you mean?"

"These computer whizzes love to explain how clever their software is, so let's ask to speak with him about security protocols. Tell him we suspect someone may have hacked into the system and knew about Hailey and Caldwell's date."

Hugo shrugged. "Worth a try. Give them a call while I get the car," he said, picking up his keys and jacket. "Because whatever we're doing, lunch is next on the agenda."

My stomach rumbled in agreement. Or it may have been the caffeine causing a nuclear reaction.

After taking a picture of the board, I looked up the number for the OC Match offices and called. As it rang, I remembered it was Saturday, and was surprised when the enthusiastic receptionist answered.

"Hi, this is Investigator Cromwell with the Orange County Sheriff's Department. We came by the other day."

"Okay," the woman answered without her usual buoyancy. So much for thinking I might have developed a rapport with her.

"I'd like to speak with Dylan Monroe, please."

"Oh, okay. Let me transfer you to his EA."

Hold music replaced her voice, and I waited for at least a minute. Probably while the receptionist called Monroe's assistant and filled her in so she wasn't blindsided by a call from the cops. In turn, the EA would tell her boss for the same reason.

"Dylan Monroe's office," came a woman's voice. "How may I help you?"

I repeated my introduction. "We'd like Mr. Monroe to help us understand a few technical details about his software as part of a current investigation."

"One moment, please, let me see when he might be available."

At least the hold music was a pleasant indie rock song I recognized, even though I couldn't recall the artist. Which I figured was a standard female brain issue rather than my weird brain.

"I can schedule a Zoom call for you in… let's see here… how about Thursday the 25th?"

"That's a month away," I responded. "This is an active murder investigation, ma'am. Dropping by and speaking with him this afternoon would be more helpful."

"Please hold," she said curtly, and I went back to feeling like I was sitting in a coffee shop on a Saturday night as the music played on.

The EA came back on the line. "Mr. Monroe can see you briefly at one p.m. if you can be here by then. If not, I'm afraid it will be next week before he's available."

I looked at my watch. It was 12:28 p.m. So much for lunch.

"We'll be there," I responded, and hung up before she could renege on the meeting.

I hurried outside, dragging my backpack with me and clutching my phone. Hugo was waiting.

"He can see us now," I explained, "but we have to hurry."

"They're working on a Saturday?" he questioned.

"It appears so. I was surprised, too."

"And you mean after lunch, right?" Hugo replied, pulling up to Golden Lantern.

"Only time he can fit us in his schedule this week is in thirty minutes."

"That's bullshit," Hugo responded. "We should have uniforms pick him up for questioning. Bring him into the station. See how that fits his damn schedule."

"Tempting," I agreed. "But we're more likely to get something out of him if he thinks he's helping us. Let him feel important for a while until we hit him with the boat question."

Hugo grunted a response, then turned onto Golden Lantern and accelerated away.

We arrived at one minute after the hour. Miss Bubbly gave us a guarded smile before leading us through the field of mostly unoccupied cubicles to an office in the other back corner of the building. Which seemed like an odd dynamic to me. The two owners of the company chose to be placed as far apart as possible, with six other offices and a conference room between them. Maybe their egos required the corner views, or perhaps their spheres of responsibilities didn't intersect often enough to worry about the longer walk. Or they hated each other. I'd never run a company, so it was all theory in my head, but Hugo and I sat opposite each other for a reason.

Miss Bubbly handed us over to a less enthusiastic-looking woman who guided us from her desk to Monroe's office. A firmly built man with thinning hair and round glasses stood from behind a bank of computer monitors. He was quite tall and more closely resembled an athlete than a stereotypical computer programmer. Dylan wasn't particularly good-looking, but maintained a closely trimmed beard, which probably improved his looks.

"I'm sorry to have you rush over, but my schedule is hectic," he said, offering us a seat at a small, round conference table.

The office was a mirror image of his sister's space, but furnished completely differently. Where she had sofas, artwork, and carefully placed books and artifacts, Dylan had computers, file folders, and coding reference manuals.

"We appreciate you fitting us in," I said after introducing ourselves. "Especially on a weekend."

"How can I be of help?" Dylan asked, taking a seat opposite us.

I knew Hugo would stay quiet, which, for once, was fine with me. He was in a lousy mood over delaying lunch, so he was queued up to be bad cop when and if needed. A role he was good at even when he was in a good mood.

"Not sure if you've spoken with your sister, who we met with yesterday, but we're investigating the murder of a woman who was out on a date facilitated through your app."

"Sienna mentioned you came by," Dylan replied. "Very unfortunate. But to my understanding, she provided all the data we're legally allowed to make available."

"She was most helpful," I replied, which was stretching the truth. "But our questions today are more about the technical side of the software."

"Okay," he responded. "I'm not sure how that would be pertinent, but I'm sure you'll explain that to me."

"Is it theoretically possible for someone to hack your system and see your client's communications?" I asked.

Dylan grinned. "You've made this meeting short and painless, Miss Cromwell," he replied. "No, is the answer. Did you have anything else?"

He began rising from his seat.

"Where were you on Wednesday night, sir?" Hugo asked.

I'd envisioned us taking longer to get to this point, but Hugo didn't like to skip a meal.

"Excuse me?" Dylan replied. "I thought you were here to ask about the software. What do I have to do with any of this?"

"Standard question we ask everyone we speak with," I quickly interjected.

"You realize I didn't know the victim," Dylan continued, evading the question. "It's not like we personally know our customers. Shit, we have hundreds of thousands of people using our app."

Hugo let out a disgruntled sigh. "If you've nothing to be concerned about, then answer the question, Mr. Monroe. Where were you?"

"It's not a concern issue, it's a personal rights and common courtesy matter," he responded. "I made time for you and answered your question, and now you're making wild accusations about me."

Hugo laughed. "Wild accusations? We haven't accused you of anything, sir. You're getting all wound up over a simple inquiry into your whereabouts at the time of the murder."

I smiled inside. Hugo was brilliant at batting a suspect around like a cat playing with a doomed mouse.

"I think I should consult my lawyer," Dylan said.

Hugo stood. "Wow. You'd rather shell out thousands of dollars to a lawyer than answer where you were on Wednesday night." He shrugged his shoulders. "No problem. It's your money. We must ask you to come with us to the station, sir."

"What?" Dylan groaned, jumping to his feet. "No way. You've got no right to arrest me."

Hugo sighed again. "Look, here's the situation, Monroe. You can answer my question, and if we're satisfied with your response, we can all get on with our day. You're a busy man with some of your staff here on a Saturday, so I'd think that would be preferential. Or you can come with us to the station where we'll wait until your overpriced lawyer saunters in, blaming traffic, while the meter's running on your dime. And option three is even less desirable. We arrest you. Same shit with the lawyer, but this time he's filing paperwork, so it's more money, and you can't be arraigned until Monday. So, two nights in jail for refusing to answer one simple question."

Monroe looked at me, his eyes wide. If this guy had the nerve to plan, put into motion, and follow through on the murder of Hailey Carter, I'd be surprised. Currently, he looked like Roger after he heard an unfamiliar noise in the house.

"Hard to understand why you're making this so difficult on yourself, Mr. Monroe," I said. "You have to see how from our side of the fence, this doesn't look like the actions of an innocent man."

"Why would I have anything to do with Hailey's murder?" he huffed.

"Hailey?" Hugo pounced. "Not 'Miss Carter,' or 'the victim,' huh?" he added, glancing at me.

I dutifully raised my eyebrows.

"This is insane," Monroe said, rubbing his forehead and pacing about.

"Might as well call your guy," I said. "He can meet us at the station."

Monroe held up his hands. "No. I'm sorry, you just took me aback with the question. I was on my boat Wednesday night."

"Anyone confirm that, sir?" Hugo asked.

"Yes, yes. I was with a friend of mine."

"We'll need the name and a contact number, please," Hugo said in a softer tone.

It wasn't common for things to go this well, but Monroe had just confessed to being on his boat when all we had was grainy video showing two figures on the flybridge. We couldn't ID him from the CCTV.

"Where's your boat kept?" I asked, as though I didn't know.

"Dana Point."

"And where did you go on Wednesday evening, sir?" I asked.

His expression tightened. "Nowhere. We stayed in the slip."

"What time did you arrive at the boat, and what time did you leave?" Hugo asked.

"Around seven until late. My friend left, and I stayed overnight on the boat."

This kept getting better.

"Leave for dinner at any time?" Hugo asked.

"We ordered in," Dylan replied.

"Perfect," Hugo said cheerily. "So you arrived around seven p.m., stayed on the boat with your friend all evening without leaving, then your friend went home at what time?"

"One, maybe closer to two in the morning," Dylan replied.

"The name, please," I asked, opening my notebook.

"Jason Browning. He's one of my software developers."

I wrote down the cell phone number he read from his phone, then flipped the notebook closed and put it in my pocket.

"I'm sorry for the confusion earlier, but glad I could help you," Monroe said, gesticulating toward the door. "My EA can show you out."

"That's okay," Hugo replied. "You're coming with us."

"What? I just answered your question like you said."

"You remember the part about answering to our satisfaction, Mr. Monroe?" Hugo asked, then continued without waiting for a reply. "Well, we have CCTV footage of you leaving Dana Point Harbor aboard your boat on Wednesday evening and returning much later that night, so you just lied to us."

Monroe's jaw quivered. "I'd like to call my lawyer now."

"That's a great idea, Mr. Monroe," Hugo grinned. "Now, are you coming along voluntarily, or are we arresting you?"

The man looked at me again. "What would you be arresting me for?"

"He'd arrest you for having a dumbarse name on your boat, but we'll probably settle on providing false information for now."

"We'll save the murder charge until Monday," Hugo added.

I backed up to the doorway and took out my camera. "Smile," I said, and snapped an instant photo.

16

———————

As Monroe had chosen to come to the station under his own free will, we couldn't leave him while we waited for his lawyer to show up. If he reconsidered and walked, we'd be chasing him all over the place to arrest him. So, we parked our suspect in a conference room and took turns keeping him company. It was mid-afternoon by the time we had sandwiches delivered to the station. If there was a word for the afternoon version of brunch, we were having it. "Lunner" doesn't have the same ring, which probably explains why no one bothered adopting the term.

Meanwhile, we'd secured a warrant to search the *Shore Code*, although the judge wouldn't extend the warrant to cover Monroe's home. Understandable, as we didn't have a stitch of evidence pointing to the man doing anything illegal, so I was actually surprised the judge let us search the boat. Or rather, Ripley and Hanson were searching while we babysat.

At 3:15 p.m., we finally sat in an interview room with Monroe and his lawyer, Jonathan Ambrose.

Hugo began speaking, "for the recording, Mr. Monroe, the reason we've asked you to come in here and speak with us today is based on the fact you told us you and a friend remained in the slip at Dana Point Harbor all evening on Wednesday night. We have CCTV footage of you and your friend leaving the harbor at 8:05 p.m. that evening, and returning at 12:15 a.m."

"You have a positive ID on who was on the boat?" Ambrose asked. "From CCTV at nighttime."

"No, we can verify there were at least two people on the boat from the CCTV," Hugo replied. "Your client told us it was he and his friend, Jason Browning, an employee at OC Match, who were the only ones aboard all evening."

"Then I believe we can clear up this misunderstanding without further delay," Ambrose responded. "My client was confused about which night was which. He was not aboard the vessel on Wednesday evening."

"Really?" Hugo responded without surprise. "So, who was aboard the boat? 'Cos it sure left the harbor and headed south toward where a young woman was murdered that night."

"My client doesn't know," Ambrose smugly replied. "He was unaware it had left the harbor."

Hugo chuckled. "Seriously? That's what you're going with?"

"My client apologizes for the confusion and will see if he can determine who may have taken the boat out, but our best guess is it was someone who took it without permission."

"Okay," I said. "Then our original question from your office remains, Mr. Monroe. Where were you on Wednesday night?"

"My client was at home on Wednesday night," Ambrose replied.

"Would you let your bloody client speak for himself?" I jabbed. "You're here as counsel, not to answer everything for him."

"Doesn't matter at this point," Ambrose replied with an annoying smirk. "Your question has been answered, and you have no reason to hold my client, so we're leaving."

They both rose from their seats.

"So when we search through the CCTV, we won't see your vehicle arriving at the harbor on Wednesday evening?" Hugo asked, standing up to stare into Monroe's eyes.

The suspect evaded the look, but his expression tightened.

Hugo laughed. "Yeah, that's what I thought."

"We're leaving," Ambrose repeated, and started for the door.

My phone and Hugo's buzzed at the same time. It was a text from Deputy Ripley.

"GPS shows boat out Wed night. Found bag of white powder. Looks like coke."

Hugo put a hand on Monroe's arm, bringing him to a stop. "You're not going anywhere."

"You have no grounds on which to hold Dylan, so we're leaving," Ambrose insisted. "Remove your hand from my client."

Hugo just grinned. "Dylan Monroe, I'm placing you under arrest for possession of an illegal narcotic—"

"What's all this about?" Ambrose ranted. "What narcotics?"

Monroe's face flushed, and his jaw quivered.

"The cocaine we just found on your client's boat," I informed the lawyer.

The drugs allowed us to hold Monroe and buy time, but we knew what was coming. He'd claim they must have been left there by whoever took the boat for a joyride on Wednesday night. Which meant we were back to scouring CCTV to place Dylan at the harbor.

Returning to our desks, I was about to contact the harbor security at their operations office when my cell phone rang from an unsaved number.

"Cromwell," I answered.

"Hi. Detective Fitzpatrick with the Newport Beach Police returning your call."

"Thanks for calling me back, detective," I replied. "I wanted to chat with you about an old case of yours. See if there are any links to one we have on our plate in Dana Point."

"Of course. Although, you have access to the file, so not sure what I can add, but I'll do my best. Is this about the drowning the other day?"

"That's the one."

"Then I presume you're asking about the Taylor Davis case."

"That's the one," I said again.

"Okay. Yeah, that was a weird case."

"Could we meet to talk?" I asked.

"Sure. I'm about done for the day, and I live in Laguna if you're up for meeting there. That'll be about halfway between Newport and Dana Point."

"Perfect. Where and when?"

"Is Laguna Coffee Company okay?" he asked. "I can be there in forty minutes."

"Beyond okay," I laughed. "See you there in forty."

I stood and began gathering my things, collecting my pictures I'd laid out.

"You leaving?" Hugo asked.

"That was Fitz… patrick," I said, catching myself and finishing his name. "I'll say hi for you."

Hugo grunted and leaned around his monitor. He did not look amused. "Better you don't," he grumbled.

***

For most of the drive north to Laguna Beach, I felt bad for leaving Hugo with more CCTV to grind through. But once I'd parked, ordered a large latte, and sequestered a table outside to wait for Fitzpatrick, my guilt quietly found somewhere else to be. I'm not sure exactly what I had in mind for Fitzpatrick's looks, but it wasn't the man who boldly walked over, set down a coffee he'd just bought, and extended a hand. He was tall, almost gangly, with curly dark hair and a stern expression.

"Fitzpatrick," he said confidently. "Everyone calls me Fitz."

"Katherine," I responded, shaking his hand. "But everyone calls me Kat. Thanks again for meeting me."

I watched him sit down. He wore a nice suit and tie, but everything about the guy was a step short of being quite right. His tie was slightly crooked, his hair a little messy, the collar on his shirt creased in an odd spot, and the left shoulder of his jacket appeared to have been scuffed on something. All things that would drive Hugo nuts.

"I assume you've read the file on Taylor Davis?" he asked.

I nodded.

"Then I'll do my best to recall anything you might deem important that didn't make those pages."

"Do you think Devin Williams killed her?" I asked, starting with the biggest question.

Fitz took a moment before responding. "It felt to me like he did, but probably because we had absolutely no one else."

"But nothing definitively tying him to the scene?" I asked.

"He's a college-educated realtor with no priors, but more importantly, he couldn't have done it," Fitz replied. "His alibi was solid. The timing meant he couldn't have killed her. Which was why as bizarre an accident as you could imagine became the only explanation."

I sat back and thought through both cases. The biggest similarity was beginning to be the fact that in neither case, the obvious suspect could have done it. And the internet date aspect, through OC Match.

"We have one of the owners of OC Match in custody. We have his boat leaving Dana Point harbor earlier in the evening and returning after midnight. Did you guys track down any boats in the vicinity?"

Fitz scoffed. "The beach is next to the seawall for the channel to Newport Bay. It's a busy traffic area for boats. We looked at the camera from the jetty, but couldn't see anything odd or suspicious. Boats came and went that evening, but nothing turned hard left toward the beach."

"What about the tides?" I asked as a thought occurred to me.

"It wasn't a king tide, but that night had a larger swing from low to high tide than normal. Best we could reconstruct, the girl went in the water around low tide and drowned when the tide came in around midnight. It's actually more likely she drowned earlier than that after becoming exhausted."

I sipped my coffee and mentally checked another box in my mind.

"How was she caught up in the line?"

"We couldn't get great pictures in the water as the surf was churning up sand, and first on scene cut her loose, anyway," he replied. "From what we could reconstruct, she'd not just become wrapped, as otherwise she'd have been able to spin the other way to get out, but the line had been threaded through its own mooring loop, which acted like a noose on her leg. Almost like she'd stepped through the noose, then tightened it when she struggled."

"Sounds more like a trap," I commented.

He nodded. "Or was slipped over her leg and tightened by someone. We worked with that theory from the beginning, but there wasn't a stitch of forensic evidence at the scene. Rope was old and covered in algae and growth from being underwater, a lot of which she'd scraped off in her struggles. But nothing under her fingernails other than from the rope, no sexual assault, and her clothes had been picked up by either somebody, or the tide. We had nothing."

"But you were still suspicious of foul play, so why close the case?" I asked, knowing I was potentially treading on the man's toes.

He looked at me for a long while, and I wondered if I'd indeed overstepped the mark.

"At the end of the day, I had nothing to follow up on, so I was handed another case. After a few more weeks, it was suggested that we close it."

Fitz held my gaze a few moments longer, which spoke louder than his words. Unsolved cases were thorns in the side of a department, and didn't look good for anyone. I could read between the lines without pushing Fitz further. He would have been under pressure from above if he had no leads and a plausible accidental death explanation.

"You're partnered with Hugo?" he asked, catching me off-guard with the subject change.

"I am," I replied.

"How's that?"

The simple question felt heavily loaded. Hugo had been tight-lipped beyond the fact that they'd had a relationship, but clearly things hadn't ended well. I was desperately curious to know more, but I couldn't afford to piss my partner off.

"Rocky start, but good now," I responded, which was the truth. I thought.

Fitz grinned, but didn't hold it for long. "Did he mention he knows me?"

I nodded, worried that if I opened my mouth, my foot might leap inside.

"What did he say?"

In some situations, I did have the ability to hide my emotions, but this wasn't one of them. He had to know I was uncomfortable, yet he'd still asked an awkward question. Which, of course, made me more uncomfortable. I thought about dumping my coffee in my lap as an excuse to leave and clean up, but naturally, I'd drained every drop from the cup.

"He mentioned you two had been in a relationship," I replied.

"So, you know?"

"Know what?"

"About Hugo."

"About Hugo being gay?" I whispered.

He nodded.

"Obviously. He told me about you two."

"I'm just surprised," Fitz replied, lightening his tone. "He guards that secret like his life depends on it."

"He thinks his work life does."

The detective shrugged his shoulders.

"You're out, I take it?" I asked.

He nodded. "It was difficult for a while, but eventually it was old news and stopped being an issue. He just needs to do the same and put it behind him."

"I'll tell him you said so," I replied.

He laughed. "No, I wouldn't do that."

In a fierce and torrid battle, which lasted no more than a millisecond, curiosity overwhelmed my good sense screaming at me to stay the hell out of this situation, and the words poured out of my mouth.

"What happened between you two?"

"What did Hugo say?"

"He didn't."

"Then I probably shouldn't, either," he replied, and finished his coffee.

My good sense picked itself up off the canvas, dusted itself off, and tossed curiosity aside in time for me to thank Fitz for his time.

Back at the car, I checked my email and saw we had Hailey Carter's phone records. Opening the file, I studied the call log, wishing I was looking at a larger computer screen instead of a phone. Names had been assigned to known numbers. I spotted several from GilTech and a couple from Enrique Gil's cell phone. Most belonged to family and her roommate.

I was switching to see the text log when my phone rang. "We have Hailey's phone records," Hugo blurted the moment I answered.

"I know. I was looking at them until you called."

"See the texts?" he asked without acknowledging my spiky response.

"I didn't get a chance!"

"Well, look at them," he snapped back.

"I can't with you on the bloody phone, so why don't you tell me?"

"Kwon," he replied. "A very upset Ryan Kwon."

"Bugger me," I muttered. "Is there anyone who *doesn't* want to be a suspect in this case?"

17

As I was already in Laguna Beach and less than half a mile from Ryan Kwon's apartment above the gallery, I volunteered to swing by. PCH was bumper-to-bumper at a little after six p.m., so I took Glenneyre Street and ran parallel the few blocks, looping around Legion to Ramona like we'd done the other day. Parking short of Kwon's place, I watched a guy I didn't recognize carry boxes and small pieces of furniture to a U-Haul truck.

I had to wait for backup from a pair of Laguna Beach police officers, who I'd requested to enter through the gallery. Now, seeing what I assumed to be a friend of Kwon's helping him move, I wondered if they'd be better served joining me up the hill behind the building. But it had taken them long enough to soldier through commuter traffic, so I was impatient to get this over with.

"This is LB531. We're in position. Over," came a voice over my radio.

"Copy, LB531. Approaching now," I replied, and got out of the car.

Forty-five minutes before the sun would set, Ramona Avenue was mostly shaded by the buildings on PCH, and I strained to make out details of the man carrying another couple of boxes to the truck.

"Excuse me, sir," I said once I was within ten feet of him. "Is Ryan Kwon home?"

The guy placed the boxes in the back of the U-Haul, then turned to face me. He was probably late-twenties, not very tall, overweight, and had dark hair pulled back in a ponytail.

"He's in his apartment, packing," the man replied in a friendly tone, which morphed into a frown as he studied me. "Why?" he added.

I showed him my badge. "OCSD Investigator, Cromwell."

He looked shocked, and I now had a dilemma. I could order him to stay by the truck, but there was no one to watch him. He could be a danger if he waited a few moments and then followed me inside. I chose the alternative.

"Mind taking me to Ryan?" I said.

"Okay. I guess," he replied, and hesitantly began walking toward the door. "What's this about?"

"What's your name, sir?" I asked instead of answering his question.

"Sean."

"Okay, Sean. Hold here for one moment," I ordered once we reached the door, which was propped open with a wooden wedge. "LB531, this is OCSD Sam 54. Come inside, please. Up the stairs to the apartment level. I'm approaching the building now with suspect's friend. Over."

"Copy," came the acknowledgment.

"What's going on?" Sean asked. "Why do you want Ryan?"

"I have a couple of questions for him," I replied, waiting a few beats for the officers to go inside and talk to whoever was in the gallery. Probably Bathrobe Lady, Camille Langley, the owner.

"Then why all the radio stuff? I'm just helping him move out, man. He's staying with me for a few days."

"That's nice of you," I responded, just to stall a little longer. "And where do you live?"

"South Laguna."

"LB531. We're on the stairs," came a hushed voice across the radio.

"Copy. Entering the building," I responded, then released the mic. "Okay, Sean. Let's go see your mate, Ryan."

The friend moved forward and started down the stairs to the apartment level. Halfway down, Sean stopped.

"Ryan! Cops are here!"

"You wanker," I groaned, and shoved Sean forward.

He quick-stepped a couple of stairs, then lost his footing and fell down the last three, hitting the landing with a thud. Kwon shot from his apartment, aiming for the fastest way out. Which I currently blocked. He raised his elbow to charge me, and I reacted on instinct.

I suppose I could blame it on too much time in my dad's gym, but my go-to defense was a right hook over the top of his elbow. I knew I'd got him good, as it hurt my knuckles something fierce. His forward momentum, combined with my solid follow-through, sent Kwon to the ground in a heap next to his friend.

The two Laguna Beach officers clattered up the stairs. I glanced over and noticed the little green lights on their body cams. I could only hope they'd not caught the altercation.

"Damn," the first officer said, looking from the groaning men on the floor up to me. He grinned. "You seem to have this under control."

I raised an eyebrow at him and resisted shaking my sore hand in front of his camera. Punching a suspect, despite being in self-defense, would still be frowned upon, so I hoped he wouldn't make a fuss. We were trained to handle adversaries with less aggressive methods, but being in the boxing gym three or four times a week apparently overrode my police training.

"If you don't mind watching Sean here for a minute," I said, helping the friend to his feet. "Then I'll have a chat with Mr. Kwon."

Ryan held his left cheek where he'd have a doozy of a shiner by the morning.

"Get up. We need to talk."

He rolled to his side, and I offered a hand, which he slapped away, getting to his feet on his own.

"What do you want now?" he said, glaring at me.

"Let's go inside your apartment. I have something to show you."

He gave me another sideways look, but complied, and I followed him.

"We'll be right here if you need anything," the first officer said.

"Yeah, cheers," I thanked him. "Moving out?" I asked Ryan once we were inside his apartment.

Boxes were strewn about the place as he appeared to be midstream of a rushed moving operation.

"Thanks to you," he muttered.

"Landlady give you the boot?"

He glared at me again, and I made a mental note to check with Bathrobe Lady and see if she'd filed a complaint against him, or had just cut her losses and moved on.

"Ryan, you told us you and Hailey were on good terms and potentially getting back together. Care to amend that statement?"

He shrugged his shoulders and shook his head a little, waiting for me to carry on. I unlocked my phone, where I'd left the text log open.

"'All you ever did was use me,'" I read aloud. "'You always think you're better than everyone else.'"

I looked up, but Kwon had turned away so I couldn't see his face.

"I should also mention the prodigious and extensive use of emojis here, Ryan. Quite impressive. Especially the devil-face one, and the broken heart."

His whole body flinched, but he continued staring out the window.

"I have to say you were firing off mixed messages, Ryan," I

continued. "'You know I still love you.' Followed shortly by Hailey replying with, 'It's been over for long enough. Move on.' You then switch gears and hit her with, 'Fuck you. You'll regret this.'"

I heard the suspect release a long exhale, and I gave him a moment. He was clearly a hothead, and while it was possible that he might slip if I kept him wound up, it was just as likely he'd try something stupid like running again. I'd prefer he resigned himself to being screwed by the evidence we had. Although, I still didn't know what the hell we had except a stalking and angry ex-boyfriend who was in Laguna Beach when Hailey was murdered.

I took the opportunity to snap a picture of Kwon in his apartment, and the whirring of the picture emerging from the camera made him turn around.

"Doesn't look good, mate," I said. "You firing off these threatening texts on the evening she was murdered."

His eyes were red, like he hadn't had much sleep, and his shoulders sagged in defeat. "I didn't kill Hailey. Those are just words, man. I could never hurt her. Besides, I was home on Wednesday night."

"After you were checking on her at Capo Beach," I pointed out.

"Yeah, but then I came home. There must be cameras along PCH. You'll see I drove back here."

"And then found your way back to Capo Beach, right?" I said, keeping a softer, sympathetic tone. "Drove all the way around the toll road, maybe. Or even by boat. Know someone with a boat, Ryan?"

He groaned. "That's ridiculous. I was home. Sure, you know I did a stupid thing and put a tracker on her car, and yes, I drove to Dana Point after we'd had the text exchange. But I was going to beg her to try again. I didn't go there to hurt her."

"I believe you, mate," I said. "I get it. Everyone's had a tough breakup or two. But when you got to Dana Point, you found Hailey out on a date, right? That had to sting."

He looked at the floor, then glanced up at me. "I didn't kill her."

I scrolled through the texts, which had ended at 7:25 p.m. The last five were from Kwon, either hurling insults or trying to get Hailey to respond. At 7:05 p.m., she'd sent her last text, which I read to myself. "'Move on, Ryan, and stop harassing me. I'm blocking your number.'"

But she hadn't blocked his number. Her date had been at seven-thirty p.m., so there was a good chance she was finishing getting ready and leaving the house at that time. Maybe she'd intended to do it later, or it was an idle threat for a guy she felt sorry for, although she no longer loved him. We'd never know.

"I need the address where you'll be staying," I said, conceding that there was little more to be gained tonight.

He wrote it down on a piece of paper, including Sean's last name, Turvey.

"If I call you, will you answer your phone?" I asked, handing Kwon a card. "It'll save us going through this goat rope every time we have a question, Ryan."

He nodded and slipped the card in his pocket.

"Running every time isn't helping your cause."

He sighed. "I know," he replied, touching the side of his face, which was already swelling up. "Still, you didn't have to punch me."

"You ran into your mate," I replied. "Right after he stumbled down the stairs."

Kwon frowned at me and went to speak, but I beat him to it.

"Accidental collision in the hallway is probably better on the report than you trying to run from the police again. Don't you think?"

He sighed once more and nodded. "Yeah. I'm clumsy sometimes."

I left the apartment and joined the officers on the landing.

"We're all done, lads. Thanks for the help."

Sean scurried into the apartment, and the Laguna Beach cops followed me downstairs. The gallery owner was in the store, so I paused a moment in the office.

"We'll need to submit a report," the first officer said, looking at me with a questioning expression as he and his partner turned off their body cameras.

"Yeah, no problem," I replied. "Report it as you saw it."

"They were both on the ground by the time we arrived."

"Yup. Ran into each other. Kwon wasn't expecting us coming down the stairs."

The officer grinned. "Kwon wasn't trying to run?"

I shook my head. "Nah. Just rushing around packing, from what I could tell."

He chuckled. "Okay, ma'am."

"Thanks again for the help, guys."

"Anytime. I have a feeling calls aren't dull around you."

They left, still grinning, and I wondered if the broad-shouldered, handsome officer was flirting with me or taking the piss. I'd never been good at knowing. Which might explain my lack of dates. Although, the last thing I needed was to date another law enforcement officer. I had enough shit to worry about.

"Hi, Mrs. Langley, mind if I have a word?" I asked, walking over to where she was straightening a painting on the wall.

"What's he done now?" she asked briskly.

"Nothing new," I replied. "But I see you've asked Ryan to leave."

"Didn't have a choice, did I?" she rebutted. "I can't have people stealing from me."

"You found what he'd been up to?"

"Not yet," she replied, and I wondered if I'd screwed the guy by sharing my suspicion. I didn't think she'd fire him without proof.

"My accountant is looking into it," she continued, "but when I confronted Ryan, he apologized. He backed up after that, but innocent people don't say sorry for what they haven't done, Miss…"

"Cromwell," I reminded her, feeling a little better about the situation.

I didn't know why I harbored any concern for a wanker who'd shoved me down the stairs and, at a minimum, stalked and harassed his ex-girlfriend. But I'd probably been out of line saying anything at all to Camille, so it would make me feel better to know he was actually guilty of something at the gallery.

My phone buzzed with a text from Hugo. He'd lined up Dylan Monroe's friend and employee, Jason Browning, to come into the station in the morning at ten. It was a fresh murder case, and we'd be working Sunday regardless of having an interview lined up, so it didn't matter.

I thanked Camille Langley and walked back upstairs, remembering to pause a moment, turn around, and take a picture of the stairwell from the landing. Kwon and his friend struggled out of his apartment door with his mattress, so I hurried up the next flight of stairs to the street to keep out of the way and walked to my car.

The temperature had dropped with the sun, and streetlights illuminated the narrow avenue. Reaching the car, I called Hugo.

"Hey," he answered, and I could hear the engine noise. He was driving home. "How did it go with Kwon?"

"Idiot tried running again."

"Tell me you had backup with you, Kat."

"I did. Calm down, Dad," I replied with a laugh.

"Well, I just spent twenty minutes with Captain Bradley. She's all over us to get somewhere on this case, so we can't afford any screwups," he snapped back.

"Alright, alright," I replied, trying not to react too defensively.

I hoped the Kwon incident wouldn't come to anything, and if it did, I'd likely be cleared as he'd come at me, but Bradley and my partner would still consider it a screwup.

"It all went fine. I had two locals with me," I added, forcing a calmer tone.

He grunted something under his breath, then spoke up. "We have harbor CCTV on Monroe from Wednesday night, so we have something to work with tomorrow. Any luck with Kwon?"

"Nothing new," I continued. "I confronted him about the texts, and he swears he was blowing hot air, would never hurt her, blah, blah, blah. We still have nothing placing him near the scene at the time she was killed. But the gallery owner has kicked him out, although she's not pressed any charges."

"Do you know where he's staying?" Hugo asked. "We don't want him in the wind."

"With a friend," I replied. "But I don't see how he could have done it, Hugo."

There was a brief pause. "I agree, unless there's something crazy we're missing," he said, followed by another pause. "Get anything useful from Fitz?"

I scoffed. "Lots of similarities, including the obvious suspect who couldn't have done it."

"Why'd they close it if he doesn't think it was an accident?" Hugo asked.

"Pressure from above to button it up, and nothing concrete confirming there was foul play," I replied.

"But Fitz thinks there was?"

I thought about my answer for a moment. "He wouldn't say it outright, but yeah, I think he believes there was more to it than a freak accident."

18

Reminding myself that the cupboards in my house were still bare, I'd ordered food from Taco Surf on the drive south, then stopped by to pick it up. My surfing friend, who worked in the evenings, handed me my to-go order across the bar.

"You're not staying?" Bethany asked.

"Gotta get home," I replied.

"Ooooh," she grinned. "Got a fella waiting?"

I laughed. "As a matter of fact, I do."

Bethany looked surprised. "You do? That's awesome, Kat. About time."

I unlocked my phone and found a picture of Roger while I contemplated how sad my life apparently appeared to everyone who knew me.

"He's a great cuddler," I said before showing her the picture.

She burst out laughing, which brought Amber, another server and friend, over to us.

"Oh, how cute is that little guy?" Amber swooned. "If you ever show this to my kids, I'll kill you. I have enough to keep up with without a rabbit. And the dog would probably eat it."

"Ew," Bethany grimaced. "What does he do all day when you're gone?"

I scrolled until I found another picture. "He hangs out in his hutch."

"That's a rabbit hutch?" Amber asked, squinting at the photo. "That's nicer than my TV stand in the living room."

"Eventually, I'll leave him out and he can cruise the living room while I'm at work, but we're building up to that," I explained.

"Won't he poop and pee everywhere?" Bethany asked.

"Uses a litter box like a cat," I replied, and showed them another picture of Roger sitting in a gray tray, munching on a pile of timothy hay placed at one end.

"That's his litter box?" Amber asked. "You put his food in his bathroom?"

I nodded. "Yup. Encourages him to use the loo. He does his business out the back while he's snacking at the front."

"Definitely a male," Bethany joked. "I don't understand how or why men have to have something else to do while they're using the bathroom."

"I know," Amber agreed. "And why does it take so long? I'm in, take care of business, and out again."

"Okay, you're putting me off my dinner now," I laughed, and scooped up my paper bag of food.

"Waves are supposed to be good in the morning," Bethany said as I made for the door. "See you out there?"

"Where are you going?" I asked from the doorway.

"Old Man's," she replied, referring to a great and popular longboard surf spot in San Clemente to the south of Dana Point.

"I might get down to Doheny first thing, but I have to work tomorrow," I replied.

"That Capo Beach thing?" she asked, losing her bright smile.

I nodded.

She nodded in return, a simple gesture loaded with understanding, sympathy, and concern.

"Take care, Kat."

"Cheers, Bethany," I responded, and hurried to my car.

Jason Browning arrived five minutes early the following morning, which was the good news. Unfortunately, he brought Monroe's lawyer along, Jonathan Ambrose, which meant their stories had no doubt been suitably meshed. That was not good news.

Hugo thanked them both for agreeing to meet, read off the usual blurb, and we began.

"Can you start by walking us through your evening this past Wednesday?" Hugo asked.

"I was at home on Wednesday evening," Browning replied.

Hugo maintained a friendly tone. "Okay, and what time did you get home?"

"Left work around six, I think, so home around six-thirty, I'd say."

"Perfect, thank you," Hugo continued, and I watched the lawyer's expression tighten. He could smell a sucker punch coming their way.

"From what we see on DMV records, Mr. Browning, you drive a 2023 Mercedes," Hugo said. "Is that correct?"

The man nodded. "Yes."

"Any other vehicles?"

"No," he replied, his voice wavering slightly.

Maybe Browning was picking up on the lawyer's anxiety, or perhaps he also sensed a trap. Either way, I was enjoying watching them stumble toward the blind side.

"Mr. Browning, were you with anyone else on Wednesday evening while you were home at 25105 Grissom Road in Laguna Hills?"

He shook his head.

"Verbal response for the tape, please," Hugo urged.

"No, I was alone at home," Browning responded, leaning toward the recording device.

I opened my laptop, making sure I still had the correct CCTV footage on the screen. Spinning it around to face Browning, I hit the spacebar. Ambrose opened his mouth to speak, but rethought whatever he was about to say and stayed quiet.

"As you can see from the timestamp in the corner, Mr. Browning," I said, watching his reaction, "this is you in your Mercedes approaching the Dana Point marina at 7:18 p.m. on Wednesday evening."

Browning sat there in stunned silence. I'm sure Monroe, through Ambrose, had convinced him everything would be fine if they stuck to the script. I turned to the lawyer.

"Your other client, currently staying with us on the drug possession charge, arrived at 7:08 p.m."

Ambrose didn't look nearly as smug as he had when he'd arrived yesterday.

"Let's take a break," he suggested. "I need to confer with my client."

"Pausing interview," Hugo said, and hit the button on the recorder.

"We're going to need your client to provide a urine sample," I said as I rose from the chair.

"That's not happening," Ambrose quickly replied.

"Mr. Browning, you should know that refusing a drug test by police when suspected of narcotic use is an automatic one-year suspension of your driver's license."

Realizing he was now considered a suspect, Browning looked even more horrified.

"He's not refusing a drug test, Miss Cromwell," Ambrose replied. "He's refusing a urine test. My client will submit to a blood test."

"I will?" Browning blurted, looking at his lawyer, who held up a hand to silence his client.

"We'll give you a few minutes to confer," Hugo said, making for the door. "Text us when you're ready."

I followed Hugo out, and we waited to speak until we were down the hall and the door had sprung closed behind us.

"Crafty bugger," I swore. "He knows we won't find it in his bloodstream three and a half days later."

"Yeah. It was pushing it for a pee test, anyway," Hugo said, and he was right.

The maximum time for finding cocaine in blood tests was forty-eight hours, and urine twice that, but neither was guaranteed. Some people's bodies metabolized the drug faster than others, and a lot depended on hydration and other factors in the time between taking the narcotic and testing. We asked the duty sergeant, who for once wasn't Martinez, to request a nurse for a blood sample, then made our way to the break room.

"What angle do you think they'll take now that we can place them both at the marina?" I asked as we poured coffees from the carafe.

Hugo chewed over his thoughts while he added creamer and sweetener to his cup. When done, he turned and leaned against the counter, slowly stirring his coffee while he spoke.

"Browning's best move is to distance himself from Monroe and claim he didn't know about the drugs. But I doubt that'll happen as Monroe's his boss, and I bet Monroe's paying for Ambrose to handle both their cases. Ambrose will know it's only a matter of time before we get another boat's security camera footage from the marina slip, which will show both men at the boat. So, I'd say he'll stall until the drug tests are complete, then try to work the charges down to a simple possession, claiming they never used the cocaine."

"It'll be a step forward if we can prove they were on the boat leaving the harbor," I said, considering our next challenge. "But we still have nothing placing them at the murder scene."

Hugo shook his head. "We know she was still wearing her watch, but we need to double-check if she had any other jewelry on her. Our best chance would be if they took a memento. We have enough for a home search warrant now."

"Have you looked at the GPS data from the boat?" I asked.

He nodded before taking a sip of coffee.

"Does it help us?" I asked.

"Not as much as I'd like. They run along the coast about a half mile from shore. Stop for a while, but it's a mile south of where Hailey was found."

"Could have anchored and taken the tender," I suggested. "What time did they stop?"

"Around eleven," Hugo replied. "For forty-five minutes."

"Timing lines up," I pointed out.

"Yeah," he agreed. "And these two would have the ability to see conversations in their dating app. But I don't know how they'd know Caldwell and Hailey would go to the beach."

"Hey," I said as the thought hit me. "What if Caldwell was in on it?"

"He made sure she went to the beach?"

"Yup."

Hugo looked at his phone as it buzzed. "They're ready," he said, but didn't move. "We need to see if we can tie Caldwell to Monroe and Browning."

"He uses their app, for one," I said.

"Obviously," Hugo scoffed. "I mean finding a connection outside of the dating software."

We walked to the hallway, where I paused a moment.

"You know what else, Hugo?"

He stopped and looked back.

"We need to see if *Shore Code* was anywhere near Newport Beach on the night Taylor Davis died."

He raised his eyebrows.

I smiled. "And we can check the GPS data for that, too."

Predictably, when we went back into the interview room, Ambrose had Jason Browning clammed up and ready to leave. We contemplated arresting him, but unless the drug test came back positive, or we could tie him to the murder in any way, he'd be out first thing Monday. We all wasted several hours waiting for an available nurse to take the blood sample before letting Browning leave.

Hugo and I were about to spend another thrilling afternoon searching more CCTV and looking into the GPS history from the Garmin taken from *Shore Code*, when Captain Bradley dropped by the station.

"Progress?" she asked.

We filled her in, putting a slightly more optimistic spin on the situation.

"You sure about cutting Browning loose?" she asked when we were done.

"For now," Hugo replied. "Looks like they're the first suspects with opportunity, but we're yet to establish if they had the means. They're software engineers, so fabricating metal structures doesn't immediately jump out as an obvious pastime."

"As for motive," I said, completing the three major aspects from which law enforcement viewed a crime, "we again have nothing at this stage, but we're working on the angle that this might be tied to the drowning in Newport Beach. If it is, we're dealing with a serial pattern."

"Okay," Bradley responded, looking less than okay about what we had. But she looked at her watch before continuing. "You two look whipped. Get out of here. Take an afternoon to recharge and hit it hard in the morning."

Maybe she felt guilty, as she was only sticking her head in the door for a few minutes, or maybe we did look that crappy. Or I looked like shit, as Hugo's appearance seemed its usual flawless self to me. Either way, I felt exhausted, and nothing we were about to discover that afternoon would close the case, so we took a few minutes to tidy up, then left.

It was almost one p.m. I drove toward the ocean and considered my options, finally calling my mum.

"Hi, darling," she answered.

"Have you two had lunch yet?" I asked.

"We were just sitting down to eat now," she replied. "Can you join us?"

"If that's okay?" I asked, a polite but superfluous question. Even if they were about to consume the last remnants of food in the house, my mum would race to the shops and buy more rather than say no. Knowing that made me feel special, but she'd also do the same for any friend or family member, so not *that* special.

"Of course. We'll see you in a few."

"Tell her not to hang about," I heard my dad's voice in the background. "I'm bloody starving."

I laughed and hung up. Dad would also welcome anyone to join them in the same scenario, except he wouldn't race to the grocery store, and would probably have eaten most of the food before the guest arrived.

Parking outside the home I'd grown up in since my parents moved to California from England when I was six, I pushed through the side gate and walked across the courtyard to the sliding glass door we always used instead of the formal front entrance.

"Hello, darling," Mum said, giving me a hug.

"'Bout bloody time," Dad greeted me with a grin. "Park your bum so we can eat."

And that about described my parents perfectly. My mum, the most empathetic, kind, and nurturing woman in the world, who taught drama at the high school after a very successful modeling career. And my dad, who'd beaten the shit out of people for a living in the boxing ring before retiring as Great Britain's heavyweight champion and became an announcer for American TV. Chalk and cheese. But I couldn't wish for two more loving parents.

"Is that a bruise on your face?" my mother asked as I sat down.

It had stopped hurting, so I'd forgotten about it. Dad busied himself with passing around a basket of bread.

"I had an argument with a stairwell in Laguna Beach," I said, using a partial truth to cover up the remaining evidence of Cisco's well-aimed punch.

Mum glared at my dad.

"Take some bread, then," he said, holding out the basket and looking guilty as hell.

19

————————

It was hard for my afternoon off to feel much like time off. On the way home from my parents', I stopped by the store and stocked up on groceries. Once home, a very excited Roger didn't seem to mind being woken up from his nap to tear around the living room while I put everything away. Next came laundry. I'd been stretching my work clothes, wearing the blouses for two days and the slacks for three, and I was completely out of clean workout gear. The two blazers I wore were both in need of a dry clean, which foiled my rotation plan and would have to wait until tomorrow.

Next came Roger's credenza. Generally, he was a clean little critter, but his hopping about tended to drag hay all over the place, and scatter litter and the little pellets he pooped. He fussed around me while I vacuumed his home, then freshened his bed and litter box, and sorted the myriad of toys he mostly ignored.

Worn out and ready to sit down, I contemplated ordering in food, but felt guilty now that I'd finally replenished the cupboards, so I made pasta. Not the fancy homemade sauce my mother would fabricate, but a slap-together job from a box and a jar. At eight p.m., I settled on the couch, with Roger joining me, and watched a few episodes of an old sitcom.

The weird dreams and nightmares that plagued me over my fiancé's death had lessened. Somewhat. They seemed to be farther apart, but even more intense when they did invade my sleep. I jolted awake around three a.m., feeling out of breath with sweat glowing on my brow. Paul had disappeared into the rough seas while a cruise ship full of people stared down at me, pointing and whispering in the swirling winds.

That was new. Not the Paul drowning part, which mimicked something close to what may have really happened, but the cruise ship and the people. I hadn't had that scenario before, and it definitely deviated from reality. We'd been alone on the water when the engine began playing up and left us stranded in the storm. Arguing. Not about the storm or the engine, but about Gabriella Castillo. Who would be in court in Santa Ana later that morning.

I spent the rest of the night in short bursts of fitful sleep between longer periods of restless agonizing over Castillo, Hailey Carter, and our list of suspects. At five-thirty a.m., I gave up, dressed for the gym, and after feeding Roger and letting him hop around for a while, left the house in the dark.

"Lower, Kat," my dad's voice boomed from across the gym. "Don't cheat 'em."

My thighs burned, and a stream of profanity hitched a ride on my exhale. I hated lunges. Everybody hates lunges.

"Whine all you want, love, but don't cheat 'em."

Apparently, my complaining wasn't as quiet as I'd thought.

"One more lap," he added.

I'd already made it four times around the perimeter of the boxing gym with a twenty-pound dumbbell in each hand. Every step now felt like my legs would explode, sending pieces of shredded Kat all over the place.

"You got this," or "Dig deep," boxers encouraged me as I passed the various workout stations and punching bags.

If they were on my side of the pain, they'd keep their damn mouths shut.

"Didn't you start on the other side?" my dad asked when I dropped the weights to the floor and collapsed next to them.

I rolled on my side and glared at him. "No! I started right here."

"You sure?" he grinned.

I nodded, my cheek brushing back and forth on the cool concrete floor. "Yup. I left my dignity right here when I started."

He laughed, along with several others who overheard me. Cisco was walking by and offered me a hand. I was more than happy to stay where I was for another hour or two, but I let him help me to my feet.

"You're strong for…" he began, but trailed off.

"For a girl?" I said, scowling at him. "Is that what you were about to say, mate?"

He grinned sheepishly.

"You're lucky I don't stop your fist with my face again," I growled at him.

For a second, Cisco thought he'd really pissed off the trainer's daughter, but then he processed what I'd said. He was a bright kid, but English was his second language. He laughed and gave me a fist bump.

"Where you going?" Dad called out as I headed toward the locker room after replacing the weights on the rack.

"Work!"

"Alright, then," I heard him say as I rounded the corner. "If half a workout's enough for ya."

I pictured his big stone-like face cracking a smile as he said it. It made me chuckle as I began stripping off for the shower.

The Central Justice Center in Santa Ana opened at eight a.m., with the first case heard at eight-thirty a.m. After stopping by PC Beans' drive-thru for a coffee and a scone, then sitting in commuter traffic on the 5 freeway, I arrived a few minutes before the judge took his seat in the courtroom where Gabriella Castillo's case was second on the docket.

Sitting in the back, I spotted Castillo's bleached blond hair toward the front. She was leaning over, listening to whatever her attorney was saying. The family's counsel on retainer, no doubt.

The judge arrived, and the mind-numbingly boring proceedings of traffic court began while I kept an eye on Castillo. Every few minutes, she turned around and scanned the seats behind them. I stayed half-hidden behind the person in front of me, though I doubted I was the one she was looking for. I had a good idea who that was.

Gabby had been annoyingly popular in high school. She was a cheerleader, drove a Porsche from age sixteen, and led a trail of disciples around like the Pied Piper. I played sports, hung out with the surf crowd, and maintained a small circle of friends. I got along with just about everyone, except Gabby and her stuck-up, bitchy friends. When I was talking about surf reports, she was showing off her latest phone or diamond-studded watch.

Her case was called, and predictably, the officer no-showed. Castillo left the court with a grin on her face when the case was dismissed. Her speeding ticket had been issued in Newport Beach. I had the officer's name, so as I left the courtroom, I contemplated calling his station to see if he was on duty today.

Unlocking my phone, I saw a text from Hugo, asking when I'd be in. I'd let him know I had something to take care of first thing and I'd be late, but I'd be pushing my luck to detour via Newport Beach.

With Dylan Monroe in custody and his friend Jason Browning high on our suspect list, we needed evidence directly tying them to Hailey's murder, or they'd both get to walk. At least on the murder charge. As I hurried out of the building, I replied to Hugo, letting him know I'd be there in thirty minutes, although I knew it would be closer to forty.

I was still looking at my phone when I heard a familiar voice.

"Well, look who it is. How's Katherine the cop these days?"

I stopped and turned around. Gabby was off to the side, smoking a cigarette, grinning at me with a condescending expression.

"Castillo," I responded. "No surprise seeing you in a courthouse."

She laughed. "You seemed to take an interest in my speeding ticket for some reason. Or are you just stalking me?"

So much for not being seen.

"You know you just spent more having that attorney by your side than the fine would have been, right?" I responded, ignoring her question.

She shrugged her shoulders. "Didn't cost me a penny."

I kept my cool, despite her smug expression, but I'd had enough. The whole idea of sitting in on her hearing now seemed pointless and a waste of time when we had a killer to catch. I turned and began walking away.

"I miss him," Castillo said, which halted me in my tracks.

Rage instantly boiled inside, along with an overwhelming desire to punch Gabriella in the face until I could no longer recognize her perfect nose and full lips. The thought that those lips had been all over my fiancé's body was too much to bear. A vision far too familiar from sleepless nights and tormented dreams.

My phone vibrated in my hand, and the distraction came at the key moment. I'm not sure what I'd been about to do, but it wouldn't have been good for my career. Or Castillo's health.

"Hey," I answered, seeing it was Hugo as I pulled myself together and walked away from the courthouse.

"We have the reports from a bunch of the metal distributors," he said. "It's a shitload of data to go through."

"Did you cross-reference our suspects' names yet?" I asked, trying to shove my anger aside and refocus.

"Of course," Hugo snapped.

I took another breath. "Yeah, sorry. Anything?"

"Nope," he replied, and I began wondering why he'd called. "Where are you?" he asked.

"Santa Ana. Leaving the courthouse now."

"What case is that?" Hugo asked, prying more than I'd like.

"Unrelated. I'm almost to my car. I'll be there soon."

The line was quiet for a few moments. "Okay," he finally said, and hung up.

As I drove out of the parking lot, I wondered again why my partner had called. Checking on me out of curiosity? He could be pissed off that I was off doing something else while he was working on the case, and he'd have a right to be. Or did he know I was keeping an eye on Gabriella Castillo?

I hoped not. The fuss and suspicion around my involvement in my fiancé's accident, as it had been ruled, was finally subsiding. I still wasn't Captain Bradley's favorite by a long shot, but she seemed to treat me the same as everyone else these days.

By the time I walked into the station, I'd purged Gabby Castillo from my mind and was ready to dive back into our case. Specifically, tying Monroe into the Corona Del Mar case. If we could place *Shore Code* in the vicinity at the time of Taylor Davis's murder, then the circumstantial evidence would all point to Dylan Monroe. At least we'd have a suspect we could focus all our resources on.

But Hugo quashed that myth before my butt had even hit the seat.

"Monroe bought *Shore Code* six weeks after the Corona Del Mar drowning," he said in response to my greeting.

"Bugger," I sighed, dropping into the chair. "Did he own another boat before that?"

"Not one registered to him," he replied. "Can you rent boats in the harbor?"

"Yeah, but they're all private," I groaned. "There isn't a boat rental company as such, just charters. A few individuals will rent out their boats, but anything big enough to be out at night and travel fifteen miles along the coast to the Newport area would come with a captain."

"Can't imagine he'd want anyone else aboard when he's planning to drown a young woman," Hugo muttered, then slid his chair over to face me. "But Taylor Davis aside, Monroe and Browning are still the best lead for our case."

It wasn't a question, but the look on his face seemed to beg an answer.

"Agreed," I said.

"Then how did they know they'd find Hailey Carter at the beach that night?"

I shook my head. The same question had been eating away at my brain since we'd brought Monroe in.

"Tracked by the app!" I responded, far louder than I'd intended as the notion hit me. "You know how apps ask whether you allow them to know your location?"

Hugo nodded, but regardless, I wasn't waiting for his reply and kept talking, "Monroe could easily follow her movements if she had that feature checked."

Hugo exhaled a long breath. "Be nice to check that on her phone."

"Yeah, but I bet OC Match can see it from their end," I replied. "We'd need a warrant and an IT wizard to find out."

Hugo scoffed. "Don't you think they would have buried or deleted any trace of incriminating evidence by now?"

I slumped back in the seat. "Yeah. Probably."

"And there's one other problem," Hugo said, shaking his head. "It still doesn't explain how they'd know Hailey would end up at Capo Beach. Alone."

"Maybe they were trolling the coast, and the opportunity fell into their laps," I replied, my hesitant tone betraying my lack of conviction.

"Right, they just cruised around sniffing coke until a young female using their app happened to be alone on a beach nearby. Then they rushed over with a metal structure and—"

"Alright, alright, Hugo. I know," I interrupted him. "So we've come back around in a full circle. Again."

"Yup," he agreed.

"Caldwell has to be involved," I sighed.

"Yup," Hugo repeated. "And we need to focus on finding the connection between the three of them."

20

We spent the rest of the morning hunting through Garrett Caldwell, Dylan Monroe, and Jason Browning's social media sites, internet presence, and any official records we had access to. Nothing appeared to connect either of the OC Match men with Caldwell. Different schools, no photos together online, and no family ties. Finally, as we began discussing lunch, I ran a comparison between social media friends of OC Match, the company, and Caldwell. It returned multiple results.

"It's something," I said to Hugo after explaining what I'd found.

"Hardly surprising, though," he countered. "I bet you and I have friends who use OC Match and may follow them on Facebook."

"I don't use social media," I pointed out. "I only have a Facebook account so I can access searches like this. My name on my page is Kitty BoxingGirl."

"I'm calling you Kitty Kat from now on."

"Try it, and you'll discover the boxing part," I replied, shaking a fist at him.

To my surprise, Hugo actually laughed, which made me laugh, too.

"I hope this hilarity reflects progress in your case," Captain Bradley said from the doorway.

Her sudden presence and comment guaranteed Hugo's sense of humor would go back into hiding for another six months.

"A very loose tie between Garrett Caldwell and Monroe, ma'am," Hugo responded. His voice was all business. "Monroe and Browning are good for the murder, but we still can't place them at the scene. We think Caldwell has to be involved, as that seems like the only way the vic was delivered to the right beach at the right time."

"We can't prosecute *seems like,*' Hugo," Bradley retorted. "So you'd better come up with more than that." She took a breath and softened her tone. "But I agree with your logic. Monroe and Browning will both be arraigned after lunch. So unless you come up with something concrete tying either one to the murder, they'll be out of our grasp."

I looked over my shoulder and across the desks at my partner, who raised an eyebrow in response. I'd been happy with him handling the boss, but apparently he was now handing over the reins.

"That'll be a stretch unless something comes back from forensics, ma'am," I said, turning to face her again. "But we understand the urgency."

Captain Bradley stared at me for several moments. "Do you, Kat?"

"Yes, ma'am," I was quick to respond.

She turned to leave, then paused. "Doesn't look that way when you're hanging around the courthouse instead of chasing leads," Bradley said without looking back, leaving me in stunned silence.

"It's the county courthouse, Kat," Hugo whispered. "What did you expect?"

I spun around and caught his eye before he slid behind his computer screen.

"And no, I didn't say a word to her," he assured me.

And I believed him. He was right. Any number of police officers or officials could have seen me, and word made its way back to Bradley. Or maybe she heard it from Castillo's attorney. But surely the captain would have had more to say on the matter if she were fending off harassment complaints. Not that I harassed Gabby. She initiated a conversation with me, but that didn't matter. I was sitting in the back of the courtroom during her case hearing, and that would be enough to throw suspicion on me. Plus, they'd be right. I *was* there to see what happened in her case, so it would be hard to deny.

"We have seven names on the list," I said, keen to move on.

Hugo rolled his chair into view. "Seven?"

I nodded. "Four females, three males."

"Low-percentage chance a woman would be involved in something like this," he responded.

"Agreed, but these people may not be involved at all. We're looking for a way Caldwell and Monroe are linked. The third party might just be a connection on the fringe of another group of friends."

"That's a rabbit hole we don't have time for," Hugo sighed. "At least, we don't yet. Let's chase the higher-percentage leads first."

I returned to my keyboard. "Sending you the link to one of these guys. I'll take the other two."

I used our internal messenger software to send Hugo the social media link, then brought up my first name. I'd barely started scrolling through the guy's feed when Hugo called out.

"Bingo. Look at this, Kat."

I got up and walked around to Hugo's side.

"This guy, Matthew McCall, has a business in San Clemente," he explained, and clicked to another internet tab.

It was the website for McCall Fabrication. The image on the banner was a collage showing decorative metalwork front gates for a large house, a man welding with a bright white glow from the gun, and a sports car atop a lift in a private garage.

"Do you have the specs on the metal used for the frame?" Hugo asked.

"Yup."

"Then I'd say this place is worth a visit."

Hugo was excited to grab lunch from a taco stand in San Clemente, or at least as excited as Hugo ever got about anything. It was out of our way, but I wasn't about to turn down tacos for lunch. Or any other meal.

It was one-thirty p.m. when we parked on North El Camino Real, one hundred yards down the street from the fabrication shop. It fronted the busy main road through town, but backed up to a narrow street called Los Abreros, which provided commercial access to businesses on either side.

"We should call the locals and have someone out back," Hugo said before we got out of the car.

"Can do," I replied, "but we'll have to wait, and it'll escalate what should be a simple chat. The guy has a couple of speeding tickets on his record, otherwise he's clean."

Hugo drummed the wheel. "He's still a suspect," he said, then looked at me over his sunglasses. "And I've noticed suspects like to run from you."

"Bugger off! Not my fault if they mistakenly think they can outrun a girl."

Which was even funnier, as I'd never seen Hugo run after anyone. His policy was to let them go and call uniforms to track them down. Hugo went to a gym and kept himself in good shape, but it was all about appearances. His concern was how well his expensive suits hung from his well-toned frame. I was more worried about avoiding being hit in the face by the likes of Cisco, so my training had a more practical focus.

Hugo got out, so I guessed he'd decided to forego the backup. We walked along the street and sized up the building. It was an older structure, like much of San Clemente, with a Spanish tile roof and a stucco finish that could have done with a pressure washing.

The mixed sounds of saws and grinders filtered from the rear of the building as we entered the front door into a small reception area.

At some point in time, an effort had been made to set the reception up as a showroom, but nothing had been maintained. The pictures were faded, and a variety of smaller examples of metalwork designs for gates and fences now leaned against each other in a haphazard fashion.

"Can I help you?" a young woman asked in a bored tone from behind an old wooden desk at the end of the reception.

She was probably in her twenties but looked more like an angst-ridden teenager. Her hair was recovering from a dark green dye job, and her eyes were bordered with thick lines of black mascara. I could hear her chomping gum from across the room.

"Is Matthew McCall available?" Hugo asked.

The young girl looked us both over suspiciously before turning in her chair. "Dad!" she yelled. "Someone here for you!"

One of the grinding sounds stopped, and a few moments later, a man appeared through a door behind the reception desk. He slid a pair of safety glasses to the top of his head and paused a moment when he saw us.

"Mr. McCall?" Hugo asked.

The man nodded and slipped the dirty workman's gloves one by one from his hands, dropping them on the reception desk. He gave his daughter a glare, no doubt intended as a warning against telling strangers he was available, but she wasn't paying attention. Her face was already buried in her phone as she blew a pink bubble until it burst with a snap.

We presented our badges. "OCSD Investigators Fuentes and Cromwell," Hugo announced.

"No shit," McCall muttered, throwing another wasted look his daughter's way. "How can I help you?"

"Somewhere we can talk, sir?" Hugo asked.

McCall shrugged his shoulders. "Go ahead."

"Maybe somewhere more private, sir," Hugo persisted.

I figured it was redundant, as the daughter wasn't interested in anything involving her father, but McCall led us into an office, anyway. I closed the door behind us and got a close-up look at Miss August on a tool company's calendar hung on the back of the door. Miss August hadn't bothered to put any clothes on before sprawling across the hood of a race car.

"What's this about?" McCall asked, taking a seat behind his desk.

The office was twice as messy as the reception, with stacks of paperwork and drawings cluttering the man's desk. He didn't offer us a seat, which would have required clearing the chairs of lock parts, hinges, and other assorted bits and pieces.

"What kind of fabrication do you do here?" Hugo asked politely.

"The metal kind. What's this about?"

"Custom welding type work?" Hugo continued. "With steel tube and what have you?"

I cringed inside at Hugo's vague attempt at discussing forms of metal fabrication and stifled a laugh when I tried to picture my partner with tools in his hands.

"That's why we're called a fabrication company," McCall replied.

"You seem annoyed at us, sir?" I asked, taking the bad-cop role for once. "Why is that?"

McCall shook his head. "I'm busy, okay? And you won't say what this is about, so you're making me nervous, that's all."

"Nervous?" Hugo jumped in.

I guessed we were going for bad cop, bad cop today.

"What do you have to be nervous about?" Hugo added.

"Nothing, man, but it's not every day two suits walk into my place and start asking questions."

I switched gears. "You're not in any trouble, sir, and sorry if we caught you off guard, but we're hoping you can help us with something."

McCall visibly relaxed.

"We're investigating a case which involved a fabrication, and neither of us took metal shop in school, so we're hoping you can talk us through the process. Maybe show us the type of machinery or equipment needed."

"Sure," he replied, glancing at his watch. "I gotta finish this job this afternoon, so as long as this doesn't tie me up too long."

"Mind showing us around the workshop?" Hugo asked. "It'll speed things along if you can point and explain."

McCall got up and opened the office door. His eyes caught his calendar, and he looked at me. "Sorry about that," he muttered.

I smiled in return. "Cool race car."

The workshop area was bigger than I'd expected, and surprisingly organized relative to the reception and office. I spotted five people working on various projects, from wrought-iron gates to what looked like one of those big bumpers that go on Jeeps. It was noisy, with various tools in use and sparks flying from an angle grinder in the hands of a man wearing gloves, a face mask, and safety glasses.

"What kind of fabrication are you talking about?" McCall asked loudly to be heard.

"Mainly box tube," I replied, and watched his response. "Cut and welded in places. The rest held together with quick-release pins."

Based on the man's reaction earlier, I'd expect him to tense up and appear nervous again if he'd fabricated the type of frame I was talking about. But instead, he moved to a large piece of equipment on the shop floor and began explaining.

"Usually cut to length with this circular saw," he said before moving to another bench-mounted device. "Then we use a notcher for round tube or a chop saw to make the corner joints on box tube."

I pictured the frame in my mind, recalling Rosa's photos from the water.

"This had what I think you call butt joints," I said, and the two men looked at me.

"That's the faster way," McCall replied. "But not the nice or best way."

"Maybe someone in a hurry?" I suggested.

"It was welded?" McCall asked.

"Most of it, yes."

"TIG, MIG, or stick?" he asked.

We didn't have a forensics report on the frame yet, beyond dusting for fingerprints, which had come up empty.

"I'd have to check," I replied.

McCall shrugged. "We have MIG and TIG here. If whatever you're talking about was constructed in a hurry, I expect they used MIG. It's a little faster."

Hugo caught my eye and nodded toward the far wall, which was filled with storage racks of metal tubing. The lengths, shapes, and sizes varied greatly.

"Do you do much work with three-inch steel box tube, Mr. McCall?" I asked, and he glanced over at the racks.

When he turned back, his expression had changed. "That's pretty specific."

I smiled. "Quarter-inch wall," I added, remembering the specs from Rosa's tech's email.

McCall frowned. "And they used butt joints? That's shitty workmanship. Not something we'd do here."

"But you carry that tubing?" Hugo asked.

McCall nodded and gesticulated to the racks stocked with a vast selection. "Probably. As you can see, we have most nominal sizes in stock," he replied, taking a step toward the office. "Now, I really have to get back to this job."

"One more thing before we go," Hugo said, causing McCall to pause. "Do you know a man named Garrett Caldwell?"

McCall thought for a moment. "Should I? Is he a customer of mine or something? Name doesn't sound familiar."

I gave Hugo a few moments to follow up, but he chose not to. So I spoke before McCall had a chance to walk away.

"Mind if I take a picture?" I asked, taking out my camera.

"I don't know, man. We're in the middle of a bunch of jobs, and some of these people don't want their custom work plastered on the internet."

"This won't go on the internet, Mr. McCall, I assure you," I replied with a smile.

He shuffled nervously and rubbed his chin with a grubby hand, taking two more steps toward the office door. I followed, then turned and snapped a picture.

"Just one," I said.

He huffed and shook his head. "I'd better not see that on Facebook."

"You won't," I replied, and then looked around the workshop one more time, wondering what it was he didn't want us to notice.

Hugo drove us away from McCall Fabrication and circled around to drive down the lane behind the shop. I noticed a man in overalls standing outside, talking on his cell phone. The man turned away as we drove by. It was one of McCall's employees, but I didn't get a look at his face.

Once we were back on PCH, I dialed Rosa and put the call on speakerphone.

"Hi, Kat," she answered.

"Hey, Rosa, I have a question."

"Shoot."

"The metal used on that frame. Can we run metallurgy tests or something to match it to a supplier or batch of steel?"

"Hmm. Short answer is yes," she replied. "Longer answer is yes, but it'll take a while. All the specification markings were removed from the metal on the frame, so it'll be harder to pin down the source. We'd have to test every comparison sample."

"Okay, but if we had a sample we suspected of being from the same batch, we could compare the two?"

"Certainly," Rosa said. "But I would imagine we're talking

about thousands of feet of stock that would also match, so I doubt this would be your smoking gun."

"Gotcha. Thanks, Rosa. Oh, and how long is 'a while' in the metallurgy-testing world?"

"Eight to twelve weeks," she replied.

I groaned.

"We use an outside vendor for those tests, and that's their usual lead time," Rosa explained.

"Come across anything else we might find useful?" Hugo asked.

"I didn't want to say anything, as it will likely be nothing," Rosa replied, and Hugo and I both leaned forward. "We have a few fibers that were half-captured in the concrete as it set in the buckets. They all match each other, so we're trying to determine their origin."

"That could be significant," Hugo said.

"Don't get too excited," Rosa responded. "They could have been in the cement powder from the factory, or an untraceable rag, but I'll keep you posted if we make progress."

"What about the zip ties?" Hugo asked. "Kat was mentioning something about pulls."

"Pawls," I corrected.

"Cheap zip ties, I'm afraid," Rosa replied. "We have a manufacturer, but they're Chinese imports, brought in by the millions and widely distributed. I doubt they're going to be your smoking gun, either."

We both thanked Rosa, and I hung up.

Hugo drove on in silence while we both thought about the case. At least, I did, and I guessed he was doing the same.

"Where the hell do we go from here?" Hugo finally breathed.

"Station, I suppose," I answered, my mind on metal tubing, fibers, and suspects.

"I mean with the case," Hugo groaned.

"Oh, right. It does feel like a bloody rollercoaster."

"One dead end to the next," Hugo grumbled.

I reached into the back and pulled my laptop out of my bag. Waking it up, I opened the software we used to track the case.

"Let's run through the timeline again," I said. "Maybe something will jump out."

Hugo murmured something I couldn't understand, but I pressed on.

"We know Hailey left work around five and crossed paths with her roommate Melissa around five-twenty. Presumably, she changed and got ready for her date, while having a heated text exchange with Kwon. She then left the house in time to meet Caldwell at Seabreeze Cellars at seven-thirty. So, around seven-ten to seven-fifteen, I'd say. Meanwhile, Monroe and Browning both arrive at the harbor at about that time."

I took a few breaths, giving Hugo an opportunity to comment. He didn't, so I continued, pleased that everything so far made sense to me, indicating my brain hadn't mislaid anything along the way.

"It's now after sunset, and Monroe leaves the harbor on *Shore Code* a little after eight, and Hailey and Caldwell walk to Surfside Grill at half-past eight. Low tide was at two minutes to nine, and the two leave the restaurant at ten, walk to their cars, and arrive at Capo Beach at 10:15 p.m."

At this pause, Hugo spoke up.

"Are we thinking the frame was put in place already?" he asked. "Before they arrive?"

"Sunset was seven-twenty, so properly dark by 7:45 p.m. That gave someone two and a half hours to set up, during which the tide was at its lowest," I responded. "So yes, I think that's most likely."

"Monroe had plenty of time in the area, right?"

I thought about it for a moment. "More than enough. It's only a short distance to Capo Beach. We know from the video and GPS data he left the harbor at 8:05 p.m., but he doesn't stop until 10:52 p.m., when the GPS stays in the same spot for forty-five minutes.

Odd that he'd spend almost three hours putting around the area before they anchored. Or at least paused for a while in the same spot."

"When did Caldwell leave?" Hugo asked.

"10:55 p.m."

"Bingo," Hugo replied. "They cruised, waiting. Caldwell texted them to say be ready. They anchor. He called them when he left, and that's when they took the tender to the beach."

"*Shore Code* then leaves at 11:41 p.m. and is on the harbor CCTV at twelve-fifteen," I said, reading from the software's timeline. "It does fit. And means Hailey was attacked and put on the X-frame between eleven and eleven-thirty."

"It's X-frame now?" Hugo teased.

"Easier to say," I responded.

"True. So, is thirty minutes long enough to assemble that thing, grab her, drag her out to your X-frame, and strap her down?"

"Not *my* X-frame," I rebutted. "And that sounds like a tight timeline to me. There's two of them, but it would probably take both of them to manhandle the concrete-filled buckets from a boat into the water and get them placed in the right spots. So they'd have to already have taken Hailey, which would use up time. Splashing back and forth through the water is hard work."

With relief, I noticed I could now easily recall my venture into the water on Thursday morning.

"And the buckets would have needed to be level to align with the upper frame they'd drop on," I added. "All takes time. So, no. Thirty minutes isn't long enough."

Hugo drove on without saying anything for a while.

"We need Caldwell's phone records," he finally said.

"Think we have enough for a warrant?"

He wrinkled his nose. "Borderline, but my guess is yes. We'll apply when we get to the station."

After several more minutes of reflection, it was me who spoke next.

"Bloody hell, Hugo," I blurted, rerunning an idea over in my mind.

"What?"

"Just a second," I replied. "I'm trying to make sure I'm not about to suggest something stupid."

"That rarely stops you," he said with a grin.

I was too engrossed in my thoughts for a witty comeback.

"What if the concrete posts were already there?" I said, trying to work through the physical logistics in my head.

Hugo looked doubtful. "The posts sticking out of the buckets are the same metal box tube, aren't they? Besides, if they'd already been there, wouldn't they be rusted and covered in sea slime?"

"Sea slime?" I frowned back at him, then shook my head. "Doesn't matter. No, I don't mean they accidentally stumbled across a foundation. I mean, they could have placed the concrete buckets and posts at their leisure. Maybe the night before, when they had plenty of time."

"So all they had to do was drop the upper framework in place and grab Hailey," Hugo said as he ran the scenario over in his mind. "We need to check *Shore Code*'s GPS for the nights leading up to Wednesday."

"Makes way more sense, Hugo," I continued as the logic fell into place. "I was trying to fathom how they'd manage those heavy buckets and posts from a tender. But they could have dropped them from *Shore Code*. Maybe even poured and mixed the cement on the aft deck so they didn't have to drag hefty structures around the dock. Explains the pins, too."

"I wonder if Rosa can tell if any parts were in the water longer than others?" Hugo proposed.

"I'll call her back," I said, but the words had barely left my lips when my phone rang.

The caller was in my saved contacts. "Sarge," I answered.

"Write this number down," he ordered, and I fished a notebook and pen from my backpack.

"Go ahead."

I wrote down the phone number he gave me and held it so Hugo could see.

"That's a Seattle area code," Hugo commented.

"Correct," Sarge replied. "Woman called here a few minutes ago. She may have witnessed something at Capo Beach Wednesday night. She's expecting your call."

"Sound legit?" Hugo asked.

"I wouldn't have given you the number if she didn't, Fuentes."

The line went dead.

I winced. "I bet he's fun at Christmas," I said as I dialed the number. "Open your gift, son!" I barked.

"You know he's into classical Spanish guitar and pottery, right?" Hugo replied.

I paused before hitting the call button. "Seriously?"

"Don't be stupid," Hugo scoffed. "He probably holds Reveille every dawn and inspects the wife and kids before they're allowed out for the day."

I laughed and hit the call button.

"Hello?" came a woman's voice after one ring.

"Ma'am, this is OCSD Investigators Cromwell and Fuentes. We were given your number by our station sergeant. He mentioned you may have information for us."

"Yes," she replied tentatively. "Well, I think it might be useful, but I'm really not sure. I thought I'd be wasting your time, but my husband said I should call, regardless."

I looked at Hugo, whose expression matched the doubtfulness I felt.

"Let's start with your name, ma'am."

"Cathy. Cathy Arnold."

"Okay, and where were you Wednesday night?" I asked.

"We stayed in the hotel across from Capistrano Beach. It was an anniversary trip for us."

"Congratulations," I said. "And what is it you saw, ma'am?"

"Well, that's the thing..." she trailed off and hesitated a moment. "I'm sorry, what should I call you?"

"Kat's fine."

"Oh, okay, Kat. Well, I didn't really *see* anything."

I looked at Hugo again, and he rolled his eyes. I shrugged my shoulders and wondered why Sarge had thought this woman had anything for us.

"But I heard something," Cathy continued.

"Okay. What did you hear?"

She took a moment. "I should explain why I think I know what it was that I heard," she rambled. "My grandson got one of those little drone things for Christmas. We took him to the local park so he could fly it around some, as we worried he'd accidentally land it over the neighbor's yard, or on the road."

I shared another look with Hugo, but this time, we were both more interested.

"So, after a week of following Daniel all over the place while this thing buzzed over our heads, I became quite used to the sound it made."

"And that's what you heard Wednesday night, ma'am?" I asked, eager for her to confirm her point.

"Yes, Kat. But this didn't sound like a little drone. Daniel's is no bigger than a lunchbox. I'm sure the one I heard was much larger. The electric motors had a deeper tone, and the whirring of the blades was more intense. You know, that whooshing sound from the wind off those rotor blades."

"But to be clear, ma'am, you didn't see anything?" I asked.

"Well, we had the balcony doors open, and my husband was watching television," she explained. "I was reading a book in the chair by the doors, enjoying the breeze. Cars would go by, but I love hearing the waves crashing on the beach, so it was quite relaxing. But then I heard the buzzing and whirring and recognized the sound. I got up and looked outside, but couldn't see anything. The drone sound began fading, and that's when I looked up higher in the sky."

She paused to either gather her thoughts or to run through her recollections, so I gave her a moment.

"Maybe it was a cloud, or a trick of the light," she said, then sighed. "Or a trick of the dark, in this case, but I thought I saw the outline of an object fly overhead towards the bluff."

"Did you hear it again after that, ma'am?"

"No. I didn't. But we closed the doors and went to bed, so I can't say for certain it didn't come back."

"What time was this?" I asked.

"A few minutes before ten-thirty p.m.," Cathy replied. "I know because I was just telling my husband about it when his show ended at ten-thirty."

"Is there anything else you can think of to mention, ma'am?" I asked. "Perhaps someone you witnessed arriving at the beach, or walking around?"

"No, I'm sorry. I didn't really pay any attention to what was going on until I heard the drone noise. Is this of any use to you, or am I wasting your time? I hate the idea of bothering you if it's not important. I'm sure you have enough to contend with."

"You've been most helpful, Mrs. Arnold. Thank you. I have your number, so if we have any further questions, is it okay if we call back?"

"Oh, yes, of course," she replied.

"Brilliant, thank you. And this is my cell phone, so if you think of anything else worth noting, don't hesitate to call."

After hanging up, I looked over at Hugo again. "And once again, the waters are muddied."

"Puts Enrique Gil back into the mix," Hugo replied. "He has metalworking equipment, and he has fancy drones with surveillance gear."

"Yup," I agreed. "And he's yet another suspect we can't place at the actual scene. A bloody drone didn't strap Hailey to that frame."

Hugo nodded. "True. But if it was his drone, then he had a keen interest in whatever our vic was up to. That wins him second place on my suspect list."

It still felt like a complete mess to me, with too many suspects in and around the area, near but not exactly the time we believed she was killed. Or at least strapped to the damn X-frame.

"Maybe Gil has a connection to Monroe we haven't discovered yet," I suggested.

Hugo raised an eyebrow. "Newly separated. Could be our government contractor was fishing in OC Match's sea."

22

———

Arriving at the station, I was surprised to run into Dylan Monroe and Jason Browning as Hugo and I walked through the doors to the reception area. We really needed these two held until we could check the GPS data again. Ambrose was with them and glanced our way before turning back to Sergeant Martinez behind the desk.

"Can we hurry this along, please? My clients have cooperated every step of the way."

Hugo paused, but I tugged on his sleeve. Using my swipe card at the door, I led him from the reception and down the hall to our office.

"We really need those two to stick around," Hugo said.

"I know, I'm texting Sarge. Start on the GPS data, and let's see what we have to work with."

Hugo sat at his computer and got to work while I sent Martinez a message that I hoped he'd see before he finished processing Monroe and Browning's release. *"Stall. Need 10 mins. New evidence."*

I stared at my phone screen, hoping for a verification, but all the message showed was "sent." Not even blinking ellipses suggesting an imminent reply. I tore myself away from the screen so I could check another box on our to-do list by calling Rosa again.

"Nothing new since the last time we spoke half an hour ago," she answered.

"Sorry, but I have another quirky question for you."

"Alright, what do you need to know?"

"Can you tell if the buckets of concrete and the posts were in the water longer than the upper frame?"

"Yes, I can tell you they were submerged longer," she immediately replied, and my excitement grew. "Because we know the frame was above the water for part of the time."

"Oh, of course," I muttered, all the air escaping my newly inflated balloon. "But wait, what about the lower legs of the frame that slip into the posts? Well, not the part that actually slips inside the posts, but the bit just above. They were submerged all the time, too, right? It was the X-frame holding the vic that was out of the water for part of the time."

"X-frame?" Rosa questioned.

"It's what we're calling the metal frame. It was used as an execution frame."

"That's a horrible name for it," Rosa replied.

"That's what Hugo said."

"But it does describe it correctly."

"That's what I said."

"Fair enough. X-frame it is," Rosa responded. "And I hear your point about the submerged sections, but I don't have an answer for you. At the moment. Let me take another look. We tried our best to treat the parts in the same manner, so any progression in decay or oxidation should have happened at similar rates, so we might still see a difference."

"Thanks, Rosa. Let us know."

We hung up, and I checked my phone for a text. Nothing. So I sat down at my desk and plugged my laptop back into the power supply and monitor connection. I was halfway through typing a warrant request for Caldwell's phone records when Hugo spoke up.

"*Shore Code* never moved the day before, but it did go out on

Monday evening. Left the harbor at 6:15 p.m. and returned to the slip at 9:20 p.m."

"Where did it go?" I asked, pausing my typing for a moment.

"Similar. Along the coast by Capo Beach."

"Did it stop?"

"Yes, but have a look. You know more about the waters than me."

I got up, walked around to Hugo's side, and looked over his shoulder.

"That's not what I was…" I trailed off.

It didn't feel right saying "hoping for." If Monroe and Browning were guilty, then let the evidence prove that, but hoping was too much like we were trying to force the evidence to fit a theory instead of the truth.

"It appears to me that they stop where they did on Wednesday night," Hugo said. "And the rest of the time, they're too far out from where the frame was placed. What do you think?"

"I see the same thing," I agreed. "The only odd thing is one deviation closer to shore for a few minutes," I said, pointing to the screen. "But they're half a mile south of where Hailey was murdered when they do that."

"Is that near enough to the beach to pick someone up, or drop them off?" Hugo asked.

"You've seen the beach there. Someone would wade up to their chest to get to a spot a boat that size could safely reach."

Hugo let out a long sigh and pushed his chair away from the desk. "Do we take another run at Monroe based on this?"

It was a tough call. I could hear the lawyer, Ambrose, kicking up a storm over us detaining his client based on nothing except doing what he bought a boat for: cruising around the ocean near where he lived.

"Screw it. We might as well try," I said. "Besides, I never heard back from Martinez, so they may be gone. Why don't you see while I finish this warrant request? I'll meet you in the interview room if they're still here."

Hugo groaned, but got up and walked out of the room. I quickly finished putting together my best version of why we needed Caldwell's phone records, and shortly after I hit send on the email, my phone buzzed with a text. Hugo had Monroe in the conference room.

"Hey," I said when I joined Hugo, Monroe, and, of course, Ambrose.

Hugo looked up at me. "Mr. Monroe kindly agreed to join us to clear up a few details."

That's why we were in the conference room and not a formal, recorded interview room. Hugo had pulled off some kind of sweet-talking deal. That was fine. We'd hoped to have damning evidence, and instead we had more vague, circumstantial garbage to work with. I took a seat.

"Can we get on with this so my client can get back to work?" Ambrose huffed.

Which was bullshit. The lawyer was happy to sit in that conference room all afternoon as his billable out-of-office hours racked up like a rock band's bar tab.

"Now that we have the confusion sorted out over which days you've been out on your boat, Mr. Monroe, thanks to your GPS data," Hugo began, "I'd like to verify which days in the prior week you were also cruising on *Shore Code*."

Monroe certainly didn't look as confident as his counsel did, and he now looked to Ambrose for support.

"Let me make this simpler for you, Mr. Monroe," Hugo said. "We know you were out on the boat Monday evening. Can you tell us for what purpose?"

"What purpose does anyone go out on their boat?" Ambrose quickly responded. "For pleasure. If this is why you've held us up, then we'll be leaving, Investigator Fuentes."

"Let me be more specific," Hugo continued, undeterred. "Can you explain why you stopped for forty minutes along the coast by Capo Beach?"

"We dropped anchor and hung out for a while," Monroe replied.

"We? Who else was with you, sir?" I asked.

"Jason," he said, but his expression looked defeated. He'd answered one question, and embroiled his friend and employee once again.

"Anyone else?" I asked.

He shook his head.

"And where did you go after stopping to hang out for a while?" Hugo asked.

"Back to the harbor," Monroe replied.

"Straight back?"

"You have the data, Investigator Fuentes," Ambrose intervened.

"Indeed, we do," Hugo smiled, impressively keeping his cool despite how little we had to work with. "So why did you move so close to shore after pulling anchor?"

Monroe shrugged his shoulders. "I honestly don't know what you're talking about."

"Did you anchor while you were stopped for a while?" I asked.

"I think so," Monroe replied.

"You think so?" I questioned. "This isn't like strolling down to the corner shops and not remembering which aisle you walked down. This is a large, expensive boat on the open ocean at night, Mr. Monroe. Were you not in command of the boat?"

"What is the point of all this?" Ambrose intervened. "You asked my client to stay in order to quickly clear up a few logistics, and now you're questioning his seamanship, which has nothing to do with anything, as far as I can see."

"First of all," I snapped at Ambrose, "operating a motor yacht while intoxicated is illegal, not to mention incredibly irresponsible, and second, we want to know why your client detoured so close to shore as it may have a bearing on our murder case."

"You've got no proof and have no way of proving my client's sobriety a week ago, Investigator Cromwell," Ambrose ripped back. "So for your records, he was sober. And he's done answering questions about this witch hunt you're on, trying to frame him for murder."

"Wait," Monroe said, and we all looked at him in surprise.

"We can leave," Ambrose said, lowering his voice. "You're under no obligation to answer any more questions or take this abuse."

"It's okay," Monroe said, making eye contact with me. "I want to answer. I remember now."

Ambrose sat back, and Monroe took a moment to gather his thoughts.

"We pulled the anchor, then while we were sorting everything out, we drifted with the swells. I realized what was happening and took us away from shore before heading along the coast back to the harbor. That was it, just a mistake."

"Sorting everything out?" I questioned. "What do you mean?"

"Just our heading. I'd started the engine and motored forward to release the tension while we hauled the anchor. While it was retracting, we must have drifted. I was getting my bearings, and it took me a moment to realize."

"Good practice is to figure that stuff out before you pull anchor," I pointed out.

"A lesson I was reminded of," Monroe replied.

"With that cleared up, we'll be on our way," Ambrose insisted, and gave his client a nod toward the door.

Hugo held up a hand. "Just one more thing, and you're good to go."

Ambrose was already on his feet, but Monroe stayed seated.

"Anything to help clear me of this murder business. I don't know anything about it."

Hugo smiled sympathetically. "We'd like to rule you out, too. But how well do you know Garrett Caldwell?"

Ambrose looked quizzically at Hugo, and then Monroe. This was new on the lawyer's radar. His client also furrowed his brow.

"Who?"

"Garrett Caldwell," Hugo repeated.

"Wait," Ambrose said, dropping back into his seat. "Would this be the guy the victim was on a date with?"

Ambrose was fishing, as Caldwell's name hadn't been released. Hugo stayed focused on Monroe.

"I don't believe I know anyone by that name," Monroe replied.

"Do you have access to the messages between people on your app?" Hugo asked.

"You mean the private messages between clients?" Monroe asked in reply.

"Exactly."

Monroe shook his head. "No. They're private."

"I didn't ask whether you did look at them, Mr. Monroe. I asked if you have access."

The suspect sighed. "Technically, yes. We could see them, but we have a strict policy against doing that."

"Who has that access?" I asked.

Monroe thought for a moment. "Only a handful of people with clearance to work on the coding. We restrict who can upload changes to the coding so no one can accidentally screw up the app."

"Okay, and who are these people with clearance?" I continued. "You, I assume. What about Jason?"

He nodded. "There's really only one other person. Priya's a coder who's been with us from the beginning."

"I'm sorry, what's their name?" I asked, just to verify I'd heard him correctly.

"Priya. Priya Verma."

I thought he'd said Priya, which I knew to be a female name originating from India. We had a girl at my school with the same name. We couldn't rule a female completely out of our inquiries, but it was very unlikely a female murdered Hailey Carter. Although I wondered how loyal Priya might be to her boss when he was suspected of the crime.

"Last question, Mr. Monroe," Hugo said.

"You already asked your last question," Ambrose interrupted. "We really are leaving now."

"Does your app have tracking capabilities like so many do these days?" Hugo continued.

Monroe nodded. "It can gather location data, but it's an option that can be turned off by the user."

"Presumably, you can see who has it turned on or off," Hugo said.

"We can."

There was a brief pause, and Hugo appeared to be done. Ambrose rose again. I pondered one more question, but realized it was best not to ask. They'd be able to see when the feature was activated or turned off, but if Monroe was guilty and had used the app to track Hailey, he'd have disabled it afterwards. Which he and Browning could lie about, and even scrub the data from the app before we'd ever get police IT techs anywhere near it.

Monroe followed Ambrose to the door.

"Can we get—" Hugo began saying, but I cut him off.

"Let me show you two out."

Hugo frowned at me, but I made a face I hoped conveyed my concern over asking what I thought he was about to ask.

Once I'd escorted the two men to the reception, I returned to our office.

"What was that about?" Hugo demanded, standing behind his desk with his hands on his hips.

"You were about to ask how to reach Priya, right?"

"Yeah. Don't you think it would be worth talking to her?"

"Absolutely."

"But we didn't need to warn her boss," Hugo added in a far calmer voice.

"That was my thought."

We both took our seats, and Hugo slid his over to face me. "After looking at the GPS data and interviewing him again, do you think Monroe and Browning could have set up the X-frame?"

I took a moment and laid my instant pictures out in order on my desk. After a quick scan of each one, I sat back and looked up at my partner.

"They had the ability to track both Caldwell and the vic. They have a boat plenty large enough to transport the frame parts, and they were in the area Wednesday night, and on the prior Monday. Assuming the GPS data is accurate, then they were never close enough to the murder site to unload anything from *Shore Code*, but they could always have used the tender."

"With difficulty," Hugo added.

"Yeah. It would have been with great difficulty."

Hugo blew out his cheeks and rocked his chair back. "This is ridiculous. We have a prime suspect who was with her, yet couldn't have strapped her to the X-frame. Then two more suspects who were right there with access, had a connection through their dating app, and still not a lick of evidence to say any of them touched her."

"And don't forget Kwon," I groaned. "Or Enrique Gil."

Hugo dropped his chair back on all four legs and leaned forward. "Who we believe flew a drone over the area at around ten-thirty p.m."

I nodded. "Right."

"Do we think he then went on to kill Hailey?" Hugo asked.

I shrugged. "He had a thing for her, but a 'I'm so mad at you, I'm going to murder you in a heinous way' thing? I don't know about that."

"Agreed. So what if we could get the footage from his drone?"

"He'd have to admit he was flying his super-secret surveillance drone there in the first place," I pointed out.

"Which could also give him an alibi," Hugo replied. "If he could verify where he was flying it from."

I nodded again. "Worth a shot."

23

———————

Despite having finally filled my cupboards with groceries, I couldn't face the hassle of cooking, so I ordered a pizza. Leaving the station, I was driving down Golden Lantern toward the harbor when my phone rang.

"Hey, Mum," I answered.

"Hi, darling. Just checking in to see if you need feeding or anything else."

"I'm fine, thanks," I replied. "Just picking up food now."

"You could have come by, darling. You know that."

My mum somehow managed the perfect tone, which left me knowing the exact feeling she'd implied. No guilt or expectation, just reinforcing the point that the option was always available.

"Yeah, I'm ready to hang with the furball and crash early."

"It's another long day, huh?"

"Yeah. It'll be more of them, too," I sighed.

"Tough progress?" she asked.

"Struggling to move this one forward," I admitted. "We keep going round in circles. We have more suspects than we know what to do with, but none of them could have done it."

"You and Hugo will figure it out," she said. "Get some rest. A fresh perspective in the morning can do wonders."

For a moment, I considered mentioning my run-in with Castillo that morning, but while I'd finally confessed to my mother about Paul's affair before his accident, I didn't have the energy to talk about it. The fact that I was even weighing the idea of speaking about it was a monumental shift from six months ago.

"I'm sure it will, Mum, thanks for the call. Love you."

"Love you, too. Hug Roger for me."

I laughed. "Will do."

Our call ended in perfect timing as I pulled into the Lantern Bay Village Shopping Center and parked in front of Stuft Pizza. Inside, a high school kid I hadn't seen before was working the counter.

"To-go order for Kat," I said.

"Cat, as in, not a dog?" he asked.

"With a K," I replied, and he looked at me quizzically.

"Kat, spelled with a K," I elaborated.

"Cool, gotcha," he said, and looked at the receipts taped to a row of pizza boxes. "I don't see one," He muttered, looking a second time. "Could it be under a different name?"

"No, I ordered about thirty minutes ago, and I gave the name Kat."

He shook his head. "I don't see it. We have one for Cat with a C, but no K."

I tried not to laugh. "What's the pie?"

"Excuse me, ma'am?" he said.

Now I wanted to punch the kid for calling me "ma'am." Being polite wasn't always the respectful thing to do. I wasn't old enough to be called ma'am. At least I didn't think so.

"What's the order under Cat with a C?"

"Oh, it's a weird one. Light sauce, extra cheese, black olives, and mushrooms."

Now I wanted to shoot him for calling me weird.

"That's mine."

He took a moment before a lightbulb appeared to go off in his head. I hoped his lack of common sense came from a little too much weed. If not, this kid had a tough life ahead of him.

"I think they wrote your name down wrong," he chuckled. "Yeah, I guess this is yours."

I took the pizza, thanked the kid, and left. Three minutes later, I parked in the narrow driveway alongside my cottage. I'd always had a wonderful sense of belonging whenever I arrived home. That feeling had wavered after Paul's accident, as I'd become accustomed to him being around most of the time when I was home. But over time, helped by the fact he'd turned out to be a cheating wanker, the old feeling had returned, and opening my front door took several levels of stress from my day.

Unfortunately, today it was short-lived.

As I often left before dawn and returned after dark, I'd made a habit since bringing Roger home of leaving a lamp on in the living room. Taking my key from the door, I was about to close it behind me when I saw the credenza. The door was open, with a scattering of hay across the rug below.

"How the hell did he get out?" I whispered under my breath, sensing something more was up.

When your brain has the kind of idiosyncrasies that mine does, it's hard to trust your memory. But I was sure I'd slid the catch over after letting him out for ten minutes that morning. Yet, the open hutch door suggested otherwise.

I softly closed the front door and looked around the room for anything else amiss. All appeared to be as I'd left it. I slipped my jacket off and hung it on the peg, then switched on the main living room light. I kept my belt on, which carried my holstered service weapon and a small flashlight.

I'd expected to hear Roger scurrying around inside the credenza if he'd gone back inside, or jumping from the couch if he'd been sleeping there. But there was nothing.

"Hey, mate," I whispered, although I didn't really know why I was trying to stay quiet. Beyond a strange sense of unease.

There was still no movement in the house. I walked across the room and kneeled down by the credenza, checking inside. Roger was nowhere to be seen. I felt a panic rising inside as my biggest fear took hold of me. I'd left the hutch door unlatched, and he'd gotten out. Why rabbits had an obsession with chewing electrical wires was beyond me, but every website and chatroom was full of horror stories and warnings about shielding all the cords in the house. Which I'd done. But I still couldn't shake the idea that I was about to find my little guy lying dead next to a wire I hadn't wrapped well enough.

As I went to stand up, I looked down at the feed strewn across the rug and sank back to my knees. Several spots of red dappled the yellowish-green hay. It was unmistakably drops of blood. Roger was hurt. Had the blood come from jumping out, or had he injured himself and returned to his hutch? I checked inside again, making doubly sure he wasn't nestled under his bed or a small pile of hay. He definitely wasn't in there.

I stood and looked around. Roger loved exploring and finding new nooks and crannies to squeeze into. Walking over to the kitchen, I kneeled down and checked either side of the range, and then the fridge. Still no sign of him. Of course, he could be behind the appliances where I couldn't see, but surely he'd have made noise by now? Unless he couldn't.

"Roger?" I said softly, and heard a sound from across the living room. It was barely anything. Maybe a bird on the roof, or a pipe creaking.

Standing, I surveyed the open living area. I'd closed the front door, and the side door beyond the round dining table was closed, as it should be. The credenza on the back wall was right next to my bedroom door, which was also closed. But the spare bedroom door was cracked open.

I always kept it shut. It was where I kept my boxes of photos, stored in marked files, and the boxes of instant photo cartridges I bought in bulk directly from the manufacturer. There was also a guest bed in there, hidden behind the stacks. I'd wrapped the wires in case my little Houdini ever found his way into the room, but I only ever went in there when I needed new cartridges. And I always closed the door. I tried to recall when last I'd done that. Keeping a small inventory in my desk drawer at work had cut down on my need to go in and out of the room.

Moving slowly, I walked across the rug toward the spare bedroom door. I unclipped the holster strap for my sidearm. I knew I was being paranoid, but training had formed a habit, and it was better to be safe than sorry. Through the crack in the doorway, I could see the spare bedroom was dark inside. Extending a hand, I was about to push the door open when another sound came from behind me. It sounded like something had smacked the rug. I spun around, hand on weapon.

Roger stared at me from under the sofa, the decorative flap of fabric that hid the framework draped over his back.

"There you are," I gushed in relief, berating myself for not checking under the furniture.

His entire body twitched, and I heard the same sound again.

"Did you just thump, mate?" I said, wondering what had alarmed him so badly that he'd made the instinctive sound rabbits used to warn each other. I'd never heard him do it before.

"It's okay, mate," I said, taking a step his way with outstretched hands. "It's only me. You're not in trouble for being out."

Roger thumped again and shot back under the sofa. For a brief moment, my heart broke as I wondered what I'd done to scare the little fellow. But a creak from the spare bedroom door let me know it wasn't me he was afraid of. But I was too late to do anything about it.

Strong hands seized me by the arms and flung me against my bedroom wall. My shoulder hit first, and I felt the drywall buckle, but then my head slapped almost as hard, and I crumpled to the floor. Instinctively, I reached for my gun, but the assailant kicked me, crushing my hand against my side.

I caught sight of the man above me. He wore a ski mask, but I noticed a flash of black and orange tattoo on the flesh revealed between his shirt and the mask. His gloved fist flew at my face, but

I raised a forearm and deflected the blow, sending a sharp pain up my arm.

Swinging a leg, I connected with his ribs, but it was a glancing blow, halted under his arm. I drew back to kick again, then saw his foot winding up to kick me once more. We were both committed, and his foot caught me in the side just below the ribs. I grimaced in pain as the air left my lungs. My kick had lost most of its power by the time it connected a split second later, but he'd bent over in his efforts, and I caught him in the ear.

The man gasped and clutched the side of his head. Breathless, I fumbled for my gun again, pulling it from the holster. I saw his foot as I raised my aim and squeezed the trigger. He kicked my hand as the gunshot rang out inside my house. In a blur of motion, he was moving away as I clung gamely to the weapon and fought to aim once more. He disappeared around the corner toward the dining table before I could squeeze off another shot, and I struggled to my feet.

I heard the side door open, but by the time I stumbled that way, he was already outside. Winded, I was moving slowly, but I followed him out the door and stood in my driveway alongside my home. The man was gone. I staggered to the road and looked both ways, up and down the hill. He'd vanished.

Across the street, I heard a gate or fence rattle. I pulled my cell phone from my pocket and dialed 911. I knew they wouldn't find the man, and my description was going to be thin, but a thought hit me as I made my way back inside the house. Closing the side door, I approached the sofa.

"Hey, Roger, it's okay now," I said softly, and a twitching nose appeared from under the sofa trim. "Come on out, mate."

I offered my hand, and he nervously hopped forward. I scooped him up and felt his little body trembling in my hands as I examined him for wounds. He appeared to be unscathed. Carrying him over to the credenza, I squatted down.

"You tried to warn me, didn't you?" I said, placing him inside the hutch.

He hopped to his bed, turned around, and sat down. I looked at the hay on the rug and the red stains, then to my left where pieces of drywall littered the floor and an indent marred the wall. I was pretty sure I knew what had happened. With sirens wailing in the distance, I looked at Roger.

"He tried to grab you, and you bit the bugger through his gloves, didn't you?"

We'd have DNA from the blood of the intruder, but I sat back and thought it over. Why would a thief mess with a pet rabbit if he was here to rob the place? I stared at the blood once more. Castillo was sending me a message. If Roger hadn't bitten the guy and ran, or I hadn't come home when I did, I suspected I'd have been greeted by… I didn't even want to think about it.

With sirens drawing closer, I had a decision to make. If the DNA from the blood led back to the Castillos, there'd be a lot of questions about my involvement with them. Outside of my family, no one knew I'd seen my ex's car outside Gabby's place. It was the sort of thing I was obliged to reveal as a law enforcement officer. But I hadn't.

As I heard a car pull up outside and the red and blue lights strobed around the living room, I reached for the blood-stained hay. Then stopped. If the DNA wasn't run, I might never know for sure if the man had been hired by Castillo.

Leaving the hay, I closed up Roger's hutch and went to the front door to greet the deputies.

24

———————

It was nearly eleven by the time the police left. I'd discharged my weapon, which meant paperwork, interviews, and handing over my gun. The intruder had cut a hole in the side door glass, so at least I could prove someone had broken in. I'd worried they'd see it as a domestic squabble escalating out of control, but no one gave me any strange looks, and I was free to continue my duties. I'd have to use my backup weapon.

But after sweeping up the drywall mess and duct-taping over the hole in the glass, I hadn't slept worth a shit. By one a.m., I'd given up, so Roger and I had watched a movie. Although, he seemed to have no problem sleeping and missed most of it. By morning, I'd caught a few hours of sleep but was dragging and skipped my daily workout. I left home concerned for Roger and adding a security system to my to-do list. I didn't think the intruder would be brazen enough to return so soon, but clearly, I needed some form of home protection for when I was away.

Ordering two coffees to go from PC Beans, bleary-eyed, I made my way to the station where word had already gotten around, and I had to relive the evening for Hugo.

Just to add icing on the cake, we were about to get to work on our case when Captain Bradley called my desk and requested a few minutes of my time.

"Are you okay?" she asked when I walked in.

"Fine, thanks, ma'am," I lied.

I had a new bruise forming above where Cisco's mark had finally faded away, and my side was turning all kinds of colors. Everything ached, and I felt exhausted.

"We have a hit back already on your intruder," she said.

I was shocked we'd gotten DNA results back so quickly. Usually, it took a murder case to receive such speedy attention.

"Law enforcement target," she said, presumably noting my surprise.

"Who is he?" I asked.

"Emilio Santiago. Goes by Milo. Twenty-eight and has a hefty rap sheet. Already served two of a three-year sentence for robbery. Paroled early. Unclear exactly how he pulled that off. Caught with another guy, but only one of them was armed, and they couldn't prove which one."

"Sounds delightful," I replied, not hearing the part I was dying to know but didn't want to discuss with the captain. "Does he have a tattoo on his neck? Black and orange."

She glanced at her screen, then nodded. "He does. He's also a known associate of the Castillo family," she added, confirming my theory. So much for avoiding that discussion.

Now that the captain had mentioned the Castillo name, my omission of Paul's and therefore my connection, no matter how tenuous, had just escalated. I could plead shock and grief were responsible in the weeks after Paul's death. But now, having been in the very same courtroom as Gabriella Castillo that morning, it looked nothing but suspicious. If Bradley put two and two together and realized I'd actually been there for the hearing.

"Criminal Investigation Bureau has been after the family forever," I commented, and the captain's gaze lingered on me a few beats longer than felt comfortable.

"Needless to say, you must remain completely clear of any investigation regarding the break-in, Kat."

"Of course, ma'am. Do we have an APB out for Santiago?"

She nodded. "Just issued. Are you sure you're okay to work?"

"Absolutely, ma'am," I assured her. "We need to wrap up the Carter case."

Bradley sat back in her chair. "That you do. Anything new?"

"We're starting to piece together how the metal framework may have been placed and prepared over several days, ma'am," I explained, glad to move on from talk of the Castillos. "And we have a new witness who heard a drone flying shortly before the murder."

Bradley nodded, then looked down at the paperwork on her desk. "Keep me posted," she said without looking up, giving me my cue to leave. Which I gladly accepted.

"Okay, Hugo. What are we doing first?" I asked as I sat down.

"I think the drone takes priority," he replied. "But how do we prove it was Gil flying the damn thing?"

I thought for a moment. "We can't," I replied. "The man makes his living building covert surveillance equipment."

"So, what can we do?" Hugo wondered aloud before continuing in a more sarcastic tone, "Walk in his office and ask him?"

I laid my pictures out on the desk and looked at the one of Enrique Gil in his office. As was often the case, details of our meeting flooded back to me. His slightly smug manner and the way he'd screened the information left on Hailey's computer. I then thought about my meeting with his receptionist and Hailey's replacement, Grace.

I'd always figured it was familiarity with the surroundings that somehow anchored certain memories more securely than others. For example, conversations at home and interviews in the station tended to stick with me. I clearly recalled how Grace had been paranoid and scared.

"Yeah, let's go ask him," I replied.

"I wasn't being serious, Kat. Why would he admit to flying the drone? We have no way to trace it, and no clue where he flew it from. Could have been anywhere in Orange County. If it was even him," Hugo scoffed. "Hell, if it was even a drone. We're going on what one old lady thought she heard."

Hugo was right, of course, but he was also correct in the fact that the possibility of a drone's presence was currently our best chance at an actionable lead. I picked up my phone and texted Grace.

"Gil in office this morning?"

A moment later, the three little dots blinked as she typed a reply. Her concern over company phones came back to me, and I wondered if she was right. Was my text just screened through sophisticated software looking for trigger terms? My question seemed benign enough. Surely that question was asked multiple times a day in a busy office. But if the originating cell phone was identified as police issue, it might raise a flag.

"Bloody hell," I muttered under my breath as I questioned whether I was putting Grace at risk. "No wonder she's paranoid."

"What's that?" Hugo asked.

My phone vibrated. Grace replied with a simple thumbs-up emoji.

"Gil's in his office," I said to Hugo. "Let's take a run at him."

"That's a major long shot, Kat," he responded.

"Got something better to chase?" I asked as I typed away on my laptop, starting a search in our Automated License Plate Reader system.

"Got a plan on how to approach him?" Hugo asked, rising to his feet.

"Working on it," I replied, disconnecting my laptop and shoving it into my backpack.

When we were ten minutes into the drive to GilTech in Laguna Niguel, I had my computer on my lap while I impatiently waited for search results. My phone rang.

"Morning, Rosa," I answered.

"Morning," she replied, her voice coming over the car's speakers. "You were right."

"I'll mark down the date and time," Hugo replied before I could say anything. "We've been waiting for this moment for a long time now."

"Check out Hugo with the comedy routine," I ribbed him. "I think you're ready for amateur open-mic night, mate."

Hugo kept a straight face and focused on the road.

"Very amusing, you two," Rosa said. "But do you want this info or not?"

"Yes, yes!" I replied. "What was I right about?"

"The legs set into the buckets of concrete were submerged in salt water for a longer period of time than the legs of the upper framework that were slipped inside and pinned in place. There is a distinct difference in oxidation between the two where they met."

"Could the upper frame legs have been out of the water at low tide, Rosa?" Hugo asked.

"Not according to our measurements and the tide data," she replied. "Now, could a trough between waves have dipped that low? Maybe, but it would have been too brief to seriously affect the rusting process."

"Can you tell how long the different parts had been in the ocean?" I asked.

"We're working on that," Rosa replied. "We'll try to recreate a timeline with a bench test of similar steel in salt water here in the lab, but I can tell you the legs were in the ocean for at least twice as long, probably more."

"This is a big help, Rosa, thank you," I said.

"Okay, back to it," she responded, and hung up.

"Feels like we're getting closer with Monroe and Browning," Hugo said. "They must have placed the footings on Monday, as you suggested."

"Feels that way," I replied as I thought it over. "But they still would have had to carry them to the site in the tender, and I don't see four of those concrete-filled buckets with steel box tube sticking out being manageable in a small inflatable tender."

"Could they float them and tow them somehow?" Hugo asked.

"We'd see something being towed behind in the marina footage," I pointed out. "Unless they towed them behind the tender once they were out there."

"What if that's why they went close to the beach after being anchored on Monday night?" Hugo suggested.

"Bugger…" I muttered. "You could be right. We need to find CCTV footage for Monday night farther down PCH. Maybe they delivered them to the beach."

My laptop dinged. My search results had finished running.

"We have ALPR hits on Gil's rental car from Wednesday," I announced as I scrolled through the list.

The amount of data could be overwhelming for a vehicle driving around a lot, but the software had a neat feature where it showed the locations on a map and built a predicted route using different colors for different trips defined by the time of day. I could see the rental car being driven from Orange County Airport to GilTech, then two sightings in the middle of the day. Most likely to lunch close by, as the license plate had been registered by the same camera location about an hour apart, but no other cameras had picked it up farther afield. The vehicle was later seen at multiple locations between GilTech and Dana Point, beginning at 6:17 p.m. The last sighting on CCTV was in Dana Point at 6:54 p.m.

"Well?" Hugo asked.

I sighed. "You want the good news or the bad news?"

"Always bad news first," Hugo replied. "End on a positive."

"The bad news is that once Gil arrived home around seven, the rental car never left again Wednesday night."

"Okay," Hugo replied, looking over at me. "So, what's the good news?"

"I don't know. I was banking on you choosing bad first so I'd have enough time to come up with something, but I'm drawing a blank."

Hugo rolled his eyes. "Maybe he took another vehicle."

"His car was in the shop, and the other must be the wife's. And they're separated," I said. "But wait a sec. He didn't need a car. Why wouldn't he just fly the drone from his house? He lives in Dana Point no more than a few miles from Capistrano Beach."

"Does a drone have that kind of range?" Hugo asked.

"I think that's a bit far for a consumer model, but the military ones have a much longer range. We're talking hundreds of miles, maybe more."

"But we still don't have any leverage," Hugo pointed out. "Especially now that it appears he was home all evening."

Once again, my partner was right. "It's certainly looking less and less likely Gil had anything to do with Hailey's murder," I said as I looked up the man's exact Dana Point address.

Hugo turned into the parking lot for GilTech as I brought up the satellite view of the Dana Point headland. Picking out Gil's house on Shoreline Drive, I found what I was looking for and closed the computer.

"I think we have an angle," I told Hugo as we got out of the car.

"Then you lead the way," he replied.

The receptionist fussed about Mr. Gil being busy, then called Grace, who came down to greet us.

"Hello," I said. "You may remember we came by last week."

Grace looked less worried once she realized I was keeping quiet about our more familiar meeting at the station.

"Hard to forget," she replied. "We're still stunned about Hailey."

"All we need is a few minutes of Mr. Gil's time. We promise not to keep him."

"Follow me," Grace replied, and led us upstairs, where we waited outside while Grace closed Gil's office door behind her.

A few moments later, she reappeared. "Mr. Gil will see you now," she said, holding the door open.

I thanked Grace, and we walked into the office. Enrique Gil stood on our side of his desk, and I presumed he was hoping to keep us all standing and hold us to our promise of only a few minutes.

"We appreciate you seeing us, sir," I said, extending a hand, which he shook.

"If you'd called ahead, I'm sure we could have scheduled something, but I have a couple of minutes before I must be in a virtual meeting," he replied, shaking Hugo's hand.

"This should be quick and easy, sir," I said with a smile. "We have a neighbor's security camera footage of you flying a drone from your home on Wednesday night, Mr. Gil. And an eyewitness who spotted the drone over Capo Beach at half past ten. We know you had made advances to Hailey Carter and were tracking her movements."

The man looked completely stunned.

"We're here for the drone footage," I added firmly.

25

Enrique Gil took a long time before he responded, and I let the uncomfortable silence hang thick in the room like a spring morning fog off the ocean.

"You'll need a warrant," he finally said.

"If that's your choice," I replied. "But we'll simply arrest you on suspicion of murder. That'll expedite everything for us and stop you tampering with evidence."

"I didn't lay a finger on Hailey," he shot back, looking as pained as he did indignant.

"So, let me ask you this, Mr. Gil," Hugo weighed in. "Seeing as we already know you had yourself a bit of an obsession with Hailey Carter, do you think what's on the drone footage will alter that fact? If it records an accurate timestamp and GPS location associated with the footage, this could actually help you establish your whereabouts."

The man walked over to the door and closed it, then returned to his desk, standing by the window and stroking his chin.

"I was home all evening."

"We think you were," I agreed. "But alone, weren't you?"

He nodded.

"So, no one to corroborate that fact."

"I ordered in food about eight."

I shrugged my shoulders. "We don't much care where you were at eight."

Gil raised a finger like he'd thought of a key point. "I set my alarm after the delivery girl left. You'll see it was armed until I left in the morning."

"Those things can be set remotely," I replied. "And it would be easy for the owner to figure out a way around the system."

Gil shook his head. "No, this is a serious security system. You can't get in or out of my home without triggering something."

Hugo looked at me. "I'm tired of this goat rope. Let's just arrest him and go through his office now."

Gil held up both hands. "No! You don't need to arrest me, dammit. That kind of stigma is hard to shake, and I can't have my government vendor clearance compromised over this ridiculousness."

He dropped to his expensive office chair, opened a drawer on his desk, and held up a small memory card.

"Here it is."

I looked at the large double monitors on his desk. "Bring it up. Let's take a look."

Gil paused again while he considered my request, then sighed in resignation. "I can put it on the room monitor," he commented, and then did something with his phone so the window blinds whirred as they closed halfway, dimming the light in the office.

The big-screen TV on the wall flickered to life, and a few moments later, it showed a dark image speckled with a handful of lights. As my eyes focused, I picked out a few more details and realized we were looking at a garden at night with landscape accent lights. The screen then switched to a green hue. With night vision, it was as though we were looking at Gil's backyard during daylight with a dark green filter lens.

The drone motors whirred into life, and the machine rose off the patio, hovering with a view of the ocean beyond the headlands.

From there, the shot rotated, and the drone gained more altitude, picking up the city lights and cars moving along the streets.

"Are you flying this manually, or using a destination input?" I asked.

"Manually," Gil replied. "But this model can be flown with a predetermined route or a waypoint."

"Cool toy," Hugo commented as the drone moved swiftly over the harbor towards Capo Beach.

Gil scoffed. "This is no toy."

The man was far from off the hook, but I hoped Hugo would chill for a few minutes until we saw what the drone footage gave us. Gil could still insist on a warrant, and arresting him would be a stretch on our part. I'd bluffed the tech genius, but we'd have to provide actual evidence for a judge.

The drone arrived over Capo Beach with the dark expanse of ocean to the right and the bluffs to the left. Olamendi's restaurant, along with the hotel and timeshare resort, was nestled into the base of the steep slope. We could see the footbridge over the railroad tracks up ahead, then the camera rotated down to show Hailey's Prius and Garrett Caldwell's pickup truck.

"Did you have a tracking device on Hailey's vehicle?" I asked, forgetting my own concerns about spooking Gil.

"No!" he responded.

"Her work cell, right?" Hugo said.

Gil was silent.

"But she didn't carry it with her outside of work, and we didn't find it at the scene or in her car," I thought aloud.

Gil went to say something, then stopped himself.

"There they are," Hugo said, pointing at the TV.

The drone had rotated to face the beach, and two figures, distinguishable as shadowed movement on the paler sand, walked slowly along the shoreline. They were halfway between the footbridge and the north end of the parking area. The drone rose and eased closer to the couple. As it did so, an object moved on the water.

"Stop!" I called out, and Gil paused the footage. "Go back a bit."

He did so, and Hugo and I moved closer to the enormous TV screen.

"That a boat?" he asked.

"The night vision is less effective with low contrast," Gil said from behind his computer. "Looks like a vessel to me, but more like a small barge than a boat."

"It's closer to the beach than *Shore Code* ever came," I said quietly to Hugo. "I think he's right. It's another vessel we didn't know about."

"Rewind one more time," Hugo ordered, and Gil obliged. "Freeze."

The closer I moved to the screen, the less clear the image became to my eyes, and I backed away.

"Is there a way to clean this up?" I asked.

"We have software to do that," Gil replied. "But to be honest, it won't help much here. The software uses predictive algorithms to determine what the image is most likely to be, and looks for changes in the pixels to determine edges, angles, and shapes. There's so little to work from in this situation, I wouldn't trust the results. It'll use the GPS data to identify the object is on the water, but from there, it'll be applying logic more than real data to build a better image."

"Meaning, it will determine it's a watercraft of some description," I responded. "Because that would make sense."

"Exactly," he replied.

"Okay, let's see the rest of what you shot," Hugo said.

We watched as the camera tilted to stay on the couple walking. They were moving at a relaxed pace, several feet apart. I couldn't see any physical contact between them, either romantic or adversarial. After a minute, the drone rose higher, turned, and flew over the bluffs before sweeping north to return home.

"That was it?" Hugo asked.

"Yes," Gil confirmed.

"You didn't fly it back to the beach?"

"No. Keep watching. You'll see I flew it to my house and landed. That was it."

I thought about the timeline. Cathy, the lady who'd called us, heard the drone at close to ten-thirty, and we knew from the PCH CCTV Hailey and Caldwell had arrived at ten-fifteen. As they were walking north along the beach, Cathy must have heard the drone as Gil flew it away. That would match her description of hearing it overhead.

"Why were you stalking her?" Hugo asked, moving closer to Gil's desk.

"I wasn't stalking her," Gil responded defensively.

Hugo laughed. "Seriously, man? We just watched you track her to the beach and film her without permission."

Gil sat back and released a long breath. "Okay, look. I'm going through a divorce after a lot of back-and-forth with my wife. It's been a difficult time, and I'd always gotten along well with Hailey at the office. I thought there might be something more between us, but I guess not."

"Meaning, she turned you down," Hugo quickly responded.

Gil nodded. "Yeah. And I didn't want to believe that was really the case. I had my head up my ass, okay? But this was all in the week before she was killed. You can see, I flew the drone over there, and I'm watching her walk the beach with some guy, and that was a reality check for me. I realized I was being an idiot, and totally unprofessional. After flying the drone home, it was all over with, as far as I was concerned. I planned to apologize to her the next morning, but of course, she never came in."

"You understand you just described a common motive for murder, right?" Hugo pointed out.

"Then you should see I'm being honest. Why would I tell you any of that if I was guilty? Besides, you just saw she was fine in my camera footage, and I was home all night afterwards."

"Except you lied to us," I said.

"No, I didn't," he responded, throwing his arms up in frustration.

"You told us you set the alarm after the delivery girl left, yet you must have disarmed it to walk outside and fly the drone a little after ten."

"Yes, yes, fine. I did, but I can pull the records from the alarm system and show you it was rearmed afterwards and stayed on all night. I was home."

"So, how did you know she was at the beach?" I asked, circling back to the question he'd avoided earlier. "You tracked Hailey somehow, and the company phone wasn't there."

Gil hesitated again, clearly torn over what to say.

"Looks like we need a warrant for the company records, Hugo," I said in a bored tone.

"She had it with her," Gil blurted. "I could track her phone."

"You can track all your company phones, right?" I asked.

He nodded.

"Pretty sure that's illegal if the employee isn't aware of that fact," Hugo pointed out.

Gil's face was turning red.

"Hailey left her company phone at her desk when she left work," I said. "Why did she have it with her Wednesday night?"

The man closed his eyes and sighed. "Because we'd been having a text exchange."

I'd arrived at GilTech fairly certain the owner had nothing to do with Hailey's murder, but the more we probed, the more he confessed, which was rapidly changing my mind.

"Let's see them," Hugo ordered.

"See what?" Gil asked.

"The texts. Show us the messages on your phone."

Gil shook his head. "I deleted them."

Hugo groaned. "Then we'll have to get a warrant for the records. Obstruction doesn't come close to covering what you've done here, Mr. Gil. Not to mention you're sitting on the weakest alibi of all time. Anytime you want to give us a legitimate and verifiable reason why we shouldn't arrest you, I'm all ears."

"I didn't hurt Hailey," Gil replied again. "I'd never. I couldn't."

"You were stalking the woman," I responded in exasperation. "None of what you've told us are the actions of a man using logic and reason. What was in the texts?"

"You're right, I get it," Gil babbled. "This looks bad, but I swear I didn't hurt Hailey. The texts were me trying to talk her into going to dinner."

"And her turning you down," I said.

He nodded. "But you'll see, it was a friendly exchange. Mostly fun and joking."

"Then why delete them?" Hugo challenged.

"Because I knew they'd look bad," Gil replied. "I panicked."

"How did you know we didn't have her phone?" I asked as the idea came to me.

"Because you didn't say anything about the texts when you came by the other day," he replied. "I deleted them after you left."

I looked at Hugo, and he curled one side of his mouth. He was on the fence as much as I was. Enrique Gil was guilty of obstructing our investigation and stalking Hailey Carter, but did he murder his executive assistant? For me, the object in the water held my focus more than Gil did. Unless he'd magically appeared at Capo Beach without using PCH, the only road access available after ten p.m., he couldn't have killed Hailey. Much like Ryan Kwon. They both had a motive, stalked her, and were in the general vicinity a short time before the murder, but neither appeared to have been able to commit the far more serious crime.

"We need a copy of that drone footage," I said, buying myself time while I processed what I thought should come next.

I looked over at the big-screen TV where the drone's footage was paused at the end of its journey, sitting on the patio at Gil's house. I took out my instant camera and snapped a picture without bothering to ask permission. Gil didn't protest, but took a thumb drive from a package in his desk and busied himself copying the file. Hugo stepped closer to me.

"We can arrest him, but all it'll do is tie us up longer," he whispered.

I nodded. "I agree. Looks like the killer took both her phones as well as all her clothes."

"Slim chance we'll ever find any of it," Hugo replied.

"Here you go," Gil said, standing and holding out the thumb drive.

I walked over and took it from him. "We'll be issuing a warrant for your and Hailey's phone records, Mr. Gil, and I suggest you stick around town while our investigation continues."

"I have a trip to Virginia scheduled for next week," he replied. "I can't miss it."

Police demanding that suspects not leave town was a Hollywood myth. It required a court order to restrict someone's travel, and a quick call to his lawyer or a simple internet search would inform Gil of such. Which was why I'd used the word "suggest."

"Email me your flight details, please," I said, which again he was not obliged to do, but I figured he would.

"We'll be in touch," Hugo said, and we left his office.

Grace looked at me quizzically as we passed her desk, and I gave her what I hoped was a reassuring smile. Enrique Gil could still theoretically be our killer, but my gut told me Grace wasn't in danger.

"How do we figure out what that other vessel is?" Hugo asked as we left the building.

"More bloody CCTV," I replied, pausing by the car door. "But I feel like we're finally onto something."

26

———————

On the drive back to the station, I used my laptop to request the phone records' warrant. We also detoured via Buena Vista Market to pick up lunch tacos, as we expected to be tied to our computers for a while. I'd already eaten one of my three before we'd parked at the station.

"Should we be looking anywhere else where a boat could have been launched?" Hugo asked as we returned to our office.

My partner wasn't a water sports or boat guy, so I thought about how best to explain the odd features of our stretch of Southern California coastline.

"You have to go all the way south to Oceanside, or north to Newport Beach, to find the next marina on either side of Dana Point. It's all beaches or bluffs without boat ramps or private piers. So the only option would be to drag a boat in across a beach. What we saw on the drone footage was too big for that. The other option would be to travel at least twenty miles along the coast."

"It's farther than that to Catalina, and boats go over there all the time," Hugo pointed out as he hung his jacket and took his seat.

While on the drive, I'd transferred the drone data to our server and marked it in as evidence, so I brought up the footage on my computer and found what I determined to be the best frame of the mystery vessel.

"True, but a relatively small-sized barge-like vessel would be a slow-moving way to cover that distance," I replied after hitting print. "Our best bet is still Dana Point."

"Okay," Hugo said. "But you already looked through that footage and came up with *Shore Code*. You think you missed something?"

"I must have," I begrudgingly admitted, retrieving two copies of the screenshot from the printer. I slid one across the desk to Hugo.

I hated the idea I'd overlooked another suspicious vessel, but logic told me I must have done so. Sitting back down, I found the harbor CCTV file on our server and opened it on my screen.

"Hey, Hugo. How about I look earlier in the evening, and you take later? When I looked before, I had *Shore Code* returning at fifteen minutes after midnight. Start just before that and keep looking later. I didn't go much past one if I remember correctly."

He grunted, so I assumed he was okay with the plan, and I started my search at sunset and went backwards as I ate my other two tacos. Most of the traffic caught on the harbor patrol building's camera comprised boats returning to the marina. I was looking for a vessel leaving. Anything with a more rectangular profile. As the sun rose back up in the sky, everything became clearer, so I was confident I wouldn't miss anything making its way out into the open ocean.

I paused for a while on a catamaran, but it was a white boat with a pilothouse. As it was around thirty-six feet long, I couldn't see how the night vision wouldn't have easily picked it up against the dark sea. Making a note of the boat name and the time, I moved on. There was nothing noteworthy as I continued in reverse, watching the clock wind backwards. At 6:35 p.m., the Catalina Express ferry returned for the night, and I wondered how much farther back I should go. I decided 5:15 p.m. seemed reasonable. Five hours before Hailey arrived at Capo Beach and over two hours before sunset. But I knew I'd reconsider if I hadn't found anything by then.

At 6:10 p.m., I paused the playback and stared at the screen. "Hugo!"

I heard him shuffle his chair back and walk around to my side. Holding the printout from the drone footage next to the screen, I compared the two.

"That could be it," Hugo said. "It's dark with a rectangular profile."

We stared at the SunChaser pontoon boat on its way to exiting the harbor. Its decking was gray, along with the seating, but the hull and pontoons were black. An unusual choice for a watercraft. One person, who appeared to be male from the rearview, piloted the vessel from the console on the boat's starboard side, and one passenger, also male by my best guess, occupied the left seat.

"Can we see it coming towards us?" Hugo asked.

"When they come back in," I said. "Otherwise, we'll have to hunt for other cameras in the harbor."

"They must have returned in the dark," Hugo replied. "We need to see their faces in the light."

"You didn't see this boat returning?" I asked.

"Not yet, and I'm at one a.m. or so already," Hugo replied.

The pontoon boat didn't have a name I could see, and even in the daylight, I couldn't quite read the registration numbers. I skipped bothering Nate again and looked up the number for harbor security. After a few selections in an automated system, the line rang four times before a man answered.

"Harbor security."

"Hi, this is Investigator Cromwell with the Orange County Sheriff's Department. Who am I speaking with?"

"Gary Craven. What can I do for you?"

"Hi, Gary. I was hoping you could help me identify a boat leaving the harbor on Wednesday evening."

"Okay, I'll do my best, but it's a big harbor with a lot of boats moving around."

"I have CCTV of the vessel from harbor patrol's camera, but I can't read the reg number. I was wondering what other cameras you have that might give us a better look, Gary?"

"Do you know if it came from a slip?" he asked.

"Good question. We don't know."

"From which way did they approach the exit, Miss…"

"Cromwell," I filled in for him. "The south end right past harbor patrol. We have them at 6:10 p.m."

"Right. Miss Cromwell. We have a couple of cameras at the end of the wharf and one on the fuel dock. It may take me a few minutes to pull those up. Shall I call you back?"

"I'll hold, if that's okay with you. This is a potential lead in a murder inquiry."

"Shit," he muttered. "The Capo Beach thing?"

"Ongoing investigation and all that, Gary, so I can't really say. But that case is our station's highest priority at the moment."

"Gotcha," he replied. "I'm putting you on hold, but I'll be as quick as I can."

Hugo had returned to his desk and now peeked around the monitors.

"Any luck?" he asked.

"My new mate, Gary, is looking for us. They have a bunch of cameras, so fingers crossed."

"I'm on fast forward here, and I don't see that pontoon coming back," Hugo said, moving back to his screen. "In fact, I don't see anything going in or out after *Shore Code*. I still think Monroe and his buddy have to be involved. Too much of a coincidence they're out on their boat Monday and Wednesday nights."

"Hmm," I responded.

My first reaction was to agree, as it made sense, but the Monday night part didn't necessarily fit for me. We'd determined the legs went in the water before the framework, but Rosa had said it was twice as long or more. If the upper frame was placed in position after sunset on Wednesday night, and pulled from the water by Rosa's team on Thursday morning, that meant twelve to fourteen hours. Twice that was twenty-four hours or more. Which meant more like Tuesday night. Surely she would have seen a far greater difference in corrosion at three times the submersion.

"Miss Cromwell?"

"Yes, Gary."

"I've pulled up everything we have at six p.m. on Wednesday night. What are we looking for?"

"A black with gray interior SunChaser pontoon with two guys aboard."

"Okay, give me a second to search," Gary replied, but came back almost immediately. "Oh, yes. I've got it."

"Can you read the registration number?" I asked.

"Let me see from a different camera."

I waited a few moments.

"Got a pen?"

"Shoot," I replied, and wrote the number and letter combination he gave me. I covered the phone and slid my notepad across the desks. "Hugo?"

He took the note and began typing on his keyboard.

"They launched that pontoon, Miss Cromwell," Gary continued. "They're on CCTV at the ramp. Two guys, as you said. Pulled it with a pickup truck."

"Blimey, what a score," I muttered, reaching across the desks to repossess my notepad from Hugo.

"What's that, Miss?" Gary asked.

"Oh, I mean this could be mega-helpful. Thank you."

"You're not from around here, are you, Miss Cromwell?"

"Grew up right here in Dana Point," I replied. "But I came over from the UK when I was six."

"You've certainly kept that cool accent."

I needed to get this back on track. I was looking for a murderer, not a date.

"Got a license plate on the pickup, Gary?"

"Oh, right. Sorry."

He read off the plate, and I quickly searched it in our system.

"Definitely a pickup truck, right, Gary?"

"Yes, ma'am. Dodge Ram crew cab."

"That plate's off a 1998 Volkswagen Jetta," I replied. "If I send uniforms by, could you give them copies of any CCTV you have with that pontoon or truck on it?"

"Sure," Gary replied. "Or, if you wanted to come by, that would be good, too."

I laughed. "If this leads us somewhere, I'll be sure to drop by and shake your hand, Gary."

"Deal," he replied. "Good luck, Miss Cromwell."

"Thanks," I replied, and ended the call.

"We might be onto something here, Hugo," I announced, finally feeling like we had momentum on the case. "Pontoon was dropped by a truck with stolen plates."

He slid his chair over and held up his own notebook. "Got an address for the pontoon owner. Dale Kinney. 33787 Via De Agua in San Juan Capistrano."

"What are the chances he's home around midday on a Tuesday?" I asked.

"I'll call and see what we get," Hugo replied, picking up his cell phone.

While he tried Kinney's house, I sat back and allowed myself a moment of guarded optimism. On the job, we'd been drilled since the beginning not to let ourselves become emotionally involved in our cases, with the victims or their families. It would burn you out. The world was full of good people, but there were also a fair few doing evil things, and in law enforcement, we dealt with them at a disproportionate rate. We couldn't cry over the victims, or develop hatred for the offenders. Those emotions distracted from the task, and wore you down.

But having stood in the water next to Hailey Carter's corpse strapped to the X-frame, I couldn't help myself from mourning her loss. From everything we'd discovered about her, Hailey appeared to have been a hard-working young woman with her life in order. An attractive female who people enjoyed being around. Which, ironically, could well have been her undoing. It seemed implausible for two men to be stalking her while she was out on a date with a third man, and a fourth man with a loose connection to her nearby on a boat, but the evidence suggested that's exactly what had happened. Could there really be a fifth entity involved?

"Mr. Arbuckle?" I heard Hugo ask into his phone, deliberately using the wrong name. "My apologies, sir. I must have misdialed."

Standing up, he gathered his jacket and pocketed his phone. "He's home. Let's go."

It took a few minutes to coordinate support through Sergeant Martinez before driving the three-and-a-half miles across town to the Reservoir Canyon neighborhood on the inland side of the 5 freeway. Deputies Ripley and Hanson followed us up the steep hill with large, older homes on either side of the street. Everything was either built up or down a slope, the development having been sculpted into the hillside. Kinney's house was a beige stucco, probably built in the '70s or '80s by the look of the dated design, but landscaped nicely with a much newer stonework retaining wall for a small, lush green lawn.

We parked in front, and the deputies used their cruiser to block the short driveway to an attached double garage. As we walked to the front door, I unclipped the safety strap on my sidearm holster, registering the different feel of my backup piece. Hugo knocked, and the two deputies hung back on the sidewalk, watching the sides of the house.

The door opened, and a woman in her late fifties or early sixties looked at us in surprise. We held up our badges, and her eyes widened, especially when her gaze drifted to the uniformed deputies outside.

"Is Mr. Dale Kinney home, ma'am?" I asked.

A small dog yipped from somewhere inside the house, but the woman was speechless.

"Are you Mrs. Kinney?" I asked.

She nodded. "Yes."

"Is your husband home, ma'am?" I asked again. "We'd like a word with him."

"Just a moment," she muttered, then pushed the door halfway closed before walking back down the hallway.

Hugo reached out and opened the door back up so we could clearly see inside. Muffled voices came from what I guessed to be a living room. The home had been updated inside with tall baseboards, a tile floor, and crown molding to what I was sure had once been popcorn ceilings.

A man appeared in the hallway with the woman in tow.

"Can I help you?" he asked before reaching us.

His voice was bold and slightly gruff. About the same age as his wife, Kinney wore slacks, a golf shirt, and brown slippers. His brow furrowed as he approached us, and I noticed he walked with a halting gait.

"Orange County Sheriff's Department Investigators Cromwell and Fuentes, sir. You're Dale Kinney?"

"I am. What's this about?"

"Do you own a 2019 SunChaser pontoon boat, sir?" I asked.

"Yes," he responded, the furrows deepening on his forehead.

"When was the last time you were out on your boat, sir?"

He shrugged his shoulders. "It's been months. What's this about?"

"So you weren't on the water with your pontoon on Wednesday evening, sir?" I continued, knowing this wasn't one of the two younger men we could see on the CCTV.

"What are you talking about?" he replied. "My pontoon hasn't moved in months. Since before my hip surgery in June."

"Where do you keep your boat, sir?" Hugo asked.

"Friend of mine has a lot down the hill. Lets me keep it there until he builds. Before I answer anything else, how about you tell me what the hell is going on?"

Dale Kinney wasn't about to drag a young woman into the

Pacific Ocean and strap her to a frame against the incoming surf, so I had a pretty good idea what we'd find at his friend's lot.

"Your pontoon boat was seen in Dana Point harbor on Wednesday night, sir," I explained. "I think we should take a drive down the hill and check on it."

"Oh my Lord," he muttered. "Let me get some shoes on."

While Dale organized his footwear, we took a step back from the front door.

"We need to check for stolen Ram trucks last week," Hugo said as we waited.

"Yeah," I replied, getting a sinking feeling in my stomach. "I think we've found the how, but we'll still be nowhere closer to who."

"We should also check for stolen boats around the time of Taylor Davis's death in Corona Del Mar," Hugo said thoughtfully. "If these two guys were responsible for both killings, and have been stealing the vehicles each time, they're bound to have left some kind of evidence."

"True," I agreed, only slightly buoyed by Hugo's optimism. "Even if it's nearby CCTV of them coming or going in their own vehicle."

Kinney came out of his house wearing tennis shoes, and his wife watched him join us in Hugo's car. The boat owner directed us down the hill to a cul-de-sac, which appeared to be a newer development. About half the lots had been built upon with large, more modern homes. Kinney pointed to a lot on the left, and Hugo pulled up to the curb. Ripley and Hanson parked behind us.

"Son of a bitch," Kinney swore as we looked at a utility trailer and a covered car of some sort on the graded lot. "It's gone."

"When was the last time you saw it here, Mr. Kinney?" I asked as the three of us got out.

He shook his head. "To be honest, it was probably before my surgery. I'd just started thinking about getting her in the water before summer's over."

"If you'd speak with the deputies and give them all the details,"

Hugo said, "they'll help you file a report so we can start watching for your boat, sir."

Kinney nodded, and Ripley took over asking him questions. I looked around. A new house was mid-construction on the right of the lot, with saws and nail guns making a clamor that no doubt pissed off all the neighbors. To the left was an enormous home that occupied two lots, by my estimate. A tall, modern white building with large, tinted windows. A matching stark white retaining wall stretched from one side of the lot to the other, breaking for a pair of ornate black metal gates.

Hugo followed as I hurried along the sidewalk, certain I was about to be disappointed. But instead, we stumbled across what would either be another crazy coincidence or a major break-through. A small plate riveted to the square steel gate post read, "McCall Fabrication, San Clemente."

27

I took a picture of the gates, then Hugo and I stood on the sidewalk, looking at each other.

"So where's the pontoon now?" Hugo questioned. "Why didn't they return to Dana Point Harbor?"

"I don't think they returned at all," I replied.

"You mean they went somewhere else? You said it was too far."

"That's not the somewhere else I mean."

"You're confusing me," Hugo replied.

I raised an eyebrow. "What do most punk kids do with a stolen car?"

"They ditch it," Hugo replied. "But how do you ditch a boat? Not like you can walk home."

"Correct," I agreed. "We need a different angle of the pontoon in the harbor. I'm pretty sure I know what we'll see."

I could see Hugo wanted to ask me more, but he refrained. I looked at the gates again. "Do you get the feeling McCall is good for this?" I asked.

"I have the feeling he has something to hide," Hugo replied.

"Me too," I agreed. "But not murder."

Hugo shrugged. "I've been wrong before. We follow the

evidence, and the current evidence leads us back to McCall. So, yes, maybe he murdered Hailey."

"Why don't we drop in on McCall and see what he has to say?" I suggested.

"I think we should," Hugo replied, walking back to the car. "Business is picking up. I'm glad we grabbed an early lunch."

I was, too, but my stomach was already growling. Which could have been my caffeine level slipping below the critically low mark.

I thanked Dale Kinney and the two deputies before joining Hugo in the car.

"Coffee stop on the way," I said in a tone I hoped inferred that it wasn't an optional detour.

"Sure. It'll take you a while to get the ball rolling on the Ram truck search, anyway."

I pulled my laptop from my bag as Hugo turned around in the cul-de-sac.

"We need to look at harbor footage from other nights, too," I said, booting up the computer. "See if the pontoon was used to place the footings."

"There's a CCTV camera at PCH and Dana Point Harbor Drive," Hugo replied. "We can check there for the pontoon on a trailer. They'd almost certainly have to pass through that inter-section."

"Blimey, I don't think I can get all that done before we get to McCall's, even with a coffee stop."

"Best quit yapping and get searching, then," he said with a hint of a grin.

For a moment, I wondered what had brought out my partner's sense of humor lately. He usually kept it well under wraps, only to be revealed on very special occasions. But I decided it was best to enjoy the moments and not worry about why they were happening.

Matthew McCall was not pleased to see us again. His daughter was potentially even more uninterested in what her father was pleased or disturbed about.

"Don't you need a warrant or something to keep coming around someone's business?" McCall asked.

"To have a conversation?" Hugo scoffed. "No. But we can caution you and take you to the station for a formal interview if you'd prefer."

The daughter looked up from behind the front counter and tore her eyes from her phone for a moment. Apparently, her father being arrested was worthy of her time. But McCall just shook his head and opened his office door, so she lost interest again. Concerns over the future of humankind raced through my head, and I wondered when I'd started thinking like my father.

"You did a job on Calle Gorgonio in San Juan, Mr. McCall," Hugo began. "A large pair of steel gates. Do you recall the project?"

He nodded. "What about it?"

"Can you tell us who worked on-site to fit those gates?" Hugo asked.

McCall shrugged his shoulders. "No. That was a month ago. I send whoever's available for a job."

"How about you give it a bit more thought, mate," I said, making sure he saw me noticing his calendar on the back of the door again. "We wouldn't be here if it wasn't important."

He sat down behind his desk, cleared a pile of papers out of the way, and logged into his computer. After a few moments, he looked up.

"Chelsea!" he shouted.

"What?" his daughter replied from beyond the door.

I opened it to assist in the communications.

"Get me the file for Rasmusson."

"Who?"

I could see Chelsea, and she hadn't moved, her eyes still transfixed on her phone.

"Rasmusson. Those big gates last month."

The daughter huffed, put her phone down, and spun her chair around to a file cabinet behind her. Yanking open a creaky steel drawer, she produced a file and shuffled into the office.

"Remember who fitted them?" McCall asked her.

"Why'd you ask for the file, then?"

"Because these two need to know who worked the job."

"Well, that ain't in the file, Dad," Chelsea replied. "You need the time cards."

"I do?"

Chelsea rolled her eyes. She mumbled something under her breath as she left the office and returned to the counter. I watched her check something in the file, then go to work on the computer keyboard.

"While we're waiting, Mr. McCall," Hugo said. "Can you tell us where you were Wednesday evening?"

McCall frowned. "Why?"

"Standard question we ask," Hugo lied.

"This is getting ridiculous," McCall muttered. "Wednesday? Home, I guess. No, wait, my other daughter had a school thing. We were at her school until about eight or so, then we went to dinner."

"What was the school *thing*?" I asked.

"A play."

"*Clue*!" Chelsea shouted.

"What's that?" McCall bellowed back.

"The play was *Clue*, Dad."

"Oh, right. Yeah. *Clue*."

"Nice one, you idiot," I barely heard Chelsea mumble. "It was only your kid's play she's worked all semester on."

"Where did you eat dinner?" Hugo asked.

"Gibroni's," McCall replied.

"That the pizza place here in town?" Hugo asked.

McCall nodded.

"When did you leave?"

McCall threw his hands up. "I don't know. Ten, maybe?"

"Eddie, Luis, Mateo, and Mason," Chelsea called out.

"Both days?" McCall asked in return. "It was a two-days installation, right?"

Chelsea muttered under her breath again and flipped the manilla file open once more. After shuffling through papers for a few moments, she returned to the computer.

"Two and a half days!" she shouted back. "Just Eddie and Luis on the first day, then all four after that."

"Thanks!" McCall shouted, then looked at me. "That what you need?"

I glanced back at Chelsea. She'd resumed her position of slouching in the office chair and surfing her phone. I had to admit she was buttoned down when she needed to be, so maybe there was hope for the planet after all.

"We need their full names," I responded, returning my attention to McCall. "And we'd like to speak with each of them, please."

"Mateo's on vacation, and Eddie's out quoting a job. He won't be back in today. The others are out back, but we're busy, man. I can't have you tying them up with questions all afternoon."

"Let me remind you, this is a murder inquiry, Mr. McCall," Hugo snapped. "If it was your daughter in the mortuary, I'm sure you'd want people to do everything they could to cooperate."

McCall nodded. "Yeah. Sorry. We're just slammed right now, which is good, but you know how it goes. I got Mateo out, so I'm a man down, and we're quoting so many new jobs, I got Eddie run ragged."

"How long has Mateo been out?" I asked.

"I don't know. What day is it, Tuesday? He was out all last week, and he'll be back on Monday. Went to see family in Mexico."

That ruled him out of at least being involved in Hailey's murder.

"Okay, let's start with one of the other two, please," I said, but McCall didn't move.

"You can't honestly believe any of my guys had anything to do with a murder?"

"Then we'll be able to rule them out quick as you like, and they'll be back to work in a tick," I replied.

He looked at me strangely as he got to his feet.

"The British comes out in her sometimes," Hugo said, and I frowned at him.

McCall smiled for the first time.

"We'll talk to them in your office, if you don't mind?" I added as the owner walked out back to get one of his guys. "Thanks a lot," I muttered to Hugo.

He shrugged. "You talk funny for someone who grew up in California."

"It's English!" I hissed back at him.

"You're in America," he retorted with a hint of a grin.

He was enjoying this far too much, and I knew better than to be drawn in, but of course, I couldn't stop myself. Which was one of my frustratingly annoying character traits. Annoying to me, that is. Amusing to my partner, apparently.

"And what bloody language do you speak?"

"American English."

"So, you took another language, threw out a few u's, and claimed it as your own?"

"I didn't, but I think you have the gist of it. The u's were superfluous, and you know how the land of excess hates waste."

Before I could decipher Hugo's deliberate contradictions, McCall returned with an older Hispanic man. His worker wiped his hands on a rag, looking nervous as he entered the office.

"Luis?" I asked.

He nodded.

"Just answer their questions, and they'll be out of our hair," McCall said, following him in.

"Give us a minute," Hugo directed to the company owner.

McCall shook his head some more, but stepped outside. I pushed the door closed, trying not to stare at the calendar model's impressive assets.

"Hi, Luis, we're OCSD Investigators Cromwell and Fuentes," I began. "We're investigating a case which had an element of metal fabrication, so we're asking a few experts about the process to help us better understand."

I was impressed with the approach I'd come up with on the fly, although Hugo gave me a sideways look. I ignored him as Luis appeared more at ease, which was the goal.

"What is your role here?" I continued.

"I'm a fabricator," Luis replied in heavily accented English.

He may have preferred switching to Spanish, but I wasn't about to put my high school language skills to the test. Or let Hugo scare the wits out of Luis.

"And what does that entail, exactly?" I asked. "Welding, cutting metal, installing jobs?"

"*Sí*," Luis replied.

"Okay," I sighed. "But do you specialize in one particular area?"

"No."

"Where were you last Wednesday night, Luis?" Hugo asked, obviously tired of my novel approach, which I had to agree was getting us nowhere.

Luis tensed once more. "Home."

"Can someone corroborate that?" Hugo asked.

Luis stared back in puzzlement.

"*¿Puede alguien confirmar eso?*" Hugo asked.

"My wife."

Hugo paused and glanced at me, so I dived in again.

"Luis, have you seen a fabrication job here which involved a box tube framework about six-foot by three-foot?"

"We use box tube a lot," he replied.

"This wouldn't have been a fence or gate. It's more like a platform with legs," I explained. "Mainly three-inch square box tube."

Luis frowned. "I don't know this job."

"Have you worked on or seen any projects in the last four weeks which utilized three-inch box tube?" I asked, already expecting another monosyllabic reply.

"*Sí*."

"And what was that job for?" I continued.

"A lift for a garage."

"So, that was a large frame, not like I mentioned?"

"It was big," Luis replied, using his hands for emphasis.

I looked at Hugo, and he shrugged his shoulders. It did feel like we were wasting our time.

"One thing strange," Luis added, and we both turned his way.

"Yeah? What was that?" I asked.

"We have enough tube to build the lift. But we go home, and next morning, we missing some tubing."

"When was this?" I asked, my interest piqued.

"Two weeks, I think."

"How much material was missing?" I asked.

He lifted his hands. "I don't know. Enough Mr. McCall must order more."

"This was three-inch box tube?" I asked, moving to open the door.

"*Sí.*"

The owner wasn't in the reception, so I walked through to the workshop where I found him talking to another worker.

"Mr. McCall, how come you didn't mention you had three-inch box tube go missing a few weeks back?"

He looked confused.

"Luis told us you had to order more to complete a garage lift job," I explained as Hugo joined me.

"Oh, I don't know it was missing," he replied. "I think the estimate and material order was just off by a bit."

"Did you order the material?" I asked.

He shook his head. "Mason did."

"Mason, as in the other guy we're about to talk to?"

"Yeah, but I guess you'll have to come back."

"Why?" I asked, looking around at the faces of the curious workers staring in our direction.

"Because Mason went home," McCall replied. "He told one of the guys he wasn't feeling good. I'm sure he'll be in tomorrow."

"Mason's last name?" I asked.

"McCall. He's my nephew."

I looked at Hugo, who rolled his eyes. I turned back to the owner.

"So, Mason was here all morning, but left after we arrived?"

"I guess. Said he must have eaten something bad at lunch."

I shook my head. "We need Mason's home address and cell number, sir. Now."

28

I put out an APB for Mason McCall, then called San Clemente's Sheriff's office while Hugo drove us to the address the uncle had given us. We cruised by the apartments, which stretched back from Acebo Street and had been built on a long, skinny, sloped lot. Stairs at the far end led to walkways for each level, and from a satellite map on my phone, parking appeared to be behind the neighboring building. We stopped at the end of the road where Acebo met Avenida Del Mar.

"Bloody hell, Hugo," I muttered as I read Mason McCall's rap sheet while we waited for backup. "He has a disturbing-the-peace charge, three speeding tickets, and get this, a sexual assault charge which didn't stick."

"Finally," Hugo replied. "We might be getting somewhere."

I nodded, but was wary of getting too excited. It seemed like we'd been here before. A suspect who appeared to be good for the murder until we discovered they couldn't have been on the beach.

Two deputies arrived, pulling up alongside us in their cruiser.

Hugo powered down his window. "The apartment block back there. Suspect rents unit eight. Middle level about halfway back."

The deputy in the passenger seat nodded. "Want us to knock?"

"Yup. Cromwell will cover the front of the street, and I'll drive up the alleyway alongside and cover the back. Once we're in place, you guys block the alley and hustle up to the unit."

"Yes, sir," the deputy replied.

"And be ready," Hugo added, handing my phone between the two windows. "He's a murder suspect."

The two deputies studied the picture I'd pulled from social media before handing the phone back. We settled on a radio frequency, ran a quick check, then I got out to walk up the hill while Hugo turned the car around. A moment later, he rolled past me and turned right between our apartment block and the one next door.

The radio crackled to life. "Front door to unit eight is open. Over."

"Copy," came the response from one of the deputies.

I strolled along the sidewalk on the opposite side of the street and paused when I came level with the far corner of the apartment building. I held my instant camera like a phone and pretended to study directions while I took a picture. It also gave me a chance to check the left side of the apartments.

One unit on each of the three levels faced the front, but the rest were right-to-left through the narrow building with a couple of windows on the wall I was looking at. From the middle level, nephew McCall would have an unhealthy drop to the adjacent building's steps.

"Fuentes in position. Proceed. Over."

I stayed across the road as it afforded me a better view of the left side of the building, figuring the entry and stairs side would be covered by the deputies. They quietly drove the cruiser up the hill and parked it across the entrance to the alley. I watched the two men get out and disappear from my view.

If the apartment door was open, it boded well for McCall to be home, but it could also reflect the haste in which he may have rushed home from work. Perhaps to gather his important possessions and head out of town. I looked around, but didn't see any obvious CCTV cameras. There certainly weren't any city-owned placements on this small residential street, and most of the surrounding buildings were apartment units.

I heard the deputies announce themselves, and my adrenaline immediately surged. Most of our time was spent behind a desk or driving around talking to people, but occasionally we became involved in more tense confrontations with suspects. As Hugo had commented, I seemed to find myself in more than my fair share, but a scrap was unlikely today. The deputies had the front handled, and the only other way was out a window from two stories up.

Muffled shouts came from deep inside the apartment, and to my surprise, a window flung open on the second level. Sprinting, I crossed the road and jumped on top of a waist-high retaining wall. Between the apartment building and the neighboring steps, a four-foot-wide concrete drainage gulley ran down the hill to where I stood, intended to guide away any rain water pouring down from the flat roof.

From inside the building, I could hear more shouts and thumping noises. McCall was already halfway out the window before he turned and saw me.

"Police!" I shouted. "Give it up, mate. You're just going to hurt yourself."

Instead of going back inside, he clambered farther out and reached for something I couldn't see. With a yank of what I figured must have been a length of twine or thin string, a knotted rope tumbled from the roof and dangled next to the window.

I keyed the radio. "Suspect escaping to roof from bathroom window. Over."

"He's got the bathroom door barricaded," a breathless deputy replied. "We're trying to break it down. Over."

Once McCall reached the flat roof, we'd lose sight of him until he attempted to descend, but I was powerless unless I shot the man, and one gun discharge was probably enough for the week. Nevertheless, I unclipped the strap on my sidearm.

"Come back down, McCall!" I shouted. "Don't make me shoot you!"

He was nimbly climbing the rope, completely unfazed by my empty threat.

"I don't see him," Hugo called over the radio.

"He's on the roof," I replied, watching him disappear from my view. "Deputies, cover the balcony side. Over."

The thumping inside stopped.

"Copy."

I ran up the drainage gulley past the apartment units until it ended at the back of the building. There, it met a narrow walkway running perpendicular between the apartments and another building to the rear. Beyond that was the next street over. I had to wonder what the easement laws were when these buildings went up in the '70s or '80s, as they were stacked almost end to end.

Hugo appeared at the other corner of the building. I glanced up to see McCall leap from his roof to the gently angled Spanish tile roof of the next building.

"Seriously?" Hugo groaned.

Leaping over a broken-down piece of fencing, I ran behind the adjacent property to the corner of the Spanish tile building, where it, too, had a narrow pathway between it and its neighboring apartment block. Keeping an eye above me in case he leaped over the gap, I sprinted to a gate, which was in better condition and required me to unlatch it to pass through. I could hear footfalls on the tile somewhere above me, but I still couldn't see McCall. The side of the building stepped back, and I ran into a parking area with garages under the apartments. I looked up again and saw the roof had dropped a level as we were now on the backside of the hill.

"No visual," Hugo called over the radio. "I've called for more support."

"Nothing with us," the deputies added.

A few tiles clattered down the roof and dropped to the concrete parking area, exploding loudly into a million pieces. I pulled out my phone and looked at the satellite view on the map I still had open. The apartment buildings had been shoehorned into long, narrow lots that wrapped around the hill. On the far side from where I stood, another block of units sat almost parallel to the Spanish tile building, but the next one was at an angle, with only one corner of the roof close enough to jump between. Beyond that was finally a broad gap to a large house.

I keyed the radio. "He's cutting across rooftops. Heading south-west. I think."

I really wasn't a hundred percent sure of the direction from my quick glance at the map, but that was somewhere close. Running to Avenida Santa Barbara, I turned right, following the street as it curved. Checking the rooftops, I still couldn't see McCall, but I could hear footfalls every now and again. Reaching the apex of the corner where Avenida Santa Barbara wrapped around to meet Avenida Del Mar, I stopped. A large jacaranda tree blocked most of my view, and I had no idea which way McCall had gone. With a fifty-fifty chance, I chose to continue around the turn, figuring he was making good time across the rooftops and would try to cover the farthest distance before clambering down.

The sound of glass smashing told me our suspect was close by, and I scanned the entry side of the apartment block. Walkways ran along each level, much like his own building. I wondered why he'd break into a unit, knowing we were so close, but then he appeared on the top level of three, peering around the corner. He must have kicked a window when he was swinging down off the roof. Our eyes locked, and he retreated out of sight.

"Suspect on third floor of pale green building," I radioed to the others, then looked at the street address painted on the curb. "10414. He's currently at far end from road."

I walked up the steep driveway to the parking area. At the front of the building, the ground floor consisted of apartments closest to the street and parking in the back half. The other two floors were all apartments. As he hadn't reappeared at the corner, I ran that way to catch where he was heading. The options appeared limited. The stairs brought him out right by where I now stood, so the roof looked like his best option. Maybe he'd even backtrack across the buildings the way he'd come. But I couldn't see him anywhere.

"What's up?" a blond surfer called down, coming out of a middle-level unit. "I thought I heard breaking glass, man."

"Police. Go back inside," I ordered, which of course he didn't do.

"Should I be worried, man?"

"Not if you go back inside and lock your door," I called back.

From somewhere above the surfer, it sounded like feet scuffing or tripping. But then silence apart from the low drone of traffic and a blend of muffled stereos and televisions from surrounding homes.

One of the deputies appeared, climbing over the tall fence between the parking for these units and the lot serving McCall's apartment block. He leaped to the asphalt, brushing the dirt and fine gravel from his hands. I put two fingers to my eyes, then pointed to the roof. The deputy shook his head. Something clattered from the street, and I whipped around.

"Cover this end!" I yelled, and ran back down the driveway.

Reaching the sidewalk, I saw McCall sliding down a light pole, which had to be at least four feet from the building. He must have lunged to the pole, three stories up, like a crazy parkour athlete. I sprinted again, but he'd already dropped the last five feet and took off with a fifty-foot head start on me.

"In pursuit on foot!" I shouted with the radio mic keyed. "East on Avenida Santa Barbara."

McCall glanced back over his shoulder before cutting right across the street, giving me the chance to make up ground on the angle. The sun was scorching off the asphalt road, and my heart was thumping, which reminded me to run a few more intervals in my training.

He shot up the tiled steps of a large villa-like home built up the slope on the other side of Avenida Santa Barbara. Most of the houses had garages at street level and steps leading to a front door on the second level. McCall kept going to where I could see a tall fence divided the rear lot line of the home.

My thighs burned as I pounded up the steps behind him, keying the mic again.

"Between… two homes… on other side… of Santa Barbara."

McCall reached the top as I passed the front door. I noticed a startled woman looking out a window at me. I didn't have time to fumble for my badge, so I'd have to come back and explain myself later. Looking up, I saw McCall stare calmly back at me before hopping up on a low wall alongside the pathway. He took two steps and vaulted over the fence.

"Bugger," I huffed as I struggled the rest of the way to the top.

Following his move, I hopped up on the wall, catching my trailing foot on the edge and almost going flying into a prickly-looking bed of cactus. Once I'd regained my balance, I ran to the fence and peered over. McCall was nowhere in sight.

"Which homes, Kat?" Hugo called over the radio.

I jumped down from the wall. "Left of the brown garage doors," I replied, catching my breath. "But he's gone. He made it over to the next street, and I lost him. Have the cars patrol every street this way."

"Copy," Hugo said, and I saw him standing at the bottom of the steps.

"Bugger," I groaned again, and threw my hands up in frustration. McCall was now our number-one suspect for the murder, and clearly there was no doubt he was guilty of something. No one has a rooftop escape route rigged and planned out unless they think they'll need it.

I met Hugo at the landing by the front entrance to the home, where the lady tentatively opened the door.

"What on earth is going on out here? Who are you?"

"OCSD Investigators, ma'am," Hugo replied. "Sorry for the disturbance."

"You were chasing someone, weren't you?" she asked, looking at me. "Did you let him get away?"

As if I didn't feel bad enough about McCall giving us the slip, a random homeowner giving me grief didn't help.

"Go back inside, ma'am," I said as I started back down the steps.

"How did he get out of his apartment building?" Hugo asked, trotting down behind me. "I thought you had that side covered."

"He'd rigged a climbing rope to the bloody roof," I replied, feeling clammy from the sweat weeping from my body and dripping down my back.

"Seriously?" Hugo replied. "He has to be our guy."

"No shit," I muttered, growing more frustrated and angry with McCall's escape.

29

———

I stood in Mason McCall's apartment and looked around. The guy was twenty-seven, but the place resembled frat-house digs. Movie and sports posters on the walls, a gaming chair in front of a large computer screen, a threadbare couch, and dishes overflowing the sink. A surfboard leaned against a corner of the living room, and a huge flat-screen TV dominated one wall.

"Unless I'm underestimating the industry, there's no chance he pays for this apartment on a fabricator's salary," Hugo said, using a pen to flick sports magazines aside on the coffee table.

His point was valid. Rents in the beach towns were insane, so for any twenty-something to afford a one-bedroom on their own was rare.

"We need into that computer," I said, verifying it was locked with a password. "And a look into his bank accounts might help us out."

The days of shuffling through someone's mail on the kitchen counter were long gone. Everything was billed and paid online.

"Peddling pills is my guess," Hugo said, moving to the bathroom.

I walked into the bedroom to be met with the smell of unwashed laundry. A *Fight Club* movie poster graced one wall, an illustrated poster of a scantily clad female superhero bound in chains another. The room had a queen-size bed, wooden wine boxes as bedside tables, and a particle board dresser with ill-fitting drawers and chips missing from the white laminate. Using nitrile gloves, I began looking through each drawer, sliding clothes aside to see what lay below. Finding nothing of interest, I moved to the closet.

Sliding one mirrored door aside revealed the smelly laundry basket full of clothes and about twenty sports jerseys on hangers. The floor of the closet was covered in tennis shoes, a couple of backpacks, and a variety of flip-flops and sandals. Moving to the other side, I slid the door open and stared at three wetsuits of different thicknesses and coverage. Next to them, jeans and T-shirts hung from the old wooden rail.

I looked up at a bowed shelf running the length of the closet. It was mostly filled with ball caps, but I pulled down a shoebox and checked inside. It was stuffed with baseball cards. They may have been worth a fortune, or less than toilet paper. I didn't follow major sports carefully enough to know any of the players. After checking to make sure there was nothing hidden below, I returned the box to the shelf.

"Anything?" Hugo asked, joining me in the bedroom.

"He's a big sports nut, so could be running book," I suggested. "Or trading baseball cards." Then I thought about both options for a moment. "Not baseball cards. Collectors have the valuable ones in little plastic containers, don't they?"

"Not my thing," Hugo replied. "But yeah, I think so."

I dropped to my knees on the carpet, which I doubted had been vacuumed in months, and looked under the bed. I discovered three shoes, a pair of socks, and another shoebox, which I pulled out to see inside.

"Ew," I groaned, discovering condom packets and a tube of lube.

As I got to my feet, I looked up at the light fixture and paused for a second.

"That's odd," I muttered.

"Having a light in the ceiling?" Hugo teased.

"No, you plonker. Look at the canopy."

"What's a canopy?" he asked.

"The decorative cover against the ceiling," I explained, pointing to the white metal part, which, in this case, was larger in diameter than normal.

"Probably took out the original fixture from the eighties," Hugo said. "You know, one of those big ugly fixtures with arms going every which way."

For a second, I pictured what I figured Hugo's home looked like. My best guess was ultra-modern minimalist in gray tones.

"What's going on here?" came a woman's voice from the living room.

A deputy was supposed to be by the door, so we both walked out to see who'd found their way in.

"Are you the police?" the woman asked when she saw us.

Dressed in business casual, she looked like she'd just come home from an office job. Probably around my age, she was freckled with red hair.

"Orange County Sheriff's Department, ma'am, and this is off-limits," I said, not seeing the deputy.

"Friend of the resident here?" Hugo asked.

The woman scoffed. "Hell, no. Is he in trouble?"

"He's wanted for questioning," Hugo replied. "What's your name?"

"Tracy. I live two doors down."

"So, you're not a fan of Mason McCall?" I phrased as a question.

She shook her head. "Seemed like an okay guy when I moved in. Plays his TV too loud, but whatever. Then he took a friend of mine out on a date and scared the shit out of her."

"How so?" I asked, moving a step closer.

"Super-pushy and expected her to come home with him that

night. She said no, and he started calling her names. She left as fast as she could. That was a few months ago, and I haven't spoken with the dude since. Except to yell through the door for him to turn the TV down."

"Anything else you've noticed about the guy?" Hugo asked. "Friends or strangers coming and going? Keeping odd hours?"

Tracy shrugged her shoulders. "He's kind of a loner, as best as I can tell. Probably because he's such an asshole."

I couldn't help but smile. "Thanks, Tracy. Now we need you to head home without touching anything, unless you want your prints in here."

She made a face like she'd tasted something awful and hurried out.

"Ma'am, you can't be in there," the deputy called out, arriving at the door.

"It's okay," I told him. "We spoke with her. Where did you go?"

"Nature called, ma'am."

"Let us know next time, and we'll cover for you."

He nodded. "Will do, ma'am. Apologies."

"We're done here, anyway," Hugo said, turning to me. "Forensics can go through the place properly."

I looked around the living room one more time, my eyes finally resting on the light fixture.

"That one has a normal canopy," I said, pointing to the ceiling. "Why would a bedroom have a fancy light fixture and the living room have a regular one?"

Hugo shrugged. "No clue."

We stared at each other for several moments.

"Fine," he grumbled. "You'll be a pain in my ass if we don't look."

We walked back into the bedroom, and I judged I could reach the fixture if I stood on the bed.

"We need a screwdriver," I said, spotting a Phillips head locating the canopy in place.

Hugo patted his hands against his pockets. "I think I left mine at home, Cromwell."

I rolled my eyes as I walked out of the bedroom. "Got a pocket knife with a Phillips?" I asked the deputy.

"Sure," he replied, and pulled a small multi-tool from his pocket.

I took it back into the bedroom, holding it aloft like the Holy Grail. "Some men are useful," I said, grinning at my partner.

Standing on the bed, I wobbled around as the mattress dipped and wallowed, but I could reach the nearest retaining screw. The second one on the far side was tougher, but I managed to unscrew it, and the canopy dropped heavily to the top of the light shade, spilling several small boxes onto the bed at my feet.

"Damn," Hugo muttered. "You're a bloodhound, Cromwell."

I squatted on the bed and looked up at Hugo. "We Brits are more like bulldogs."

He shook his head. "Open them, then. Let's see how McCall pays for this place."

I picked up the first of the cardboard boxes, which was about the footprint of a cell phone, but several inches tall. Something flopped inside, and I realized right away what it was. I had a box about this size in my desk drawer. I lifted the top off to reveal business cards. Probably half the original quantity was left.

"Business cards?" Hugo scoffed. "That wasn't on my bingo card."

I handed him one and looked around the bedroom at the posters once more, especially the illustration of the female superhero. Bound.

"'Proud Kings,'" Hugo read aloud. "'Are you ready to take back your world?'"

"He's a bloody misogynist," I said, letting out a breath. "That's his motive for executing Hailey? Male superiority?"

"It fits," Hugo responded. "The only contact is a website. ProudKings-dot-com."

"Let's get to my computer in the car," I said, checking the

second box, which was more of the same. "There's no question this lunatic built the X-frame."

Hugo sighed. "But we still have to place him at Capo Beach on Wednesday night. All we have is him working next door to where a pontoon boat was stolen from, which was on the water Wednesday night."

"Yeah, and don't forget we still have to catch the wanker," I pointed out before taking a picture with my instant camera.

No one had reported seeing McCall, despite deputies continually sweeping all the streets in the area around his apartment. We had McCall's picture on our website, social media, and running on the local news channels. No credible sightings. I brought up the Proud Kings website as Hugo drove us back to McCall Fabrication. I tilted my screen towards the driver's side.

"It's behind a paywall," I said, showing him the simple but professional homepage.

The background was an illustration of medieval knights on horses, charging through a village with adulating women cheering them on. There was no menu, links to anything else, or other information. "Proud Kings" was emblazoned across the top of the page, and "Join us in taking back our world" underneath. Below that was a payment form.

"Subscription is $19.99 a month," I read, turning the computer back to face me. "I guess we've found how he paid for his apartment."

"A hundred subscribers would be two grand a month," Hugo said, parking outside the fabrication shop. "Not a fortune, but it would fund the site and pay most of his rent. I just can't understand how he'd reach a hundred people willing to throw down twenty bucks a month for this."

"We don't know what they're getting for their twenty dollars," I replied.

"I guess we need to join and see," Hugo said, pausing as he got out of the car. "Get the computer guys involved."

I looked across the roof at him. "Agreed. But we can't wait around on them."

Hugo raised an eyebrow. "I'm not putting my credit card details into that website."

"Let's head back to the station after this and get Captain Bradley to authorize a way of paying," I replied. "We have to see what he's offering."

Hugo nodded, and we walked inside.

"Are you two responsible for all this chaos in town?" Chelsea asked, tearing herself away from her phone.

"Your cousin is," I replied. "Your dad here?"

She swiveled in her chair.

"Dad! The cops are back!"

I hoped that didn't send her father and his staff running out the back of the building. My guess was that Matthew didn't know what his nephew was up to, but there was still a chance his crew could be involved.

"You ever hang out with your cousin?" I asked Chelsea while we waited.

She looked at me as though I'd just accused her of culling baby seals.

"Why's that?" I pushed.

"He's a fucking weirdo."

"Weirdo how?"

She shrugged her shoulders. "I don't know. He just gives everyone the creeps."

"Are his parents in town?" Hugo asked.

She shook her head. "My uncle drives long-distance trucks, and my aunt married some dude from Germany and lives over there now. She hasn't talked to Mason for years."

"Why's that?" I asked.

Chelsea looked at me as though I'd now asked the dumbest question possible.

"Because he's a fucking weirdo?" I queried.

She lifted a finger to acknowledge my correct answer.

"What now?" Matthew asked, striding through from the work-shop. "I'm now two men down and getting further behind today. I can't have you coming by every five minutes, man."

"Your nephew and employee is now the prime suspect in our murder inquiry, Mr. McCall," Hugo responded. "So we don't really care how much your day is disrupted."

"No shit?" Chelsea whistled.

Her father scowled at her, but rightfully decided her swearing wasn't the most important topic at the moment.

"Where would he have gone?" I asked. "He ran on foot from his apartment. We need to know any friends or family he might go to."

Matthew rubbed his chin with a dirty hand as he thought it over.

"What about your house?" I asked. "If you're his only family in town."

He shook his head. "The wife won't have him in the house. Mason has some strange ways about him."

"Which you could have mentioned when we'd been here before," Hugo snapped.

"Hey, man. I'm just trying to give the guy a break, and maybe he'll straighten out, alright? He's my sister's kid."

"Okay, so he wouldn't go to your house," I persisted. "Where else could he have gone? Anyone in the shop hang out with him?"

Matthew and Chelsea both shook their heads.

"There was some dude from Laguna or Newport who picked him up from work one day," Chelsea offered.

"There was?" Matthew said, looking at his daughter.

My heart rate picked up at the mention of Laguna Beach.

"Yeah. I noticed him cos he was kinda cute."

"Jeez, Chelsea. He was probably Mason's age," her father groaned.

"I just said I noticed the guy. That's all, Dad. Don't have a meltdown."

"Do you remember the car?" Hugo asked as I hunted for a picture on my phone.

She shrugged. "Like a bimmer or something nice."

Hugo turned to me, and I held up the picture of Ryan Kwon I'd been looking for.

Chelsea shook her head. "That ain't him."

My heart sank. I'd thought the mention of a BMW meant it was certainly Kwon.

"Wait," Hugo said, looking at Chelsea. "How did you know he was from Laguna or Newport?"

"I overheard him. He was pissed he'd had to drive down from something beach; I missed which one. When I asked Mason about the guy the next morning, he was a dick, like usual. I figured anyone who hung out with Mason must be a fu..." she checked herself. "A weirdo, too, so I didn't mention the dude again."

"It could have been Newport you heard?" I asked, thinking of someone else.

"It could have been Pismo Beach," Chelsea replied. "They were hammering out back, and I didn't hear what he said."

Finding the picture I was looking for, I held it up for the teenager to see.

"Shit, yeah," she said. "That's the dude. See, he's cute."

My mind raced as I tried to put the pieces together. I turned my phone for Hugo to see.

He took the device for a closer look. "Damn, Kat. Is that Devin Williams?"

"Yeah," I replied. "I think we just tied the two cases together."

30

"So McCall's your guy, and he was home when you got there, but you let him get away?" Captain Bradley asked, her stare firmly on me.

"Look, lady, the wanker had an escape route planned out, so I'd like to see what you would have done," was on the tip of my tongue as my anger welled.

Fortunately, Hugo spoke up before I had a chance to say anything. "We're confident he was working with Devin Williams, the suspect in the Corona Del Mar case from earlier this year. Which explains how they accomplished so much in a short period of time in Hailey Carter's murder. We have two men launching the stolen pontoon boat, which we believe was used to set up the X-frame."

"X-frame?" the captain asked.

"It's what we've called the framework in the ocean, ma'am," Hugo replied.

"And you think they're all involved with this Proud Kings male supremacy website?" Bradley asked.

I nodded.

"Yes, ma'am," Hugo replied. "We have the cyber group on it now."

The captain sighed. "Alright. What else do you need to wrap this up?"

I looked at my watch. It was a few minutes after five.

"Finding these two is priority one," Hugo replied. "Uniforms already went by Williams's work and his apartment. He left his office after lunch, and he's not home, so we have an APB out for him as well. Hoping to get a hit from the license plate of his BMW."

Bradley walked around her desk and sat down, thankfully signaling that our debrief was over. Hugo and I turned to leave.

"A word with you, Kat," the captain said, and I watched Hugo continue out of her office. It felt like the last life raft had just left the *Titanic* with me still aboard the fated ship.

"Close the door," she added, and I reluctantly did so.

Drawing in a few deep breaths and sternly warning myself to stay calm, I wondered exactly which part of the day's events she was about to pick me apart over. I didn't know why I reacted so fiercely to being challenged; maybe it was my father's boxing blood. But Bradley already had me pegged as a hothead, so I didn't need to fuel that fire. You'd think my mother's sweet nature would provide balance, but apparently they'd provided whole genes in two halves rather than a pleasant blend.

My neurological issue probably also played into it. Not that the condition itself made me volatile, but the feeling of being weird and different. I'd grown up worrying about my brain failing me, leaving me looking stupid amid a class full of laughing kids. That fear had never completely gone away.

"Kat?" the captain was saying.

"Yes, ma'am?"

"I was saying they interviewed Emilio Santiago."

"Sorry, ma'am," I replied, "I was thinking about our case."

Talk about my brain letting me down. The functioning part was even screwing with me.

"Did he confess to breaking into my house?" I asked.

"Denies it completely and offered up an alibi," she replied.

"We have his DNA at the scene," I huffed.

"I heard you have a rabbit in the house," Bradley said. "Like a house pet?"

"Yes, ma'am. Litter box-trained. Turns out he's a decent guard dog, too."

The captain allowed herself a brief smile. "Well, Santiago was released on bail, and the DA's office will decide whether or not they'll pursue charges. It's DNA at the scene versus what I'm told is a strong alibi with multiple witnesses."

I wasn't sure what to say. His blood was on my rug. There was no question in my mind that the alibi had been bought or coerced by the Castillo family. But how far did I want this to go? On one hand, putting one of Castillo's thugs away would do the world a favor, but it also brought more attention to my connection with Gabriella. Or, more accurately, my dead ex-fiancé's connection, which in turn implicated me. Until I knew for sure what Paul had been up to behind my back, I didn't need any focus on my attachment to the situation.

"Hopefully, they'll catch him nearby on CCTV, or a witness will come forward," I said, because it was what I should have said.

Bradley nodded. "We'll see. But do I need to remind you to stay clear of the investigation?"

"When would I have time to even think about it, ma'am?" I responded.

She locked eyes with me for several uncomfortable moments.

"You and Fuentes need to bring these two guys in, asap. Okay?"

"Yes, ma'am," I replied, and hurried out of her office.

"What was that about?" Hugo asked me as I sat down at my desk.

"Follow-up on the break-in at my house," I replied, wishing I had a decent cup of coffee in front of me.

"They get the guy?"

"Yeah. But he'll probably walk."

"Sorry," he said, and slid his chair over to face me. "You okay?"

I nodded. "Yeah. When this is over, I need to get a security system installed."

"Probably better than relying on your attack bunny," he said, and grinned.

I laughed, and it felt good to let a little of the tension flood out of me. For a few moments, I relaxed and cleared my mind. Then I unlocked my computer screen and stared at the picture of Mason McCall. The tension returned, but in a different way. More urgently.

"We're still missing something," I said, looking at my partner.

"The two suspects," he scoffed.

"I know that, but I feel like we're still missing a piece of this puzzle."

Hugo thought it over and glanced at the whiteboard we hadn't touched since Saturday when I'd started a list. He got up and walked to the board, picking up the solo working dry-erase marker.

"Caldwell," he said, pointing to the first name on the list. "He still has an alibi, and we've never found a motive."

I nodded, so Hugo moved on. "Ryan Kwon. We know he was still hung up on Hailey and stalked her. He's been embezzling from the gallery, which explains him running, and we have him on CCTV in Laguna. No way he could have been in Capo Beach at the time of the murder."

I slid my chair closer.

"Enrique Gil was home and flying his drone over the beach, also stalking Hailey, but didn't capture anything after their walk."

"There was an email from Sarge earlier. He had someone double-checking CCTV in town, and there's no sign of Gil's rental anywhere after we know he went home," I commented.

"Okay, so his alibi holds up," Hugo replied. "Which brings us to Dylan Monroe and…" He paused while he added Jason Browning's name by Monroe's. "His buddy. We know they were on the water that night, but can't place them at the actual scene."

IIe added a question mark next to where I'd written "opportunity" before.

"We had Devin Williams on here, and we now believe he was involved with Mason McCall," Hugo continued, adding McCall's name to the board, and Proud Kings.

He stood back a moment, wagging the marker at the list. "So what is it we're missing?"

I rolled my chair back to my computer. "Something we didn't check yet," I said as I checked a date, then typed a search into our database.

"Nine vehicles were reported stolen in Orange County the day Taylor Davis drowned in Corona Del Mar. Two trucks and four SUVs capable of towing a boat. Doesn't say whether or not they had a tow hitch."

"What about boats?" Hugo asked.

"None."

"Check the next few days."

I broadened the boat search to include the following week.

"Four days later, a tender was reported missing in Newport Back Bay. Taken off the back of a motor yacht at Newport Dunes Marina."

"They ever recover it?"

"Not that's been reported," I replied. "Case still open."

Hugo looked puzzled. "But if they took it from a yacht, they didn't need to tow it anywhere, right?"

"Exactly, so they didn't need to steal a truck."

"Then how did they get there?" he asked. "If they drove, then they had to return somehow to get their car back. I suppose someone could have dropped them."

I nodded. "Perhaps. Or..." I checked the case log and found where Sergeant Martinez had entered new CCTV footage the security office had provided from Dana Point Marina. Opening the file, I looked at the notes from the helpful security guard, Gary. He'd written times and referenced video file numbers. I opened the one I was looking for, and a camera angle looking at the boat ramps from the parking lot played. I moved the slider in the player along to the timestamp Gary had given me.

"Look at this," I said to Hugo as I watched the screen.

It was hard to make out either man clearly. They wore plain hoodies and kept their faces down. One man reversed the trailer into the water while the other stood to the side and helped direct him. What the camera view did allow was a good view into the pontoon boat.

I pointed to the screen. "That's how they returned to shore on Wednesday night in Dana Point, and how they reached the tender in Newport."

"Are those surfboards between the seats?" Hugo asked.

"Stand-up paddleboards," I replied. "And look in the stern. That's a tarp covering what I bet is the X-frame."

"So they scuttled the boats and paddled in?"

"Yup," I replied.

Hugo walked to the whiteboard and wrote "SUPs" at the bottom of the list, then turned to me.

"We didn't see paddleboards at McCall's, did we?"

I shook my head. "Only a surfboard. I'll call Fitz and see if his guys who went to Devin Williams's place found any there."

Hugo thought for a moment. "That's okay. I'll call him."

I figured that was probably a good thing, so I didn't bother Hugo with a comment, but I did wonder if it had something to do with my partner's improved spirits. Returning my thoughts to the details of the case, I pulled the now thick wad of pictures from my pocket. Spreading them out on the desk next to my keyboard, I studied them once more. What was I missing?

If Mason McCall had been the one to take the tender in Newport Beach, then did he drag Taylor into the water and tie her to the old mooring alone? He'd have to have done, while Williams made sure he had an alibi. So why were McCall and Williams both launching the pontoon in Dana Point harbor? Because the frame took two to manage?

I stared from instant photograph to instant photograph, letting the scenes roll vividly through my mind. Until I stopped on the one of Hugo standing outside the front door to Caldwell's place. The suspect and his roommate were in the shot. I shoved my chair back and leaped to my feet.

"Hugo!" I called out, and ran to the little conference room where I guessed he'd sought privacy for his phone call.

He frowned at me and pointed to his cell phone, holding his other hand up.

"Put Fitz on speaker," I insisted, and pulled the door closed behind me.

Hugo grumbled, but did as I asked.

"Kat?" Fitz asked.

"There's three of them," I gushed. "Not two. Caldwell is part of it."

"Caldwell was the date for your girl, right?" Fitz asked. "Didn't he have an alibi?"

"Same as Williams did for you!"

Hugo's face lit up as he followed along.

"Caldwell had a silver chain with a pendant," I explained. "It had the letters P and K on it. I figured it was a bloody sports team or an ex-girlfriend. But it's Proud Kings."

"Jeez, Kat, how the hell did you remember that?" Hugo asked.

I shrugged. "I recall things in crazy detail up until…" I stopped as I remembered Fitz was on the other end of the phone. "Well, you know."

Hugo nodded. "So maybe the three of them rotate roles," he offered. "That way, the obvious suspect always has an alibi."

"If there's three of them," Fitz said tentatively. "Do you think the plan was for each of them to serve up a date? If so, they've got one more to go."

The breath left my lungs, and I fumbled with my phone, bringing up my surf app.

"To fit the MO," Hugo said. "They'd need another tide with a big swing, wouldn't they? Don't those tides occur months apart?"

My throat went dry. "Yeah. They do. But sometimes they come in pairs, only a week or so apart."

"No…" Hugo muttered. "Don't tell me…"

I felt my shoulders sag. "It's tonight."

31

To her credit, Captain Bradley didn't hesitate when we barged into her office and relayed our new theory. She immediately alerted all coastal town police departments from Newport Beach to San Clemente and set Sergeant Martinez on task to bring in every available deputy.

Once we'd started the wheels in motion with the captain, Hugo and I jumped in the car and headed for Garrett Caldwell's house. We turned down backup to free up bodies to patrol the beaches, which I was surprised Hugo agreed to.

Blocking the driveway with the car, we knocked on the front door. While we waited, I cast an eye to the west where the sun was lowering in the sky. Sunset was an hour away at 7:15 p.m. Bradley had ordered all available helicopters in the air, but I had a feeling they needn't bother until dark. The suspects knew it would be exponentially harder to spot activity in the water with nothing more than searchlights, and wouldn't show themselves until then. If they were actually up to anything at all.

The door opened. It was Caldwell's roommate, Brandon.

"Aren't you the cops from the other day?" he asked, eyeing us as though we smelled of rotten eggs.

"Garrett home?" Hugo asked.

"No."

"Mind if we come inside?"

"Yes."

"And why would that be a problem?" Hugo asked.

"Because it's our home, man. You've got no reason to be in here."

"Helping us investigate a murder isn't good enough for you?" Hugo challenged.

"Got a warrant?" Brandon snapped back.

"I have a pair of cuffs and a jail cell for obstructing our investigation."

"I ain't obstructing nothing, man. I'm just not letting you in without a warrant."

"So you're a member of Proud Kings, too, then," I said, and watched his expression tense.

"No clue what you're talking about, man."

I shook my head. "That's a load of bollocks, mate, and you know it."

He gritted his teeth. "We're done here."

Hugo jammed a foot in the doorway as Brandon tried to slam it closed, but I took his arm and nodded to the driveway. Hugo removed his foot and let the door bang closed.

"His car's gone. He's not here," I said as we walked away.

"Bradley should have a search warrant for the house and car," Hugo said, looking back at the home. "But roomie will have the place stripped of evidence by then."

I paused with the car door open. "I'm guessing he's not involved in the murders, or he'd be in the wind as well."

"Probably right," Hugo replied as he, too, paused by the car. "So, how much time do you think we have, based on the tides?"

I instinctively looked at my watch, despite being well-aware of the time.

"Low tide tonight is around one-thirty a.m.," I said, visualizing the chart. "There's over a five-foot swing from high to low, and high tide is about 7:25 a.m. Figuring they'll want their next victim tied to whatever they're using when the tide is at the midway point, they'll have a window from about ten tonight until four-thirty in the morning."

"That window opens in three and a half hours," Hugo said, rubbing his forehead.

"Yeah, and based on what they did at Capo Beach, their victim will drown around five-thirty a.m."

"To be on display when the tide goes out," Hugo muttered.

I nodded and got in the car. Taking out my cell phone, I brought up the contact number we had for Dylan Monroe, but stopped myself before hitting the call button and looked at my partner.

"How do we know Monroe isn't involved in this, too?"

He turned the car around in the street as he thought it over.

"Shit. We don't, do we? Maybe he didn't actually help them drown her, but he still could have been involved. Maybe he helped match the dates, or was filming it all from a distance. Or just watching with night-vision binoculars."

"We need the cyber guys to get us a member list from McCall's computer," I replied. "Although, he doesn't strike me as being the web designer type."

"No, more likely it's Caldwell or Williams," Hugo said. "Hell, all three could be fanatics and followers taking things to the extreme and have nothing to do with the organization itself."

"McCall had all those cards," I pointed out. "I think they're all part of it. It also explains how McCall's paying his rent."

"True."

"One way to find out if Monroe's in on it," I said, hitting the button.

The call rang through the car's speakers. And kept ringing until it went to voicemail.

"You've reached Dylan. Leave a message."

"Dylan, this is Kat Cromwell with the Orange County Sheriff's Department. I have an urgent question. Please call back on this number the moment you get this. Thank you."

"No way he's calling back," Hugo scoffed.

He was probably right, but I texted Monroe's number just to double up the effort. *"Please call back asap. Important."*

"Try the sister?" Hugo suggested.

"She's the business side. We need access to the app code."

Hugo grunted, and my phone rang. Optimistic, I answered it before checking the caller ID.

"Got a sighting," came Sergeant Martinez's voice. "Devin Williams's car was picked up on CCTV on the 73 tollway heading south."

"When was this, Sarge?" I asked.

"Thirty minutes ago."

"Could be heading to meet up with Caldwell and McCall down this way," Hugo commented. "Or hitting the 5 and running for Mexico."

"We have cruisers looking for him. I'll let you know if we get anything else," Sarge responded, and hung up.

"There are so few CCTV cameras set up for live processing," I grumbled. "Once he clears the last one on the toll road, we've lost him again."

My phone rang again, and this time I noticed the number wasn't saved in my contacts.

"Bloody hell, it's Monroe," I said to Hugo, then answered. "This is Kat." I figured I'd roll with the friendly approach.

"This is Dylan Monroe. What's so urgent, and why aren't you going through my lawyer?"

"Because your lawyer can't help us, Dylan. You can."

"How?"

I glanced over at Hugo, who shrugged his shoulders. I took his response as agreeing we should go for it. "We've tied the Capo Beach case to another murder earlier this year and pinpointed three suspects who we believe will make another attempt tonight."

"Wow. Okay," Monroe replied. "And how does this involve me?"

"Because they're using your app to target the victims," I explained, then waited while he took a few moments to respond.

"Well, I hate that's happening, but I'm still not sure how I can help you."

"We need to know who's on a date tonight," I replied, knowing the implications of my request.

"That would violate our users' privacy, Miss Cromwell. I think you know that."

"Yeah. I do. But a woman's life may well depend on it, Dylan."

"You're asking me to break the law," he replied. "Pretty ironic after the way you guys raked me over the coals. I have a drugs charge hanging over me."

"We'll get a warrant, but I don't know that we can get it through the system tonight," I said.

"I have an idea," Hugo said, surprising me. "If we give you a name, could you tell us yes or no, whether they are in conversation with someone today?"

The line went quiet for several beats.

"You're going to bring me a warrant tomorrow, right?"

"Yes, sir," Hugo responded.

"It'll take me some time," Monroe explained. "I need to be in front of my computer. This isn't information I can see over my phone."

"How long?" I asked.

"Give me an hour."

Hugo and I exchanged a glance. The sun would have set by then, and everything would become more difficult.

"Make it less if you can, Dylan," I replied. "Time is not on our side."

"I'll do my best," he said, then paused for a moment. "If I help you here, will you pay me back in my drugs case?"

I rolled my eyes. "It'll be paid back in the satisfaction you may help save a woman's life."

"Of course," he muttered. "I just thought…" He didn't bother finishing his sentence.

"We'll put in a good word, Dylan, but I can't promise you it'll make a difference."

I heard him sigh. "Give me the name."

"Mason McCall," I replied.

"You said there were three men involved," Monroe formed as a question.

Hugo shrugged again when I looked his way.

"Garrett Caldwell and Devin Williams," I replied.

"I'll see what I can do," he said, and hung up.

I blew out my cheeks. "I don't know if we just tipped off an accomplice, who now knows exactly who we're after, or if he'll really help us."

"Fifty-fifty, I'd say," Hugo replied.

He took us the long way back toward the station, using Palisades Drive. Carved into the bluffs, the steep road ran across the face to reach Pacific Coast Highway. As we sat at the light, waiting on traffic to make the right turn, I stared off into the distance where the sun would soon hit the ocean. I pictured the enormous amount of coastline we had to cover and wondered if the three suspects knew the odds were stacked heavily in their favor. I hoped not.

"We should grab something to eat," Hugo said as he spotted a gap in the traffic.

"I don't know that I can," I replied, but I realized I was hungry.

"Olamendi's," Hugo suggested.

One of my favorite Mexican restaurants was up ahead on the right, almost directly across from the beach where Hailey Carter was found.

"Sure," I replied, hoping the location might inspire an epiphany rather than depress me even more about the case.

We parked in the lot beside the restaurant, walked inside, and ordered food to go. While we waited, I stepped outside to the patio and felt my anxiety rise as the sun appeared so much closer to the water. By the time they called Hugo's name to let us know our food was ready, the sky was a gorgeous array of orange and purple hues.

I couldn't help but wonder if somewhere, a young woman was enjoying the sunset, full of hope and anticipation for her date that night through OC Match.

"Ready?" Hugo said from behind me, having returned with two bags of hot food.

We walked to the car, and as I was opening the passenger door, my phone rang. It was Monroe's number.

"What did you find?" I babbled, desperate for a lead we could pursue. All we needed was a name to track down. A phone number to call and warn an unsuspecting victim.

"None of those names have been active in the past three days," Monroe replied. "In fact, Williams closed his account earlier this year, and Caldwell closed his last Thursday. There is no account for a Mason McCall."

"Bugger," I groaned, trying to think of another angle or question to ask. But I had nothing. "Hey, thanks for looking."

"You'll still get a warrant tomorrow, right?" he asked. "I don't want this coming back on me. I've got enough shit going on."

"Yeah, we'll get your warrant," I replied. "You'll be fine."

I hung up and dropped into the passenger seat. Hugo started the engine, but we both sat there, staring out the front window at the colorful mural on the side of Olamendi's building.

"Do you think he's covering for them?" I asked.

Hugo shook his head. "I really don't know. I feel like he would've never called you back if he was involved, but I wish we had the manpower to tail him and see where he goes tonight."

"He'd be an idiot to take his boat out," I scoffed.

Hugo drove us back to the station, where Martinez reported he had no new sightings of our suspects. Back in our office, we dragged our chairs to the end of the desks and plucked our dinner from the bags. I'd ordered my usual fish tacos, which were cool enough to eat after the drive. Staring at the whiteboard, I ate in silence, running down the list over and over, but nothing new was coming to me.

Stuffing the rest of the first taco into my mouth, I wiped my hands on a napkin, then took my pictures out again, spreading them across the table. My focus fell on the one of McCall's bedroom, where we'd found the business cards under the light canopy. The picture captured half of the room. And one of his posters.

I scrambled to redial Dylan Monroe.

"Yes?" he answered wearily.

"How many people sign up in a week?" I asked.

"To the app? It can be a few hundred. Our average is thirty-nine new clients a day, and then we lose a few as well."

"Bugger, that's a lot," I said, deciding on a different tack. "Can you search for another name?"

He sighed. "Okay, let me get back to my computer."

"Are you in the office?"

"No," he replied. "I'm at home. I work from here at least half the week."

I waited until I heard tapping on a keyboard.

"How do you verify ID, Dylan?"

"We have a state-of-the-art biometric facial recognition system using eighty nodal points—"

"Okay, okay, spare me the tech talk, mate. What else?"

"We match their cell phone records."

"So, if I said I was Scarlett Johansson and my cell phone was registered to a Scarlett Johansson, I'm good to go?"

Dylan hesitated. "I suppose, but you'd have to have shown the cell phone company an ID matching the name."

Hugo scoffed. "Right, and the zit-faced kid selling iPhones knows a fake ID from a real one, right?"

"Well…" Dylan stammered.

"Try Edward Pitt," I said, interrupting while he hesitated.

"Edward Pitt?" Hugo whispered next to me. "Who the hell is that, Kat?"

"We have one Edward Pitt who used to subscribe. He's sixty-four and lives in Anaheim. Didn't renew about six months ago."

I ignored Hugo. The wind was rapidly being ripped from my

sails as another theory was coming up empty, and I didn't feel like saying it out loud.

"Okay," I sighed. "Try Brad Norton."

Hugo picked up the instant photo I'd been staring at with the *Fight Club* poster in the background.

"Seriously, Kat?"

"We have two Brad Nortons," Dylan said. "One hasn't been active in ten months. The other signed up last week, and he's been active today."

"No shit?" Hugo grunted.

"Text me a picture," I said, and held my breath.

A moment later, my phone vibrated, and I switched to messages. Hugo and I stared at Dylan's screenshot. It was unmistakably Mason McCall.

"You recognize that guy?" Hugo asked Dylan.

"No. But I don't know 99.99 percent of our subscribers."

I understood why Hugo was asking, but at this point, I was more concerned with a potential victim than the slight chance Dylan Monroe was involved.

"Who's he been matching with?" I asked.

"This is pushing outside what the warrant will cover," Dylan said. "I really can't—"

I didn't let him finish. "Don't be a wanker, Dylan, give us the bloody name!"

"Okay, okay. There's three."

"Any meeting him?" I practically yelled down the phone.

"Looks like he's arranged to meet Abigail Roberts at eight p.m. No, wait, he moved it up to 7:45."

Hugo and I both looked at our watches. It was 7:58 p.m.

"Where?" I gasped.

"Sidewalk Café on Avenida Del Mar."

"Abigail's phone number?"

He read it off, and Hugo punched the numbers into his phone and called. Agonizingly, it rang and rang, until a perky voice read out a message.

"Hi! You've reached Abbie. You know the drill, and I'll get back to you."

"Abigail Roberts, this is Orange County Sheriff's Investigator Hugo Fuentes. It is imperative you call us back as soon as you get this."

"Thank you, Dylan. Send me Abigail's picture. We have to go," I said, and hung up.

Hugo and I both jumped up, running out of the office to the front desk.

"Sarge!" I called out, and he looked up. "Have the San Clemente guys send a car to Sidewalk Café on Avenida Del Mar! I'm texting you two pictures. One is Mason McCall using an alias, Brad Norton. Second is Abigail Roberts. She's their next victim."

"I'm trying her again," Hugo said, hitting redial.

This time, the call went straight to voicemail.

32

It took us fifteen minutes to reach the restaurant where the deputies had already established that neither McCall nor Abigail Roberts were there. They'd already shown the pictures to the staff and asked if they'd seen them. Nobody had. Hugo and I moved from table to table, asking the same of the patrons.

"Let me take a closer look," a younger woman said to me, and I handed her my phone.

She looked at her date sitting opposite and showed him the picture.

"We saw her walking this way as we arrived," the woman said, looking at her boyfriend.

He shrugged his shoulders. "Maybe."

The woman rolled her eyes. "You should know. You stared at her long enough."

The young man blushed.

"This is very important," I urged. "We believe she's in danger."

The young man nodded, then looked down at his meal. "I'd say that's her."

"What time was this?" I asked as Hugo finished his half of the room and joined me.

"Around seven-forty," the woman answered.

"Okay, thanks," I responded. "And this is very important. Did you see anyone else close by?"

She thought for a minute, then shook her head. "No one that I recall."

"A car pulled up as we walked into the restaurant," the young man hesitantly added.

His date's glare reflected her recognition of his last look back at another woman. For once, I was glad of a man's wandering eye.

"Notice a make or color?"

The young man shook his head.

I tried to keep my patience as the clock ticked loudly in my head. "Was it a bright color? Dark color? Something in between?"

"Between, I think."

"Okay, that's good," I said, trying to sound encouraging. "Big? Small? Pickup truck? SUV?"

"I guess it was a car, kinda nondescript, you know?" He replied. "Sorry, I didn't get a good look."

"That's okay, I get it," I said. "You were busy checking out the girl."

He blushed again, and his date gave him another hard stare.

Hugo and I moved outside to the sidewalk, where the deputies waited. I took an instant photo before I forgot, which garnered the usual curious looks from both deputies.

"Any city CCTV around here?" I asked.

They both shook their heads.

"There's a chance our vic was picked up by a suspect in a mid-size car right here in front of the restaurant," Hugo explained. "Check with the businesses close by and see if anyone has a security camera that views this spot."

"Sir," the two deputies acknowledged, and split up to cover both sides of the street.

I looked at my watch. It was already 8:38 p.m. Abigail had been gone for almost an hour. If she'd been picked up in a car, we had a fifty-mile radius they could have traveled.

My cell rang. It was the station.

"Sarge," I answered.

"Both McCall's and the vic's cell phones were turned off in the vicinity of the restaurant," he said with his usual lack of preamble. "The other two suspects powered down their phones in the early afternoon."

"Okay, thanks," I replied. "One witness here noticed Abigail approaching the restaurant, but I don't think she ever went inside. Possibly picked up by someone in a car. We have the locals checking for CCTV."

"No reports of boats missing today, but we've posted an alert online for people to check," Martinez added.

But we both knew only a tiny percentage of boat owners would happen to look at the sheriff's department social media page.

"Has someone knocked on Abigail Roberts's door yet, sir?"

"San Clemente Sheriff's have someone there now, talking to a roommate," he replied. "She's given us a description of what Roberts was wearing when she left. Check your email for details."

"Thanks, Sarge," I said, and we hung up.

"What now?" Hugo asked, rubbing his chin. "If he has her in a car, then we're still searching beaches from Newport to San Onofre."

I thought for a moment while I found the email with details of Abigail Roberts's outfit. Ripped blue jeans, a pale pink sleeveless blouse, platform sandals, and a small clutch purse. Absorbing her look, I returned my focus to running through what we knew, searching for patterns.

"Each time, it's been in the dater's hometown," I said as the thought struck me. "Whoever's turn it is to secure a date on OC Match, then the murder has been close by. McCall's should be San Clemente."

"True, but that was when they had time," Hugo replied. "We've thrown them off their game."

"Have we?" I asked. "It's the perfect tide tonight. Maybe they'd planned on waiting for the next one in a few months' time, or they could have had this lined up for tonight all along."

Hugo nodded. "Perhaps."

"The first murder was crude in comparison to Hailey's," I continued. "They've upped their game. I don't think it's a stretch to think they planned two murders five days apart."

"I'd say we've still disrupted whatever they had going on," Hugo replied. "But you're right. We don't know if they have pilings already set somewhere for another X-frame-type killing."

I growled in frustration, imagining a terrified Abigail Roberts being dragged into the ocean to meet a prolonged and agonizing death. My phone ringing startled me.

"Sarge," I said, seeing the caller ID.

"Park ranger just found a shoe and a purse on the trail to the beach at Trestles."

"They match our description?" I asked.

"Best as two men can describe such things to each other," he replied. "I'll email pictures in a few minutes."

"We're on our way," I said, and hung up, looking at Hugo. "We're going to Trestles."

By the time we reached the surf spot south of San Clemente, a police helicopter was already running a search pattern along the coastline, and at least a dozen law enforcement officers hunted for more signs of the vic. The helo's rotors throbbed loudly overhead as its powerful searchlight played across the dark water. A deputy showed me the items the park ranger had picked up, and they seemed to match the roommate's description. The clutch was empty apart from a small packet of tissues, a mirror, and a lipstick. No phone. No wallet, ID, or credit cards.

"Only one reason I can think of to bring her here," I said to Hugo as we walked closer to the water.

"Agreed. But why can't the helo spot her?" he questioned.

Trestles, named after the railroad trestle bridging a creek running to the beach, was a favorite surf spot, and remote. Parking was half a mile south in the San Onofre State Park or farther north in town. Mostly, surfers rode bikes to the beach with their boards under their arms. At night, the place was usually deserted.

"Over here!" a deputy shouted from fifty yards north of where we stood.

We ran over, desperate for a lead. A clue of any kind to Abigail's whereabouts.

"Does this look like drag marks?" he questioned, shining his flashlight on the sand.

It was hard to tell as there'd already been a lot of footprints added by the officers, but I could make out what might have been scuffs leading to the water. The helicopter swung around our location, and the searchlight momentarily swept across the beach where we stood. Seeing a larger area made the marks far more obvious. Someone had attempted to brush them away but hadn't done a thorough job. I quickly snapped a picture while the site was fully illuminated.

"They dragged an inflatable across here," I said as my eyes struggled to readjust once the searchlight moved away.

"Dammit," Hugo breathed.

"Yeah," I agreed. "That just opened our search area back up. No wonder we can't see them here."

I couldn't help myself from continually looking at my watch, which, in turn, made my anxiety soar as time slipped away at an alarming rate. It was now 9:45 p.m.

"I need a bloody coffee," I groaned, watching the helicopter continue its search along the coast.

"We're wasting our time standing here," Hugo said. "Let's get back to the car and regroup."

I followed him as he trudged ahead, swearing about the sand in his shoes. We headed for the path over the railroad tracks. I couldn't think of a reason to stay, either, but leaving felt like we were abandoning Abigail somehow.

When we reached solid ground at the trailhead beyond the railroad, we both slipped our shoes off and brushed the sand away. I was operating on autopilot while my brain whirred in a congested flow of processing and reprocessing the evidence we knew to be true.

I dialed Sarge once again as we started along the narrow, dark trail.

"Martinez," the sergeant answered.

"Don't we have drones, sir?"

"We do."

"Are they in the air, too?"

"No."

"Because?"

"Because the primary officer who operates it is out, and the reserve pilot, or whatever you call the guy who wiggles the damn sticks, says a software update came through, and now the stupid thing won't fly, and he doesn't know why."

"Bloody hell."

"Exactly."

"Okay, thanks," I said, and ended the call.

"What are you thinking, Kat?" Hugo asked.

"I'm thinking we'd feel more like we were doing something if we had a bloody drone."

"We know a guy with a pretty trick drone."

"That's the other thing I was thinking."

"I bet he has one of those really cool Italian coffee makers in that fancy house of his, too."

I broke into a jog.

I waved to the security camera above the front door of Enrique Gil's sprawling home on Shoreline Drive in Dana Point. We both held up badges as I rang the doorbell again.

"Contact my lawyer," came Gil's voice over a small speaker.

"We need your help, sir," I replied.

"It's ten-thirty at night. Contact my lawyer, and we'll make an appointment."

"We apologize for the late hour, sir, but a young woman is in great danger, and we believe you can help us."

"Seriously? You now think I have something to do with another missing girl?"

"No, no, sir. Not at all. We're asking for your help."

Hugo stepped forward. "We need your drone, Enrique. Now, come and open the damn door."

Everything went still for what felt like forever until the door finally opened, and Gil stood there in boxer shorts and a T-shirt. Despite the circumstances, I couldn't help myself from giving him a quick look-over. He was handsome, but in great shape, too. I caught Hugo doing the same.

"What on earth is this about?" Gil asked.

"Is that fancy drone of yours here?" I asked.

He nodded.

"Then let's get that little bugger in the sky."

He frowned at me, but stepped back and let us into the house.

It took a little more explaining as we walked through his entrance hall, with guest suites on either side, to the main house and living room with an ocean view. I recognized the patio beyond the floor-to-ceiling sliding glass doors from the earlier drone footage.

Five minutes later, we all stood outside, with Gil's high-tech drone before us.

"Watch for the helicopters," I warned him. "There are a couple running up and down the coast."

"Then why do you need me?" he complained.

"Because they haven't found them yet, have they?"

"Not sure I will, either. You realize this is a needle in a haystack?"

When I nodded toward the drone, Gil shook his head, but worked the controls, lifting the drone vertically off his backyard before it disappeared into the night. For a while, I could see the red and green LEDs on the device, but it wasn't long before they melted into the darkness.

We all sat down at a patio table where Gil had set up a laptop for us to watch the live stream. He monitored the drone's progress from a smaller screen on the controller. He tilted the camera down at a forty-five-degree angle, and we watched the lights of the harbor pass by below. My phone rang again.

"Sarge," I answered.

"Update from the cyber unit."

"Hold on a sec, sir. I'm putting you on speaker so Hugo can hear."

Pausing my finger over the touchscreen, I caught Enrique Gil's eye. I lifted the finger to my lips, and he nodded his acknowledgment. I didn't need to be explaining to Martinez that we were using a civilian to help us with our search. Especially a civilian who'd been on our suspect list.

"Go ahead, sir."

"Cyber unit are into McCall's computer. If he's behind the website, it's not from that laptop, but they were able to log into Proud Kings from his account. Doesn't give us much except that these guys are misogynistic bigots. Cyber guys said there are levels of subscription, and the top tier requires a second login, which wasn't a saved password on the computer. It also requires approval to join, so our people couldn't get in under the fake account they created."

"So, no way to link Caldwell and Williams?" Hugo asked.

"Not from that laptop," Sarge replied. "The domain is registered to a company called Womhats, which they're trying to hunt down. The domain was registered overseas was all I could gather from their techie rambling."

"Were computers found at Caldwell's and Williams's homes?" I asked.

"Yes. They're on their way to Santa Ana now, and the cyber guys know this is highest priority. No one goes home until we have Abigail Roberts safe."

"Okay. Thanks, sir," I said, trying to hide my disappointment before hanging up.

I looked up at the screen. The drone was about to clear the harbor and head over Doheny Beach and the state park.

"Wait a second," I blurted. "Hold there a moment."

Gil put the drone in a stationary hover. Hugo looked at his watch.

"What, Kat? It's gone eleven. This is their window, according to what you saw on the tides."

"I know, but think about this for a moment. There's no way McCall is the brains behind the website with layers of encryption, right? Caldwell works in PR, and Williams is a realtor. Neither went to school for anything to do with computers."

"Okay," Hugo replied. "So, what are you saying?"

"I'm saying Monroe is a bloody computer genius. I know it didn't feel like he was involved, and he helped us earlier, but let's take a moment and make sure his boat is in its slip."

"You'll need to show me where it is on a map," Gil commented. "There are hundreds of slips."

Hugo unlocked his phone. "It's in the case files somewhere. I'll see if I can find it."

I knew that would take a while. I found a number in my call history and dialed.

"Miss Cromwell?" came a sleepy voice.

"Hey, Gary, my apologies if I woke you."

"That's perfectly okay," he said, rapidly waking up and sounding enthusiastic. "You can call me anytime. In fact, I was thinking I should—"

"I need the slip number for *Shore Code*," I said impatiently.

"Oh," he replied in a deflated tone. "Umm, G dock in the East Basin, I believe. Don't recall which slip."

"East or west side of G?" I asked.

"East. About halfway down, I think."

"Okay, thank you, Gary."

"But, hey, are—"

I hung up and searched for a map of the marina showing slip letter and number designations, pointing to G dock for Gil to see.

"I think you left poor Gary hanging there, Kat," Hugo joked.

"I'll apologize tomorrow," I said, watching Gil maneuver the drone over the harbor once more.

"Am I close?" he asked after a few moments.

"One more to your left," I said, looking between the map and the screen.

We all watched as Gil took the drone from the boardwalk side and followed G dock along until we could see the end. Only one slip was empty. Halfway along, on the east side.

"Watch the sailboat masts," I warned. "But get a little lower so we can make sure."

Gil did so and made another pass, lingering over the empty slip from where the camera also showed the two spots on either side. Two of them had sailboats, one had the rectangular profile of a catamaran, and the fourth looked like a converted tugboat.

"*Shore Code* is gone," Hugo growled. "That bastard."

I couldn't speak, I was so angry. My knuckles turned white as I clenched my fists and just about crushed my phone. Fighting to calm myself down, I dialed another number. To my complete surprise, Monroe answered, and I put the call on speaker.

"More names?"

"Where the hell are you?" I snapped.

"Home."

"Bullshit, you're on your boat."

"I'm not on my damn boat. I'm sitting in my living room about to go to bed!"

"Then who the bloody hell's on your boat?"

The line was silent for several beats. "No one."

"So why's it not in your slip?"

For a second, I felt a wave of panic as I wondered if I'd misdirected Gil from the map, but looking again, I was sure I'd found the right spot. Although, Gary could also have been mistaken. I had woken the guy up and surprised him.

"Seriously?" Monroe asked.

"What boats are on either side of yours?" I asked, my uncertainty knocking the sting from my voice.

"This really cool, old converted tugboat on one side, and a nice Beneteau on the other."

I had the right slip.

"Who else has access to *Shore Code*?"

"Just me," he replied. "Well, Jason knows where the hidden key to the salon is, but he'd never take the boat without me."

My stomach tightened, and I looked at Hugo.

"Let me ask you a strange question, Dylan. Does the word 'Womhats' mean anything to you?"

He laughed. "Is this a joke?"

"Not even a little bit."

"Oh," he stammered. "Well, it's a stupid term Jason uses sometimes. You have to understand he's terrible at dating. He doesn't really mean anything by it."

"Mean what, Dylan?" Hugo demanded. "What does it mean?"

Dylan cleared his throat. "It's short for 'woman haters,' you know, like 'He-Man Woman-Hater.' But I swear he doesn't mean anything by it."

"Bugger!" I hissed, barely resisting throwing my phone. "How did I miss this?"

"Monroe," Hugo said. "Don't bullshit me. What was Browning doing last Wednesday night when you two were out on the boat?"

"Nothing. We just chilled."

"And you were with him the whole time?"

"Pretty much. I mean, he had these night-vision binoculars he was screwing around with for a while."

"Try calling Browning," I snapped. "Right now, Dylan. Put me on hold."

"Okay," he replied, and the line went silent.

I set my phone down on the patio table, and Gil nudged my arm.

"Where to with the drone?"

"We have to find the boat," I replied.

"Straight to voicemail," Monroe said, coming back on the line.

Hugo threw up a hand in frustration. "He's turned it off like the others."

"So, where are we looking for this boat?" Gil asked.

I buried my face in both hands. "Anywhere between here and bloody Mexico."

33

—————

It was well after midnight when Hugo and I left Enrique Gil's house. Hugo had been right. The man did have a very fancy coffee maker, and I'd have preferred to make his kitchen our base of operations for the night. But Captain Bradley insisted we all convene at the harbor patrol building in the marina. It made logistical sense, but their coffee was crap.

"We have our interdiction boat on the water," Sergeant Wills from the harbor patrol explained once we'd all gathered. "It has radar and can easily outrun that sport fisher."

"Anything on radar?" Bradley asked.

"Three obvious vessels. One has AIS and has been ruled out," he replied.

"What is AIS?" Bradley asked me in a whisper.

"Automatic Identification System, ma'am," I replied. "A transponder required on large commercial vessels. It's optional on pleasure craft, but a good idea, especially at night, to help avoid collisions."

Wills waited for us to stop conversing before continuing. "The second appears to be returning from Catalina, so we're focusing on the third."

"And where is it?" Hugo asked.

"Approximately seven miles due south of this building," Wills replied, referring to a large satellite view map on the wall. "About level with San Onofre Beach, heading south."

My Mexico comment made in frustration may have been more accurate than I'd thought.

"Our vessel, 311B, was involved in tonight's search along the coastline, so they were already south of San Clemente Pier," Wills continued. "We expect an intercept in approximately twenty minutes or sooner, providing the suspects don't change course."

It was promising that harbor patrol had them in their sights, but the waiting was agonizing. My mind kept flashing to the sight of Hailey Carter strapped to the frame in the water and imagining what may lie in store for Abigail Roberts.

"Can you fill us in on who we're expecting to encounter?" Wills asked.

Bradley and Hugo both looked at me.

"Okay, I can take that," I said, frowning at Hugo as I moved to the front of the room where printed pictures of the suspects and our victim were pinned to a board. "We believe Jason Browning is the coder behind the website, and he's friends with the boat owner. Browning has nothing on record, no gun permit, and we wouldn't expect him to be violent. The other three who might be with him are Garrett Caldwell, Devin Williams, and Mason McCall," I said, pointing to each of their photographs in turn. "Of the group, I'd expect the most trouble from McCall. He's already proved tricky to catch."

"What about the woman they took?" Wills asked.

"Abigail Roberts," I replied. "It's possible she's aboard, but more likely she's still along the Orange County coast somewhere."

"What makes you think she's not on the boat as a hostage?" Captain Bradley asked me.

"Timing, ma'am," I replied. "We checked the CCTV when we got here and found *Shore Code* leaving the harbor at 7:35 p.m. We believe Abigail was taken to Trestles after she was picked up in San

Clemente. A gray Honda Accord has been found parked near the trailhead, and when deputies called the owners, they found their car was missing from the parking lot where they'd left it. Abigail was taken at around 7:45 p.m. So, we think she was put in an inflatable we estimate they launched from Trestles around forty-five minutes to an hour later, given the drive, the walk with a resistant hostage, and getting the boat in the water."

I paused to align my thoughts and make sure my unpredictable brain hadn't dropped anything from the timeline. Hugo gave me an encouraging nod. Which was good, as I had no way of knowing if my memory was hiding anything from me. Except for an uncomfortable feeling that sometimes warned me, but as I was already at my wit's end, my gut couldn't be trusted.

"If they'd motored straight out and been picked up by Browning in *Shore Code*, then they'd be down near San Diego by now. So it fits that they spent several hours setting up whatever they had planned for Abigail, and then all bolted in *Shore Code*."

Bradley gave me a questioning look. "But we've been patrolling the beaches on foot and by air since, when?"

"About eight-thirty, ma'am. Which is close to the time they would have left Trestles."

"So why haven't we seen at least one man and a hostage in an inflatable boat motoring along the coast?"

"It's dark, and there's a lot of water to cover, ma'am," I replied. "Based on the prior murder, we think their window to set up this one opened around ten. So the timing all fits."

"What window?" she asked.

"When the tide is going out but is low enough to put their victim on the frame so they'll be drowned shortly before dawn," I replied, and looked at a room full of horrified faces staring back at me. "The trickier part would have been the rendezvous with *Shore Code*," I added, quickly moving on. "But if they timed it right and took the inflatable straight out a mile or so, we wouldn't have seen them."

Bradley nodded. I wasn't sure she entirely bought my reasoning, but she seemed open to the possibility.

"How did they coordinate all this if their cell phones are turned off?" Wills asked. "They must have communicated somehow."

"Probably a bunch of burner phones," Hugo finally contributed.

Reports from along the coastline had grown quiet, which concerned me. The officers could be losing hope and enthusiasm. They would have heard the radio calls to the harbor patrol boat in pursuit, and may well have assumed Abigail was also aboard. I hoped she was, but I doubted it.

It felt like forever before the patrol boat reached *Shore Code*, at which point they went radio silent while attempting to stop the sport fisher. It wasn't like pulling over a car, where a cruiser could maneuver a speeding motorist off to the side, or to a place where the vehicle could no longer travel. A boat had 360 degrees of options. If the boat captain didn't succumb to the threat of being fired upon, the situation could become a stalemate, unless the police had cause to actually open fire.

We all sat in the meeting room sipping terrible coffee, nervously looking at the radio set.

"Target apprehended," came the radio call, and I breathed a sigh of relief. "Four adult males in custody. No one else aboard. Over."

"We need them back here as soon as possible," I blurted, and Sergeant Wills nodded.

"311B, this is Dana Point. Returning with suspects is priority. Question suspects about the woman. Over."

"Dana Point, this is 311B. Returning asap. Suspects requested legal counsel. Over."

"They've lawyered up, dammit," Hugo fumed.

"Sounds that way," Wills replied. "But we'll have them here in less than half an hour."

"Ask your guys to bring up tonight's trip on the GPS," I said. "We can see where *Shore Code* has been. And get the lawyers' names. We'll send cars to their houses and drag their arses here.

There's four of them. All we need is one suspect to turn on his mates."

Hugo and I both checked our watches. With Abigail still missing, I felt even more confident our theory was right and she was already in the water. We were racing the tide.

Wills nodded and got back on the radio. A few minutes later, his man in the field responded with the lawyer's info.

"What about the GPS? Over," he asked.

"It's been smashed," the deputy replied, and my heart sank once more.

We ran around like idiots for the next hour and a half, rousting the suspects' counsel and getting everyone to San Clemente Sheriff's station. Their location had several interview rooms, where we only had one in Dana Point.

Standing outside the room where Jason Browning sat with a bleary-eyed attorney at his side, I checked my watch. It was 3:14 a.m.

"How long do you think she's got?" Hugo asked.

"If their setup matches Capo Beach, the water will soon be rising above the level it was when Abigail was placed in the water," I replied. "The tide will continue coming in until she can't keep her airways out of the ocean anymore. Somewhere around five or five-thirty is my best guess."

Hugo blew out his cheeks. "We're running out of time."

"Browning seems like he'd be the weakest member of the herd," I replied. "I wish I could hold their heads underwater until they talked, but I guess that's not an option."

Hugo pushed the door open, and we went in.

"No comment," Browning answered to our first five questions.

His lawyer was Jonathan Ambrose, the same guy who'd represented Monroe. Ambrose sat in silence while his client did as he'd obviously been coached.

"Okay," I finally said. "Let's try it this way. We have CCTV and physical evidence to go with what our cyber team is accumulating, associating you with the other three. Who we know murdered

Taylor Davis and Hailey Carter, as well as abducting Abigail Roberts tonight. From what we can see, your involvement is on the website, and taking Monroe's boat to help the other three escape. You're an accessory at best. Abigail dies, too, and we're coming at all four of you. First one to give us a location on Abigail is the only one who gets a deal."

Both Browning and his lawyer stared at me. Ambrose remained emotionless, but Browning's expression was full of confusion. If we were right, once we'd closed in on the others today, starting with McCall, a panic would have rippled through the ranks and forced them into a new plan. I was betting that Browning had never believed he'd be tied to any of it, and was likely coerced or threatened into taking *Shore Code*.

Ambrose looked at his client, who hadn't spoken the words he'd been told to reply to every question.

"One gets leniency. Three are going away for a very long time," Hugo said. "We're not talking some cushy white-collar place, either. This'll be the real deal with murderers and rapists. You won't last five minutes."

"Don't threaten my client," Ambrose said, finally speaking up.

"Not a threat. A fact," Hugo responded.

"Those three have one bloke representing all of them, so they're circling the wagons, mate," I continued. "What's it going to be? Go down with your 'He Man Woman Hater' buddies, or save Abigail and get a deal?"

Ambrose leaned over and whispered in his client's ear. Browning nodded.

"I don't know where she is."

Hugo and I both got up out of our chairs.

"I swear, I don't know!" Browning shouted.

"Please," Ambrose insisted. "Hear my client out."

We both turned.

"I know where I picked them up," Browning said. "She'll be somewhere near there."

"On another frame in the water?" I asked.

He shook his head. "I honestly don't know. I had nothing to do with what they were up to. They went too far. They threatened me this afternoon, which was the only reason I took the boat."

"Bullshit," Hugo snapped. "You watched Hailey Carter through night-vision binoculars."

Browning's head dropped to his chest, and his voice broke. "That's when I knew I needed out. But those three are fanatical."

"Okay, where did you pick them up?" I demanded.

"About a mile and a half off San Clemente Beach."

"You gotta do better than that, mate. There are miles of beach."

"I don't recall the coordinates, but I know it was straight out from those tall Mediterranean-looking condos. I could see the lights."

"Vista Pacifica Villas," Hugo said, and I was surprised he knew them. San Clemente wasn't his town. "I've been there a few times," he whispered to me, and I got what he meant.

I was glad Bradley had insisted we use San Clemente's station. The drive to the beach was much shorter. We concentrated our search north of the pier, along the stretch of beach in front of the villas built on a small bluff overlooking the water. Distance and direction from a boat to shore could be very deceptive unless the person was looking at a compass. Especially at night. I was worried we were putting all our eggs in too small of a basket, but we were out of time and short on resources for an expanded search.

Hugo and I stood with Sergeant Martinez on the sand, watching the helicopter run back and forth, lighting up the water in search of anything breaking the surface.

"How could we have missed her?" Hugo huffed. "Especially at low tide."

"Maybe we pressured them into panicking," Martinez suggested. "They just dumped her, tied to a heavy weight."

The thought gave me chills, but everything about this case had been unsettling. I looked to the south where the 1300-foot-long pier, originally built in 1928, stretched out into the Pacific Ocean, its wooden deck lit by occasional lampposts. The multitude of tall pilings supporting the pier were mostly lost to the darkness.

"The pier's been checked, right?" I asked, already knowing the answer.

"Multiple times," Martinez verified. "harbor patrol boats have carefully checked the pilings several times and reported they're clear. They would have spotted a body strapped to a piling."

At a loss for what else to do, I pulled my pictures from my pocket and began shuffling through them, one by one. The clear imagery that flashed through my mind helped realign my thinking and allowed me to make sure my temperamental brain hadn't skipped a vital detail.

"What is it with you and those instant photographs, Cromwell?" the sergeant asked.

He'd asked me that question before, and I'd always avoided a straight answer. This time, I simply ignored him while I stared at Hailey Carter's body strapped to the metal frame.

"Why did they change their technique from the first to the second killing?" I proposed, looking at my partner.

"Built a better mousetrap," he replied.

I nodded. "Yeah. So maybe they've done that again."

"We shouldn't be looking for an X-frame," Hugo said, following my thoughts. "Something more spectacular, perhaps?"

"Maybe they have her underwater on a scuba rig that'll run out of air," Martinez suggested. "That's dramatic."

"No," Hugo and I replied at the same time.

"They want the spectacular reveal tomorrow morning," Hugo added, and Martinez looked slightly embarrassed to have missed what appeared to be the obvious point to us.

"Look," I began, thinking aloud. "If Browning isn't lying about the location, and if they didn't set up another X-frame, then what are their options?"

The two men both looked at me.

"I guess it's a blessing that I don't think like a serial killer," Hugo said. "I'm at a loss."

I looked again at the pier. "You use the resources available," I muttered, and began jogging down the beach.

"It's been searched top and bottom, Cromwell," Martinez called after me, but I kept running.

There was no powerful urge pulling me that way. It was all about simply doing something. Anything but standing on the sand, watching time pass by. Leaving them behind as they both briskly walked, I upped my pace, struggling as the sand took the power from each stride. Reaching the paved boardwalk, I picked up more speed and turned right between the two darkened restaurants at the entrance to the pier. My tennis shoes thudded on the well-worn wooden planks.

It had been years since I'd last strolled down San Clemente Pier, a bold attraction that had been refurbished and repaired many times over the past century. The ocean end widened into a larger square from which people fished daily from around eighteen feet above the ocean, depending on the tide.

Out of breath, I arrived at the end and turned to look back at all the flashlights on the beach. To the north, the helicopter made another fruitless sweep, spotting nothing but empty sea in its bright searchlight. The view started me thinking about the answer we'd given Martinez. The three men wanted to make statements with their victims. If they'd stuck with their torturously slow drowning theme, where would a body get the most attention? The beach was busy on either side of the pier, but to the north was the large, brick lifeguard building where people with binoculars regularly scanned the waters.

I moved to the north side and looked over the railing. Incoming swells sloshed against the pilings below me, barely visible from the dim accent lights of the lampposts at night. I walked along the side until I reached the corner where the square end cut back to meet the pier. Twenty feet of pier and the pilings below faced the beach, clearly visible during the day.

Hugo and Sergeant Martinez arrived, both looking at me.

"Well, Kat?" Hugo asked. "What are you thinking?"

I scoffed. "This case has driven me bloody bonkers. I think I'm clutching at straws."

Beneath the thick wooden boards, I felt something through the thick wood, and heard a clunk.

"What—" was the only word Hugo managed before a loud splash reached us from below.

I grabbed the railing and looked over. It was too dark to make out much, but I swore a swirl of frothy water widened in a circle before the next swell collected it in its path.

Pulling off my shoes, I threw my jacket at Hugo and dropped my belt to the ground.

"Kat, we have divers on the beach!" Martinez shouted.

"Tell them to hurry," I replied, ripping the buttons on my blouse in my haste to get rid of it. I nearly tripped stepping out of my slacks.

Grabbing the small flashlight from my belt on the ground, I took one step and, without further thought, vaulted over the railing.

The drop was far longer than I'd anticipated, accompanied all the way by Hugo and Martinez shrieking at me. The impact into the cool Pacific water was also much more violent than I'd been ready for, and with a vaulting start, I hadn't organized myself into a classic feet-together entry. Awkwardly hitting the ocean knocked the wind out of me, and I almost dropped the flashlight.

Pulling and kicking at the water, I struggled to the surface where I managed one gulped breath before a swell smashed against the pilings, hitting me in the face. Spluttering, coughing, and wiping the stinging salt water from my eyes, I struggled to turn on the flashlight. Barnacle-covered pilings creepily towered over me, and the ocean rattling through the hundreds of round supports was much louder than I'd expected. Voices rained down from above, but I couldn't make out a word they were yelling.

As I gathered my wits, I started thinking I'd made a ridiculously impetuous decision, and the scolding words Captain Bradley would have for me began echoing in my head. But then my flashlight beam fell upon something else running from above me into the water. It was a heavy marine rope. Two of them, in fact.

In a flash, everything came to me. The bastards had rigged something to release by a trigger or timer, dropping Abigail from the underside of the pier where the patrols hadn't seen her. The line would have been carefully measured with a weight on her feet, to hold her under until the tide receded later that morning and revealed her to a crowded beach full of people.

And I had nothing with me to cut the rope. Even worse, if I did cut the line above the water, she would be dragged to the bottom by the weight.

I had to reach her. Taking a deep breath, I dropped below and pulled myself down the line.

Barely a few feet below the surface, my hands brushed over what felt like hair before meeting Abigail's head, which was violently jerking in panic, along with the rest of her body. Pulling myself down her naked torso, I found the harness around her waist. Reaching below, I could feel her legs were held taut by the weight. I could release the harness, but all that would do was allow the ballast to drag her into the depths.

The ocean tried pushing me away as another swell rolled over us, and my lungs burned as my brain cried out for a fresh breath. I was already feeling like I was running out of air, so I could only imagine Abigail's terror after suddenly plummeting through the night into the cold water.

Reeling myself down her slender legs, I found the strap around her ankles and fumbled in the pitch black, trying to fathom its fastening. Above me, I felt Abigail's flailing lessen, which, in her panicked state, could only mean one thing. She was running out of oxygen and losing her fight against the water. A human body's natural mammalian dive reflex, which slows functions to require less oxygen, was being overcome by her sheer terror. It reminded me to slow myself down and move deliberately, but my lungs ached, and my instinct for self-preservation was screaming at me to swim to the surface.

Wrapping my hand around her ankle, I instantly recognized her restraint. My dad had them in the gym. Despite my bitter complaining, he made me use them sometimes. Soft weight pouches filled with lead pellets wrapped around the ankle, secured by straps through a loop, which then Velcroed to themselves.

Yanking the strap of her first ankle free, the weight quickly unthreaded the strap from the loop and sank toward the bottom. Reaching for her other ankle, I sensed her body had stopped writhing altogether. My lungs were about to explode, and logic told me not to drown myself over a corpse if Abigail was already gone, but gritting my teeth, I fumbled for the other strap and ripped it from its fastening. The weights fell away, and I kicked like crazy for the surface, pushing Abigail's limp, naked body before me.

Looking up, the surface had become a bright white light, and the strength in my limbs was draining away until my foggy brain could no longer tell if I was moving at all.

Something firmly gripped my wrist, and a moment later, the pressure of submersion subsided as fresh air hit my face. Roughly dragged over what I guessed to be the smooth, round side of an inflatable boat, I slumped to the deck and coughed until I thought I'd pass out.

Struggling to open and focus my eyes between retches, I heard a man speaking close by.

"We have them both in the boat. Over."

"Alive?" came a voice I recognized as Captain Bradley's.

"Yes, ma'am. Both breathing."

34

———

"The other left," my dad chuckled from below me.

I adjusted the small security camera in the opposite direction from what he'd previously told me.

"Better," he said. "Oh, bollocks. It disappeared off the screen now."

I looked down from the stepladder. "What?"

"This software's pretty naff," he mumbled.

"Your sausage-like fingers are the problem," I said, coming down to where he stood outside my side door.

With a couple of clicks, I reopened the window showing the live view from the third camera we'd installed. Every door and window now had a sensor, and the doorbell contained another camera to cover the front of the house. Each camera recorded and uploaded to the cloud, and I could live-view any of them from my phone or laptop.

I wasn't sure if having the system made me feel safer, or made me worry more about why I needed one. Of course, I hadn't told my mum and dad the real reason for installing the system, but made up a story about a few local break-ins that had occurred during the day while people were out. I'd had the glass pane replaced, and I'd fixed the drywall on the first few days of my leave from work.

"Should be all set now," Dad said, folding the stepladder and returning it to my detached garage, where it hung from hooks he'd installed several years ago.

I knew he was torn between happy that I now had security around me and disappointed that I felt the need to have protection in our sleepy beach town. I struggled with the same thoughts, but my fear of crime came from a far more targeted adversary.

He closed the side door behind him, and we joined my mum in the living room. She was on the floor playing with Roger. "Fetch" was not a perfect description of the game my rabbit would play. It was more like "get this stupid thing out of my way." If you threw a toy near him, he'd pick it up with his teeth and toss it aside. But my mum seemed entertained, so at least one of them was getting something out of it.

"We surfing in the morning?" my mum asked as the little bell in the toy jangled with another launch from Roger.

"Sure," I replied, although I wasn't completely certain I was ready to get back in the water.

In the four days since I'd leaped from San Clemente Pier, my nights had been interrupted by nightmares about drowning. While in many ways, the shift away from visions of my fiancé's death was a welcome respite, I worried about how I'd feel to be back in the water. Surfing meant everything to me. Not only as a fun pastime I'd enjoyed my whole life, but it had always been my happy place where the demons left me alone and my thoughts calmed and gained perspective.

The idea that I might now harbor a fear of the ocean was terrifying.

"Let's go now," I blurted.

My mum looked at her watch.

"It's nearly lunchtime," my dad said, also checking the time.

Mum looked at me, and despite my efforts to give nothing away, I watched her expression warm, and she nodded.

"Be good to catch a few before lunch," she said. "Work up an appetite."

"I worked up a bloody appetite already," my dad complained, which garnered him a stern look from his wife.

"Have some hay with Roger to tide you over 'til we're back," I told him, rushing to the bedroom to grab my swimsuit.

With Dad still grumbling, we loaded my board into my 1979 Volkswagen bus, and I pulled down the drive beside my house with Dad giving us a wave from the side door. I turned right, and from the hillside, the familiar peek of the ocean appeared between the homes and the palm trees lining Copper Lantern. Mum chattered away as the wind rushed through the open windows while I drove to their house to collect her board.

As usual for a Sunday in the summer, Doheny was busy, but we got lucky with a car leaving, allowing us to grab a parking spot. Tugging on our wetsuits, we eyed the waves, as every surfer did in every beach parking lot around the world. It didn't look great, but that didn't matter today. In her typical way, my mum never mentioned the smaller, inconsistent waves, the crowded parking, or the busy lineup of newbies and tourists trying their hand at surfing. She kept the conversation light, letting me work through whatever it was I was dealing with.

My first steps from the sand into the cool water reaching the beach felt inviting and gave me hope. A slight sense of trepidation made me tense when we paddled out and ducked under the first real wave. Immersing myself completely for a few seconds sent an odd tingle and hesitation through me, tightening my grip on my nine-foot Wingnut board.

Weaving between the kids and first-timers, we joined the lineup, and several regulars said hello or waved. Turning, I straddled my board and gazed at the packed beach, full of families enjoying a California summer's day. A startling contrast from a dark night pierced with searchlights as we'd hunted for a missing woman.

I wondered if Abigail Roberts would ever set foot in the ocean again. Maybe not, but at least she was alive with a chance of regaining a normal life for herself. Unlike Hailey Carter and Taylor Davis.

"Wakey-wakey, dreamboat," my mother said, smiling at me and nodding behind us.

A decent wave was closing in, and we both began paddling. Feeling the swell lift the tail of my board, I pulled hard with my arms as the roller pushed me toward the shore. It's a wonderful feeling as you sense you and your board becoming one with the power of the wave, now progressing together, as though you're cradled in the arms of a mighty creature.

Popping to my feet, I knew my mum had caught the same wave, and would stay far enough right of me to not interfere with my ride. Turning the nose along the face of the wave, I could now see her doing the same, and she glanced back, laughing with child-like joy. I envied my mother's inner peace and the way she had compartmentalized pain, stress, and turmoil. Things that seemed to perpetually fill my world.

But not in that moment. Riding a wave in the California sunshine was still my escape, and for a few moments, the emotional pollution stripped away, leaving nothing but unadulterated pleasure. Until I looked farther ahead, where three young girls were attempting to paddle out on rented foam boards. My mum would clear around them, but they were too close together for me to cut between them, and too spread out to avoid. Whipping left, I turned into the breaking wave and dove over the backside of the swell.

The leash pulled taut against my ankle, with the powerful swell still dragging my board in its path. The breaking wave pummeled me into the spin-and-rinse cycle. I tumbled inside its grasp, my leash wrenching at my leg. For a moment, the dark, unforgiving water below San Clemente Pier came flooding back to me. Fear consumed me like the cocoon of turbulent water holding me pinned beneath the surface. As quickly as the terror surged through my mind, a second wave of calm took its place. The familiarity of the surroundings overwhelmed the fear. As teenagers, my friends and I had spent afternoons after school when we played in the waves, just to be spun and tossed around like we were on a rollercoaster. We'd come up laughing and brushing sand from our hair.

"Sorry!" I heard one of the girls call out as I surfaced and gathered up the leash.

I waved. "No worries."

Slipping back onto my board, I rode the white water into the shallows where my mum stood with a look of concern on her face.

"You okay?" she asked.

I knew her question had nothing to do with my physical well-being, as she could see I was fine.

I grinned. "Yeah, I'm good. Let's go have lunch."

She put an arm around my shoulders as we walked up the beach, picking our way between families sitting on large towels, staking out their slices of paradise for the day. Even though I'd fallen off the horse I'd only just climbed back on, I'd learned what I needed to know. The ocean was still my second home. My oasis in a vast desert of violence, deceit, and grief that filled my days as an Orange County Sheriff's Department investigator.

I'd forgotten I'd invited Hugo to drop by for Sunday lunch. In fact, I'd thrown out the invite when he'd called to check on me a few days back, then never given it another thought. Hugo and I didn't socialize outside of work. I'd politely invited him to several gatherings in the past, none of which he'd shown up for. So when my mum asked whose BMW was parked out front as we drove up Copper Lantern, it took me a moment to realize it was my partner's personal car.

I parked in the driveway, and we got out, wearing damp T-shirts over our wet swimsuits. Hugo appeared from his BMW and looked at me from across my tiny front yard.

"Did I get the time wrong?" he asked.

"No, not at all," I replied. "Perfect timing." I turned to my mother. "This is my partner, Hugo."

"So nice to finally meet you," she said, walking his way.

My dad must have heard the voices as he came out the front door. Hugo shook hands with Mum, and then with Dad as he met him in the driveway. I wasn't sure what to do. I needed to wash down the boards and wetsuits with fresh water, but changing into dry clothes seemed like more of a priority.

"Thanks for coming," I said, choosing to pretend to know how to be a host.

I had no clue. Couples Paul knew used to come over for dinner sometimes, but he'd handle everything. Since I began living alone again, the only people who visited me were my parents, and my mum usually took over doing anything that resembled taking care of guests.

Hugo looked at me and smiled. "Back in the water?"

I nodded. "Yeah. Felt good to get that out of the way."

He blinked softly and widened his smile. "Good."

"Come on inside," I said, ready to follow my parents into the house.

"I hope this is okay," Hugo said, his tone strangely hesitant.

"What's okay?" I quizzed, turning back.

It was then that I saw a man getting out of the passenger side of the BMW. Fitz smiled and waved at me as he finished a call, slipping the phone into his pocket as he joined us.

"Of course it's okay," I replied, stunned.

"I didn't realize your family would be here," Hugo said, and I read the concern on his face.

"They'll appreciate the three of us involved in the case raising a glass," I replied.

Hugo looked at the other man.

"Sounds good," Fitz said. "One step at a time, right?"

Hugo nodded. "Eventually. But not today."

I laughed and was about to continue to the front door when I noticed a car rolling slowly down the street. Normally, it wouldn't get my attention, but a shiny black SUV with ridiculously oversized chrome wheels wasn't the standard Dana Point ride. A Hispanic man stared out the open driver's window, which froze me in place.

I recognized Milo Santiago from his mugshot. Leaning forward in the passenger seat, Gabby Castillo looked over at me with a broad grin.

"Friends of yours?" Hugo asked as the SUV continued down the hill.

I swallowed hard and fought back a mixture of anger and fear.

"Not so much," I muttered.

"Want to tell me about it?" he said, creasing his brow in concern.

I forced my jaw to relax and looked at my partner.

"Eventually. But not today."

Don't forget to grab the next book in the series,
The One Who Ran

ACKNOWLEDGMENTS

My heartfelt thanks go to:

My incredible wife Cheryl, our family, and great friends for their unwavering support, love, and encouragement.

The fine folks at the Orange County Sheriff's Department who met with me, emailed, Zoom called, and provided their wonderful advice and knowledge. Any variances from procedure and law enforcement facts are strictly on the author by error or to enhance the story.

Peter Carey of Capistrano Boxing Gym for taking the time to help me with the boxing scenes. Again, any errors in this regard are solely on the author.

My marvellous editor Chelsey Heller for her diligent and detailed work.

My beta reader group for their wonderful support, feedback, and keen eyes, which make each book better before reaching you, and my ARC group for their amazing support.

Above all, I thank you, the readers: none of this happens without your choice to spend precious time with my stories. I am truly in your debt.

LET'S STAY IN TOUCH!

To buy merchandise, find more info, or to join my newsletter, visit
my website at
www.HarveyBooks.com

If you enjoyed this novel I'd be incredibly grateful if you'd consider
leaving a review on Amazon.com
Find eBook deals and follow me on BookBub.com

Catch my chat show, The Two Authors' Podcast with co-host
Douglas Pratt

Visit Amazon.com for more books in the
Investigator Kat Cromwell Mystery Series,
Nora Sommer Caribbean Suspense Series,
AJ Bailey Adventure Series,
and collaborative works:
The Greene Wolfe Thriller Series
Tropical Authors Adventure Series

ABOUT THE AUTHOR

A USA Today bestselling author, Nicholas Harvey's life has been anything but ordinary. Race car driver, motorsports professional, adventure traveller, divemaster, and since 2020, a full-time novelist. Raised in England and resident in America for many years, Nick and his amazing wife, Cheryl, now base themselves in Grand Cayman from where they travel the globe in search of new plots for his novels. He is the author of the Nora Sommer Caribbean Suspense series, Investigator Kat Cromwell Mysteries, and AJ Bailey Adventure series, along with multiple collaborations.

For more information, visit his website at HarveyBooks.com.

www.ingramcontent.com/pod-product-compliance
Lightning Source LLC
Chambersburg PA
CBHW020741310726
48969CB00002B/366